THE CLUB
OF MASKS

THE CLUB OF MASKS

ALLEN UPWARD

WILDSIDE PRESS

Originally published in 1926
Published by Wildside Press LLC.
wildsidepress.com

CHAPTER 1

ON HIS MAJESTY'S SERVICE

I had only just let myself into the hall of the quiet house in the respectable street beside the British Museum when my ear was startled by the subdued shrilling of the telephone bell overhead. Whether this was the first time it had sounded, or whether that alarming call was being repeated for the second or third time, I had no means of knowing, as I turned hurriedly to fasten the front door behind me. Cautiously, and yet as swiftly as I dared, I shot the bolts and began speeding on tiptoe up the two flights of stairs between me and safety from detection. The night telephone was placed beside my bed on the second floor, but Sir Frank Tarleton slept on the same landing; and unless I could reach my room and still that persistent ringing before it penetrated through his slumber I ran the risk of meeting him coming out to find why it was not answered. And not for much, not for very much, would I have had the great consultant see me returning to his house at an hour when daylight was already flooding the deserted streets of the still sleeping city.

There was something ominous in the continuous peal that sounded louder and louder in my ears with every step I made towards it. It seemed as though the unknown caller must know of my predicament and be bent on exposing me. I clutched the rail of the banisters to steady myself as I panted up those interminable stairs in the darkness, and my feet felt clogged like those of one in a nightmare as I lifted them from step to step; all the while racking my brains for some excuse to offer for the breach of duty I had been guilty of in spending the night elsewhere. For my real excuse, the only one that could have tempted me to betray my chief's confidence, could never be disclosed.

The darkness all around me seemed to be vibrating with the merciless clamour overhead as I toiled through those tense moments. My knees trembled under me, and my heart well-nigh stopped beating, as my head reached the level of the last landing and I turned my eyes desperately to the physician's door in search of any sign that he had been aroused.

No sign as yet, thank Heaven! Five more stairs, three lightning strides to my own door, and he would never know of the secret errand that had taken me away from my post that night.

At last my agony was ended. I stood breathless on the topmost stair, darted past Sir Frank's room, not daring to pause and listen for any movement from within, and clutched the handle of my own door, summoning all my nerve to open and close it again so rapidly as to permit the least possible sound to escape. An instant later and I had reached the telephone and silenced its urgent voice, and was beginning to draw my breath freely for the first time since I had reached the house.

Then, after a few deep gasps, I hailed the caller.

"Inspector Charles of Scotland Yard speaking," came grimly over the wire. "Who is there?"

There was nothing to startle me in the fact that the police were calling so imperatively. Tarleton was the greatest living authority on poisons; it was to pursue his researches in their mysterious history that he lived in the unfashionable neighbourhood of the Museum; and the Home Office treated him with a confidence which they placed in no other of their advisers. Neither was there any cause for uneasiness in the Inspector's cautious question. Very many of the calls that came to that unpretending house in that quiet corner of London had a certain character of furtiveness, and the callers showed the same anxiety to make sure whom they were speaking with.

My usual response came to my lips mechanically. "This is Dr. Cassilis, Sir Frank Tarleton's confidential assistant. The doctor is asleep."

There was a pause before the caller spoke again. There was nothing alarming to me in that, either. I had grown accustomed to the pause during my first few weeks under the roof of the great consultant. Few of those who needed his services liked to disclose their business to a deputy.

"Please have him waked immediately. He is wanted as soon as possible—on His Majesty's service."

The request was peremptory, nevertheless I was not inclined to give way to it at once. The police formula made no difference to me. I was His Majesty's servant as much as my chief, and it was for me, and not for the Inspector, to decide which of us was to take the case. At the same time I began casting off my clothes so as to be ready to go in and rouse Tarleton if it became necessary; and one hand was busy with my necktie and collar while the other held the telephone mouthpiece to my lips.

"My instructions are not to disturb Sir Frank unless I am satisfied that the case is urgent, and that I can't deal with it myself," I said firmly. "I must ask you to tell me something more."

There was another pause before the caller spoke again, and I took advantage of it to wrench off my collar and throw my waistcoat after my coat onto the floor. When the wire buzzed again the first words that reached my ear nearly caused me to drop the tube from my fingers.

"I am speaking from the Domino Club, Vincent Studios, Tarifa Road, Chelsea. There was a masked dance here this night, and one of the dancers has been found dead, apparently poisoned."

And now I might well find myself trembling all over, and have to lean against the wall to recover myself. I only just succeeded in keeping back a cry of consternation. For it was to go to that underground club, with its dark reputation, and its strange character of mingled fashion and depravity, that I had been tempted to quit my post that night. I had been one of those masked dancers, jostling with I knew not whom under the shadowy lights and in the curtained recesses of the pretended studio in London's nearest approach to a Quartier Latin. I could recall the scene in the after-midnight hours, the sea of black silk-covered faces thronging under the crimson lamp-shades, the bizarre confusion of costumes, monks and Crusaders, columbines and queens, the swish of silk and tinkling of swords and bracelets, and the incessant flood of whispers that had made me think of the scene in Milton's pandemonium when the assembly of fallen angels are suddenly deprived of speech and changed into hissing serpents.

I had used the greatest precautions in coming and going. I had no reason to think that there was any real likelihood of my presence there being discovered. But a cold fear laid hold of me as I steadied my nerves to deal with the Police Inspector who had so unexpectedly conjured up a spectre on the scene of that past revelry. It was doubly imperative now that I should make no mistake, and above all that I should get rid of every sign that I had not passed the night in my own bed.

I was fast unbuttoning my shirt as I spoke again to the waiting police officer.

"I'm afraid I can't awake Sir Frank for that. It seems to be a case that he will expect me to attend myself. Is there anything peculiar about the medical symptoms? What does your local surgeon say?"

Inspector Charles at last revealed the true reason for his persistence in demanding the attendance of my chief.

"I haven't called in our local surgeon. There doesn't seem anything mysterious about the cause of death. It looks to me like a simple case of opium-poisoning, very likely a suicide. But the case must be disposed of *in camera* if possible, for the sake of the people in high places connected with the club. My information is that there was a royalty present at this dance, the Crown Prince of—"

Whether purposely or not, the speaker let his voice drop so low that I failed to catch the final word. But I had heard enough. There could be no more doubt that Tarleton must be informed. It was a bare possibility that the victim might prove to be the foreign Royal Highness himself. Failing that, it might at least be someone who had been mistaken for him by the assassin. In any case I could thank my stars for the intimation that the case was likely to be hushed up on his account. Provided that I could efface every sign of my nocturnal expedition, I ought to have nothing now to dread.

I bade the officer wait, and tore off my remaining garments, slipped into my sleeping-suit and dressing-gown, and rumpled my hair to give myself the look of one just roused from sleep. Then and not before, I ventured out upon the landing to face my chief.

As I did so I was chilled by another shock. I saw a thin line of light under the door in front of me. Sir Frank Tarleton was awake.

I don't think I can be accused of cowardice for feeling as I did during those desperate moments. It was not only my worldly fortune that was at stake; there were peculiar circumstances which made it doubly shameful on my part to be false to the trust put in me by the great specialist. They went back to the day when I began to attend his lectures on forensic medicine at the University College in Gower Street. I had already taken my medical degree in the University of London with a view to becoming a public analyst, and I had been anxious to profit by the Professor's unique knowledge of poisons. From the first I had attracted his favourable notice; my papers had won his praise; and he had invited me to call on him, and admitted me to his friendship. Then, at the end of the year's course, he had overwhelmed me by an offer so much beyond my hopes that I could scarcely yet believe in my good luck.

I can see him now, the whole scene is clear before me, the brisk figure with its face of intense thought, crowned by a shock of unkempt gray hair, standing over me on the hearth-rug of his dingy consulting-room on the ground floor in Montague Street. He was following his quaint habit of swinging his magnificent gold repeater in front of him by its shabby scrap of ribbon, while he gave me the amazing news.

"I've decided to take an assistant, Cassilis. I have passed my sixtieth birthday, and though my work interests me as much as ever, I mean to spare myself a little more in future. I don't intend to turn out in the middle of the night because a bilious duchess fancies that someone has bribed her French maid to poison her. And I've told them at the Home Office—I suppose you know I'm their principal consultant—that I won't be sent down to Cornwall one day and to Cumberland the next every time a coroner lets himself be puzzled by a simple case of strychnine or arsenic. It's work for a younger man."

He waved the watch towards me as he went on.

"Sir James Ponsonby—that's the Permanent Under Secretary—has consented to my having a deputy, and I'm submitting your name."

I recall my sensations as he stopped abruptly and bent his keen eyes on me from beneath their bushy roof of eyebrow to see how the proposal struck me. I had gasped for breath then as I was gasping now. At the age of twenty-five, only just qualified for my profession, I was to be lifted at one step out of the struggling crowd into a position which was already success, and which I should only have to make proper use of to attain in time the same eminence as my patron.

My answer must have been incoherent. But Tarleton interrupted it with a jerk of his gold repeater, which, I can remember, almost made me duck my head.

"I'm paying you what most of the men in our profession would consider a doubtful compliment when I tell you that you seem to me to be a young man with imagination, Cassilis. And that is what's wanted in my work. It isn't doctor's work really so much as detective's. It's not only symptoms I have to look for, but motives. There was a touch in your very first paper that showed me you could think for yourself, and speculate. And speculation is the master key of science, although all your second-rate men decry it. It's the old fable of the fox who had lost his tail. Not having any imagination themselves, they would like to forbid it to everyone. The Trade Unions rule the world today, and they are all trying to reduce the intelligence of mankind to the lowest common denominator."

He had spoken with a certain bitterness which it was easy for me to understand. Eminent as he was, unquestioned as his authority had now become, I knew that Tarleton was not popular with the medical profession. His baronetcy had been given late, and given grudgingly. Perhaps he had recognized in me something that reminded him of his own youth, and had taken a generous resolution to help me in consequence. Certainly his treatment of me since had been more like that of a father than an employer.

He had said a good deal more that I hadn't forgotten and that I was least likely to forget just then. His manner had been very grave as he dwelt upon the confidential character of a great deal of his work.

"If you are to assist me in my most important cases, and to qualify yourself for succeeding me later on, as I hope you will, you must learn to be more discreet than in almost any other line of life. You will find yourself in possession of secrets that compromise the honour of great families; men in the highest positions will hold their reputations at your mercy; the safety of the State itself may sometimes depend on your silence. I know of at least one man sitting in the House of Lords who owes his peerage to an undiscovered murder; and what is more, he knows of my knowledge. I make it a rule if possible never to go into any company where he is likely to be present, and he takes the same care to avoid me. But if he ever thought it necessary to his safety, that man would no more hesitate about taking my life than he did about taking his nephew's—a boy twelve years old."

No doubt Tarleton had gauged my disposition pretty well before he chose me for his assistant, and he knew that I should be more attracted than repelled by such hints as that. My blood tingled at the prospect opening before me. The days of Richard III and the Bloody Tower seemed to have come again. And I was to be behind the scenes tracing the midnight assassin at his work in the heart of modern London, and in the very purlieus of her palaces. It was enough to sate the greediest imagination.

"I mustn't conceal from you," my kindly chief had gone on to tell me, "that I have had to overcome strong objections to your appointment. Sir James Ponsonby considers that you are very young to be entrusted with such serious responsibilities. You can't wonder if the Home Office has taken some precautions. I submitted your name a month ago, and I only received permission to make you the offer yesterday. I have very little doubt that you have been under observation most of the time between."

This was the part of the conversation that had come back to me most vividly that night when I was struggling frantically towards the accusing bell.

For the whole sting in the communication that my memory thrust so pitilessly before me was in the last condition, the very condition I had been driven to break that night.

I had been less dismayed than most men of my age perhaps—particularly most medical students—would have been by learning that my life had been under the microscope for a month. I had nothing very serious to reproach myself with. The memory of a secret love affair, an unhappy one, alas! had served to keep me clear of the most dangerous of all the snares that life sets for youth. It was my good luck never to have tasted, and never to have felt the wish to taste, anything in the way of alcohol, and to be able to sit with nothing stronger than a cup of strong coffee in front of me in the midst of the most riotous company. I believe it was this exceptional merit that turned the scale in my favour with Sir James Ponsonby. Gambling had equally little appeal for me, and I took no interest whatever in that noble animal the horse. My real vice was love of excitement for its own sake. One prize-fight had more attraction for me than a hundred cricket-matches. It was in search of sensation that I was drawn into the night life of London. I was haunted by the mystery of silent streets and shadowed courts. Like Stevenson, I felt that life ought to be a series of adventures beginning in Leicester Square. The Press Club and the Chelsea Art Club were the two poles of my romantic sphere, and I revelled in the society of men who seemed to me to be leading lives more mysterious than mine.

It appeared that this was the weakness which stood in my way with the Government Department I was to serve. Tarleton had ceased to swing his watch, and had given me a very meaning glance as he came to the decisive point.

"Sir James has made it a condition of your appointment that it shall be a resident one. You will have to take up your quarters with me. I shall have a telephone installed in your room for you to take the night calls. And I shall depend on you not to trouble me with them unless I am really wanted."

My face must have fallen as I listened to this stipulation, for I saw an answering shade on the doctor's brow. I felt that a good deal of the gilt would be taken off the gingerbread if I had to surrender my personal freedom and abandon my favourite haunts to lead a regular life under my employer's roof, and under his surveillance; for, of course, that was what it came to. My chief inducement to take up the career of an analyst instead of a general practitioner had been the greater freedom I should enjoy. I had dreaded the idea of having to settle in a provincial town or a prim residential suburb, where I should have to keep regular hours, go to church in a black coat on Sundays, act as sidesman, and generally put on all the airs of respectability. It would be almost as great a wrench to give up my artist and journalist friends, in whose company I had had such jolly times, and go to bed every night just as the real day was beginning, under the watchful eyes of my chief.

I fancy Sir Frank himself felt some sympathy with me, though he was too wise to express it.

"A man must expect to be judged to some extent by the company he keeps," he had hinted. "You can't expect the head of a Department like the Home Office to feel easy at the idea of entrusting important secrets to a young man who spends his nights, I won't say in disreputable company, but at all events in circles where a good many adventurers are found. These people"—the bitter note came back into his voice—"these people hate the shoulders on which they have climbed. They govern the empire which the Raleighs and the Clives have gained for them, but they don't want any more Clives and Raleighs. They threw Burton away; they wouldn't use Gordon till it was too late—Faugh!" He swallowed his disgust with an effort, and became almost stern. "Now, my boy, this is a great opportunity for you, and you must take it. You must forget that you are a genius, and put your neck into the collar for a few years. At the end of that time you will have a reputation, and you can do what you like within reasonable limits. I expect you to trust yourself to me."

And, of course, I had. He had taken me to the Home Office and formally presented me to the Under Secretary, and I found myself appointed an

Assistant Medical Adviser, detailed for duty under the orders of Sir Frank Tarleton, with a salary that seemed riches in advance.

Perhaps I had found my work a little disappointing since. The night calls had not been numerous, and they had grown fewer after the first month or two, as though Tarleton's clients or patients, I hardly know which to call them, had found out that it was no use expecting him to turn out any longer, if the case was one that I could deal with. Most of my time was passed in the laboratory in Montague Street, carrying out analyses under his directions, and improving my knowledge of rare poisons, of which he had formed what was probably the finest collection in the world. But of really sensational cases, involving criminal suspicion and mystery, there had not been one before that fateful summons from the Domino Club.

But I dared not hesitate longer in delivering it. Every moment now would only make matters worse. I crossed the landing and knocked firmly on the closed door.

The answer was instantaneous—"Come in!"

I obeyed, to find myself in the full glare of the electric light over the bed, in which Tarleton was sitting upright, his beloved repeater in one hand, while he gazed at me questioningly from beneath his knitted brows.

"I first heard the telephone nine minutes ago. You have taken some time to answer it."

CHAPTER 2

THE EVIDENCE OF MADAME BONNELL

Instead of excusing myself I thought it the best plan to plunge into the account of what had taken place at the Domino Club, in the hope that it would absorb his mind. The alert physician made only one comment as I finished.

"A case for Inspector Charles is pretty sure to be a case for me; but you didn't know that." He was out of bed the next moment.

"Please tell him I am coming at once, and order round my car. And be ready yourself as soon as you can."

I needed no injunction to make haste. I was in a fever to be back at the scene of that masked revel, and find out what had happened there. I congratulated myself on the care I had taken to cover my own tracks. I had left the doctor's house and returned to it in my ordinary clothes. Not a soul in the Domino Club, except the member from whom I had obtained a ticket of admission, could have the least idea of my identity. So far as I could see I was absolutely secure from discovery. But it had been a dangerous game to play, and Tarleton was a dangerous man to play against. With all his kindness for me I trembled at the thought of coming within the range of his uncanny powers of detection.

As soon as I had dispatched his messages, and put a pot of coffee on to boil over a little spirit stove, I sluiced my head in cold water, and got into my clothes again as quickly as I had got out of them. I was ready with a steaming cup of coffee for my chief as he came out of his room, and was rewarded by the heartiness with which he gulped it down. His square leather bag, fitted with everything likely to be needed for the treatment of a poisoning case, was always kept ready in his bedroom, and he had it in his hand. I relieved him of it not presuming to bring my own; and we found the car waiting for us when we opened the front door.

As we rolled through the streets, just beginning to show signs of life, Tarleton acquainted me with the personality of Inspector Charles.

"He's a retired Army man; he likes to be called Captain Charles. He's also the younger son of a peer but he doesn't like that noticed. His family are silly enough to object to his being in the police, and he drops the

Honourable on their account. But of course it's known in the Yard, and he gets most of the society jobs in consequence. I suppose they think he's more likely to know his way about among the big people. But if you ask me, I think an experienced valet knows ten times more. You'll find Charles straight, and you'll find him thorough, but you needn't expect him to see an inch beyond his own nose."

This was comfortable for me. But the next words of my chief gave me an awkward jar.

"By the way, you ought to be able to tell me something about the place we're going to—what is it?—the Domino Club. It sounds like the sort of night haunt the Home Office objected to so much when I asked for you as my assistant."

I had to make up my mind in a hurry. To tell the truth was out of the question. It was not only my own honour and safety that were at stake; there was another for whose sake my presence at that fatal dance must be concealed. I was on the point of denying all knowledge of the club when it struck me that I might be betrayed into some unconscious movement in going through the premises, or some thoughtless remark, which would reveal to a keen intelligence like Tarleton's that I had been there before.

I made an effort to seem as if I had been searching my memory.

"Yes," I said slowly, "now you speak of it I remember having been there. But I am not sure that I am free to say anything about it. My impression is that there was an implied pledge of secrecy. Everyone wore a mask and a disguise of some sort. It was supposed to be a place where people in very high positions could let themselves go in security. I was told there were sometimes judges present, and I rather think Cabinet Ministers, as well as peeresses, and so forth."

The specialist nodded gravely. "I expect the authorities knew what they were doing when they told Charles to call for me. We shall see whether he has found out who the man is that has been poisoned."

"He didn't say it was a man," I ventured to suggest.

Sir Frank pursed his lips, but made no answer. He took out his gold repeater and began swinging it slowly, a sure sign that he was following out some train of thought.

In another quarter of an hour the car drew up in one of the old-fashioned streets of Chelsea between King Street and the Fulham Road, at the entrance to the curious building or group of buildings that bore the name of Vincent Studios.

The place resembled a rabbit warren. A short flight of steps led down from the street pavement into a dark, cavernous hall with doors opening out of it on three sides. Behind most of these doors were the studios of artists—one or two of them known to me—studios as cavernous if not as dark as the hall, and ending in glass doors that opened on mysterious gardens or garden yards overgrown with nasturtiums and other plants that seem to love the grime and cinders of suburban London. In the background one was aware of gray piles of timber, as of a mountain range closing a landscape. Some forgotten builder, perhaps, had died, leaving those stacks behind him, and his heirs had never discovered their existence, so that they had been left to the possession of the rats.

At the far end of the entrance cavern two doors side by side still bore the name of artists, one of whom had lately blossomed into an Academician and been transplanted to the sunnier region of Bedford Park, while the other had exchanged the brush for some more promising weapon in what, I fear, had been a losing fight with Fortune. Only the initiated knew that the door still bearing the name of J. Loftus, A.R.A., was now that of the Domino Club; while its companion, from which the name of Yelverton had been roughly effaced, served as a back door for the use of the tradesmen and servants of the club, and also for such members as had reasons of their own for not coming through the streets in fancy costume. For their benefit a row of small dressing-rooms had been fitted up, in which they could transform themselves from sober moths into bright artificial butterflies and back again.

In front of the club entrance an officer in plain clothes was stationed who recognized Sir Frank with a respectful salute.

"You will find Inspector Charles inside, sir," he said, opening the door for us.

We found ourselves in a dark narrow passage empty of everything but cloak- and hat-pegs. A door at the further end opened straight into the dancing-room.

The former studio had been decorated in a fashion evidently meant to recall the Arabian Nights Entertainment. Vistas of Moorish arches and fountains playing among palms and oleanders had been painted on the walls. At intervals wooden columns had been set up to support curtains of gauze embroidered so as to afford a half concealment to the nooks that they enclosed. The whole place was still suffused with the lurid glow of a series of red lanterns hanging from the roof. But a glass door at the further end had been thrown open to admit the daylight, and where it reached the crimson glow became haggard and spectral and the whole place had the air of an old woman's face from which the paint had peeled in streaks, revealing the wrinkles and sharp bones beneath.

Inspector Charles, tall, upright, and looking the personification of law and order, stood beside one of the curtained alcoves close to the garden door, and invited us with a solemn gesture to approach.

This was the moment I had been dreading. I endeavoured to keep my face passive, and give no sign of recognition, as I came behind my chief and took my first glance at the spectacle the Inspector had to show us.

Within the curtains, stretched at full length on a low divan, was a figure attired as an Inquisitor. The black robe was folded carefully round him, but the peaked hood with its two eye-slits had been thrust back over the head, so that the face was fully exposed. It was a striking face in every way, the face of a man of fifty or thereabout in the full possession of his powers. The forehead was intellectual; the eyes, wide open but glazed in the death stare, must have been full and penetrating in life; the nose and chin were strongly carved; only the lips showed a certain looseness, as of over-ripened fruit, that seemed to hint at something evil underlying the dignity and strength manifested in the rest of the face.

I scanned that prostrate figure with painful curiosity. The costume was only too familiar; I had had ample opportunity of observing it during the night that had just elapsed. But the face was as strange to me as it was to either of the other two who stood and gazed beside me. Even the eyes, unnaturally dilated by the drug, seemed to bear little likeness to those that had peered through the holes in the black hood when I last looked on the sombre shape in life.

The Inspector spoke briefly, addressing himself to my companion.

"This is how he was found when they came in to put out the lights after everyone was gone as they supposed. They thought at first that he was in a drunken sleep, and tried to rouse him by shaking. When they failed, they went to bring Madame Bonnell, the proprietress of the club. They dared not uncover the face without her authority; the rules of the club are so strict on that point. She laid back the hood herself, and saw at once that he was dead. After that she rang us up, and saw that the body was not touched till I got here. I thought it best not to touch it myself till you came."

Clear, succinct, containing the bare facts and nothing more, such was the report of Inspector Charles. It was evident that no better man could have been put in charge of an affair in dealing with which prudence was the most essential requisite.

The great physician received the statement with a nod of satisfaction.

"You suggested to Dr. Cassilis over the wire that it looked like a case of opium-poisoning," was his first remark.

Captain Charles favoured me with a cautious glance, in which I read some disapproval of my youthful appearance.

"I thought an opiate must have been the cause of death, Sir Frank, because there was no sign of a struggle nor of any suffering. He seemed to have died in his sleep."

Again the consultant gave an approving nod. All this time he had not once removed his eyes from the pallid face on which a leaden tinge had become visible. Now he turned to me.

"What do you say, Cassilis?"

I shook my head. There was something in the case that puzzled me.

"I agree with Captain Charles to some extent. The appearances are consistent with opium-poisoning. But—" I turned to the Inspector—"can you tell us the hour at which the body was found with life extinct?"

Captain Charles consulted his watch. Tarleton's fingers were already pinching the shabby ribbon of his repeater, and it was going to and fro with the slow movement of a pendulum.

"It is now half-past six. I got here soon after five. It must have been about half-past four when the body was found."

I looked questioningly at the great specialist.

"Unless the opiate was given very early, in which case the effect would surely have been noticed by someone, it must have been a very powerful dose to produce death so soon. I should be inclined to suspect some weakness in the heart, or some other derangement, to account for such rapid action. I don't like the colour of the skin."

"Ah! You see that?" Tarleton bent over the dead face in grave scrutiny for some moments. Then he straightened himself up.

"And now, who is this man?" he asked the Inspector.

"His name is Wilson, so the proprietress says. But she seems to know very little about him."

"Wilson?" The doctor repeated the name with a sceptical intonation. "That is the sort of name that man would be likely to give himself in a place of this kind, I should think. Can I see the proprietress?"

Captain Charles went out in quest of her. He was no sooner gone than my chief whispered quickly in my ear, "Not another word about the cause of death before anybody else. I blame myself for asking your opinion. I underrated your powers of observation. Hush!"

I looked round to see a capable middle-aged Frenchwoman dressed in black silk, emerging from a portière across the room. Very capable and businesslike she looked, with her well-arranged hair and commanding black eyes, and well-preserved face and figure, and that amazing air of respectability which only a Frenchwoman can keep up in an atmosphere charged with evil. In Madame Bonnell's presence vice was deprived of its impropriety, and even murder took on the character of a business mischance about which the less fuss made the better.

Madame had obviously employed her time since the discovery of this particular mischance in making the best of her personal appearance. She greeted us with affability.

Even Tarleton, I thought, was softened by her graceful and yet digni-fied deportment. In a moment we seemed to become four friends engaged in a confidential talk over a matter of common interest. It was Madame who induced me to sit down.

"You understand, no doubt, Madame, that we are not here with any hostile purpose," the representative of the Home Office began. "If it is pos-sible to dispose of this matter privately, without involving you or your es-tablishment in any scandal, I shall be glad."

The explanation seemed unnecessary. Madame Bonnell by her man-ner refused to perceive the possibility of her being involved in scandal, or in anything else inconsistent with the character of a respectable business woman.

"You have identified the deceased, I understand, by the name of Wil-son. Have you any idea whether that was his real name, or an assumed one?"

Madame Bonnell had no idea. Madame Bonnell was desolated by hav-ing no idea, since the amiable Sir Frank seemed to wish her to have one. Monsieur the late Wilson had introduced himself to her originally under that name, and she had never inquired if he had any other.

Madame succeeded in conveying to us that she was not in the habit of inconveniencing her patrons by inquiries of any sort, or of distracting her own mind by curiosity on any subject except their ability to pay her.

Under the polished surface of indifference I nevertheless thought I could detect in the proprietress of the Domino Club a consciousness that she was being examined by the representatives of the law about a serious business, and that it would not be prudent on her part to withhold any mate-rial information. It must have been clear to her that candour was her best policy, up to a certain point at all events.

To Tarleton's next question, how she came to make the acquaintance of the dead man, she made a pretty full reply. Monsieur Wilson had introduced himself to her a year or two before, when she was managing a small restau-rant in Soho, in a street in which there is more than one small restaurant, and the restaurants are patronized by more than one class of customers. It was Monsieur Wilson who had proposed to her that she should exchange her position there for the more profitable one of proprietress of a fashion-able night club. Monsieur had offered to provide the funds required for starting such a club, and had undertaken to make it fashionable, and in both respects he had kept his word. All the first members of the club had been brought by him, and he had gone on introducing others since. Madame avowed that she was under a debt to Monsieur Wilson, which she could not easily repay. She made an effort to repay it, as she spoke, with tears for his fate, but the dividend forthcoming did not strike me as a heavy one. By this time, doubtless, the Domino Club was fairly on its feet, and in no great need of the dead man's further support.

Madame Bonnell's evidence so far had only served to deepen the mystery instead of lightening it. Who was this unknown Wilson? Why should he have wanted to start a night club, and what was the influence that had enabled him to fill it with so many members drawn from the highest social ranks? The chief part in the examination had been taken by the physician, Inspector Charles intervening mostly to secure dates and addresses for his note-book after the meticulous fashion of the law. At length I took advantage of a break to put a question which had been in my mind for some time.

"These people whom Wilson, if that was his name, brought into the club must have been his friends, apparently. So far as one can see the club was entirely composed of his personal friends and other friends of theirs. Doesn't that make it more probable that he took poison himself than that anyone else gave it to him?"

I threw out the suggestion generally, and my three companions all turned and stared at me as though it took them by surprise, although it was an obvious alternative. The physician said nothing, but the compression of his brows told me plainly that he had rejected such a theory. Captain Charles made a fatal objection.

"After he had founded the club and done everything to make it a success, why should he have come to it to commit suicide—the very thing that would damage it most?"

Madame Bonnell became genuinely agitated for the first time.

"But of course that will not be known!" she exclaimed sharply. "You sir," she appealed to Tarleton, "you will know how to contrive that this unfortunate shall be taken elsewhere. Think of the scandal if it should be known that a crime was committed in the presence of the Crown Prince!"

Evidently His Royal Highness was a strong card in Madame's estimation, and one which she could rely on to win her game. Perhaps it was not the first time in her business experience that she had found the police disposed to shut their eyes to awkward incidents in which great personages were involved.

The consultant of the Home Office looked by no means yielding.

"I have not yet decided what course I shall recommend the authorities to take," he said. "Have you anything to say in answer to Dr. Cassilis? Is he right in assuming that everyone present here last night must have been Wilson's friend?"

Thus pressed, Madame Bonnell presented the appearance of an unwilling witness, who hesitates to speak for fear of the consequences to himself.

"As long as I believe that no proceedings will be taken against the Club, which is my property, everything I know, my suspicions even, are at the service of the police," she replied cautiously.

It was a bargain which the astute Frenchwoman was proposing openly to the authorities. Tarleton shrugged his shoulders. He was the last man to commit himself to anything of the kind.

"The moment I am satisfied that you are withholding any information that bears on the case I shall advise the police to close this place, and apply for your deportation as an alien, Madame Bonnell."

The capable Frenchwoman saw that she had made a false step. She retracted it immediately in admirable distress.

"But Monsieur must pardon me! I am bewildered by the situation in which I find myself. I do not understand the Britannic law. I am ready to throw myself on Monsieur's consideration. What is it that he would have me say?"

The physician looked at his watch.

"I am waiting for your answer to Dr. Cassilis."

Madame Bonnell gave me an appealing look, of which I thought it best to take no notice. I had seen nothing of her during the time I had spent at the dance, and I was confident that she was quite ignorant of my presence at it. She found herself compelled to speak without assistance.

"The Doctor Cassilis is mistaken," she said at last, with an air of weighing each word before she uttered it. "Monsieur Wilson was acquainted with the people whom he introduced here, undoubtedly, but they were not all his friends. On the contrary, some of them were his enemies, and he went in fear of them. Even in mortal fear."

It was the revelation Tarleton seemed to have been anticipating. He gave the short, satisfied nod I knew so well.

"Go on," he commanded. "Explain how you knew this."

"In effect I knew it because he told me so himself. He took me into his confidence in order to ask for my protection. He feared this very thing that has happened. He instructed me to pour out everything he was to drink with my own hands, and to send it to him by the waiter he thought he could trust—Gerard."

"Now I think we have some real information," the specialist observed. "Be good enough to send for Gerard, if you please."

CHAPTER 3

THE EVIDENCE OF THE DEAD

At this point I began to feel a touch of nervousness. I had faced the proprietress of the Domino Club without any, because she had not seen me even in my disguise. But the waiters had been going to and fro throughout the night. I had given orders once or twice, and I could not feel certain that my voice would not be recognized. I told myself that my fear was fanciful, and that the last thing that could occur to anyone's mind was that a representative of the Home Office, engaged in the investigation, had himself been present on the scene of the crime, if crime it was. But none the less I resolved to do nothing to attract the waiter's notice, if I could help it.

I saw Tarleton frown as Madame Bonnell returned with her servant. He gave her an authoritative nod.

"Thank you, Madame. I won't detain you while I am questioning this man."

The prudent Frenchwoman concealed any vexation she may have felt, and instantly retired, leaving Gerard alone with us.

He was as much the type of the discreet waiter as Madame was of the discreet manageress. If he had only possessed side-whiskers he would have been the perfect waiter of the French stage. But he was a good deal younger than Madame, and showed less self-possession. His eyes searched us nervously in turn as though he were looking for someone to propitiate. The physician read his rather white face with one swift glance, and came to his relief.

"You are not under any suspicion, Gerard. Provided you tell the truth, you have nothing to fear."

The waiter braced himself up with a visible effort. Not, I fancied, that he had any objection to tell the truth, but that it was a rather novel exercise for him. From that moment he neglected the Inspector and me to concentrate his efforts to propitiate on Sir Frank.

"I hear that the man who is dead trusted you. Did he trust you with his real name?"

"Never, sir." Gerard spread out his two hands to show their emptiness of knowledge. "I knew nothing of him except what I learned from Madame."

"And that was?"

The waiter looked apprehensive. No doubt the idea crossed his mind that it might be awkward if his account contradicted hers.

"That was very little indeed, sir. She told me to treat him as proprietor. He never paid for what he consumed. I supposed that he was Madame's partner."

"Were you the only man who waited on him?"

"For the last four months or six months, yes, sir. He made it his request to Madame and to me that I should bring him everything he ordered."

"Did he tell you why?"

"Yes, he said to me that I was to carry his glass of wine or his cup of coffee very carefully. 'See that you do not spill it, and see that nothing is spilled into it by the way'—those were his words, sir, as nearly as I can recollect."

"What did you think when he said that?"

Gerard's expressive hands mutely protested that it was not their business to think.

"I do what I am ordered to do, sir, without thinking too much. But Monsieur Wilson himself explained his motive to me. He said, 'I do not like to have practical jokes played on me, and I fancy there are some practical jokers in the *cercle*.'"

"Did he say *cercle* or club?"

"Monsieur, he always spoke to me in French. He had spent much time in Paris, he told me once. I believe—" Gerard interrupted himself, as though doubtful whether his belief would be acceptable as evidence. It struck me that he had been a witness in a court of law at some time or other.

Tarleton threw him a friendly nod. "Go on; tell me what you believe."

"I think," Gerard corrected himself, "that perhaps Monsieur Wilson founded this club in order to escape the necessity for going to Paris to amuse himself."

The examiner moved his head doubtfully.

"You think he had some business, then, which made it necessary for him to remain in London."

"But I am sure of it!" The waiter's tone became confident. "Business that assisted him in establishing the club, even. The great people who came here were his customers rather than his personal friends; such is my idea."

Tarleton turned an approving face to us.

"I think that this man knows what he is talking about. We are dealing with something very daring and very dark. Did you ever guess what the business was?"

The question was darted out suddenly. But the little Frenchman manifested no uneasiness. The doctor's praise seemed to have given him confidence.

"I supposed sometimes that it was not a lawful business, sir." He lowered his voice a little and glanced behind him as if to make sure that his employer was not within hearing. "I fancied that Monsieur Wilson might be the proprietor of an establishment for the reception of ladies who did not wish to become mothers."

I could not resist a slight shudder as the gruesome hint came glibly from the lips of the pasty-faced waiter. He did not look the kind of man who would have made any objection to a post in such an establishment.

"Some of the ladies whom he introduced here had the air of being afraid of him, I thought," Gerard added by way of confirmation.

Inspector Charles had begun to take notes of this evidence. He now straightened himself up, and looked at Tarleton.

"Wouldn't it be well to search his clothes, Sir Frank? We might find an address, perhaps?"

"In another minute. Is there any question you would like to put, Cassilis?"

I had to make a call on my courage, as Gerard faced towards me in readiness to be addressed. His figure was not less familiar to me than that of the masked Inquisitor had been. I was now to see whether my voice would sound familiar to him. I dared not modify my usual tone with Tarleton's keen ears listening.

"We have heard that a royal personage was here last night," I said slowly and distinctly, and then paused to note the effect.

At my first words Gerard's watery eyes grew wider for an instant and I feared the worst. Some note must have been struck in the echoing cells of his memory. But the next moment reassured me. Out of the many hundred voices with which a waiter's memory must be stored, how should he be able to identify one which he had heard say scarcely a dozen words? The man's face was a perfect blank again before I went on.

"Can you tell us if there were any other strangers present?" I asked boldly. And turning to my chief and the Inspector, I explained, "It seems to me just possible that an attempt may have been planned on the life of the Crown Prince, and that this man may have been mistaken for him."

Tarleton did not reject this suggestion so decidedly as the theory of suicide. I saw a thoughtful expression come on his face, as though he was engaged in trying to adjust the idea with another one previously in his mind. Captain Charles took up the scent quite eagerly.

"Do you know what disguise His Royal Highness was wearing?" he demanded.

The waiter hesitated and then shook his head.

"I had my suspicion, sir, but Madame can tell you for certain."

The Inspector was satisfied with the answer. But Tarleton's voice rang out sharply.

"Let us have your suspicion, please."

Gerard had the air of a man who had committed himself, and regrets it.

"Milor,"—he had been sharp enough to notice the Inspector's use of a title in addressing the consultant—"I particularly noticed one person who appeared to me a stranger who did not very well know his way about the club, and who appeared to have some business with Monsieur Wilson."

"Ah!" Tarleton's deep breath told me that he felt himself on a real trail. "And how was this person disguised?"

"The disguise was an extraordinary one, milor. It was that which first attracted my notice. It was at once the costume of a man and of a woman. That is to say, the upper part was that of a warrior in armour, and the lower part was a woman's skirt."

"Joan of Arc," exclaimed Charles.

The Frenchman shrank in horror. "But, monsieur, it could not have been Sainte Jeanne! For instance, the helmet was Roman."

"Neither did she wear a skirt with her armour," the physician added quietly. "It must have been meant for Zenobia."

The Inspector's face showed so clearly that he had never heard of the famous Queen of Palmyra that I should have been amused if I had not been on the rack of suspense. Fortunately, Tarleton was now engrossed in his new line of inquiry.

"In spite of this feminine disguise, in spite of the skirt, you recognized that this stranger was a man, it seems?"

The eloquent hands protested again. "But no, milor; I said I had my suspicion, that is all. Madame—"

The doctor cut him short.

"You thought this person, Zenobia, had some business with Wilson. Tell me, how many persons knew that Wilson wore that disguise last night?"

He turned and pointed to the dead body which lay full in view from where we were seated. Gerard let his eyes follow the gesture and withdrew them with a sickly twinge.

"Everyone knew it, I think. It was the disguise he wore invariably in the club. It was as if he came here to meet his clients, and it was necessary for them to know that they were speaking to him."

Sir Frank Tarleton nodded more than once this time. He evidently felt himself to be getting a firm grip on the problem. I admired the sagacity he had shown in transferring his examination from the proprietress of the club to the waiter. Gerard was proving a much easier witness to deal with than Madame Bonnell. He had not so much at stake.

"And now," the consultant pursued, "perhaps you can tell us if there were any other persons who showed a desire to meet Wilson last night?"

Gerard brightened up visibly.

"But certainly, milor. There was one in particular who never seemed to take her eyes off him. She danced with him time after time, and when she was not dancing with him herself she watched those who did."

"And how was she dressed?"

"Milor, she was hardly dressed at all." Gerard may have feared another irreverent guess from Captain Charles, for he added quickly: "I heard Monsieur address her as Salome."

The Inspector was again busy with his note-book. But Sir Frank struck me as not being quite so deeply interested in Salome as he had been in Zenobia.

"And there was also a lady whose costume it is not easy to describe." Gerard was going on of his own accord now, as though his interest had been kindled in the inquiry. "Part of it was a leopard skin. And she wore a necklace composed of claws of the same beast, as I imagined. In my own mind I called her the Leopardess. Without doubt, her costume was that of an East Indian princess."

Tarleton's interest seemed to revive again at the description of the Leopardess. Yet it was impossible to be sure that he was not playing a part to conceal his true opinion of all this from the witness.

"And this lady, did she dance much with Wilson?"

Gerard gave his head an emphatic shake.

"She did not dance with him at all, although he asked her more than once. I am sure of it. I was surprised, for it was not often that he was refused. I saw him speaking to her very earnestly, even threateningly, but it was no use. And she left early, long before the dance was over."

The examiner shrugged his shoulders. I wondered that he did not point out to the man that a woman who had left early could hardly have played any part in the tragedy. But I was beginning to grasp that it was his method to listen much and speak little when he was face to face with a mystery.

The next moment he had dismissed Gerard abruptly, and risen to his feet. He crossed over to the corpse, followed by Charles and myself, and gazed intently on the exposed face. The slight leaden tinge I had remarked was more noticeable already, and in addition there was a slight roughness of the skin which I understood still less. I took care this time not to make any remark on it.

The specialist's attention was concentrated on the features and expression of the dead man. After a moment or two he slowly shook his head.

"No," he pronounced, "that is not the face of a man degraded enough for such a business as the waiter supposed. It is not the face of an adventurer. This was a man of the world, in a good position, able to meet with the people whom he brought to this place on a footing of equality. His motives were not sordid, perhaps, in the first place. We are dealing with a Tiberius rather than a Tigellinus, I think."

I don't fancy those names had much more meaning for Captain Charles than Zenobia's. But he acquiesced respectfully in the judgment.

"From all that we have heard about the Domino Club at Scotland Yard there has never been the slightest suggestion of crime about it," he observed. "One of the judges of the High Court is a member of it. He has the reputation of being pretty fond of women, but he certainly wouldn't be mixed up with anything shady."

"Shaded, but not shady, eh?" Tarleton returned with a curl of the lip. "But come, it is time to see if the dead has any evidence to give about himself."

Thrusting his gold repeater carelessly into his pocket, he deftly stripped the body of its long Inquisitor's robe. Underneath was revealed an evening suit of fine material and faultless cut with a white silk waistcoat and soft-fronted shirt. They were the clothes of a man of good position, as Sir Frank had said, and a man accustomed to respect himself. A Bohemian would scarcely have troubled to dress himself so carefully beneath a domino.

Captain Charles viewed this correct attire with the approval of a military man. "A gentleman as you guessed, Sir Frank."

"As I inferred," the doctor responded sharply, "I never guess." His capable fingers were already exploring the pockets of the corpse. Most of them seemed to be empty, but presently he extracted a silver matchbox from the waistcoat, and opened it. A low sound like a suppressed whistle came from his tight lips as he shook out on the palm of his hand two pellets the size of small peas.

Of all my experiences on that eventful night, or rather morning, this was the most amazing. Only by a strong effort was I able to keep my astonishment within due bounds. Although I had thrown out the suggestion of suicide, the last thing I had expected was to find poison on the dead man's person.

My chief passed me one of the pellets, and put the other first to his nostrils and then to the tip of his tongue.

"Well?" He motioned to me to imitate his action.

There could be no doubt about the result of the test. "Opium in a highly concentrated form, and soluble," I whispered hoarsely.

We exchanged looks of intense surprise. The Inspector on his part was evidently surprised by our attitude.

"Then Dr. Cassilis was right after all," he said, staring at us. "It was suicide?"

The great consultant smiled at him indulgently.

"I am sure that this discovery has made Dr. Cassilis renounce that theory," he answered. "A man who was accustomed to take opium in such doses as these would have to take a terrible quantity to kill himself. And this box, is nearly full."

My brain was buzzing while he spoke. Utter darkness seemed to be settling down on my mind. I gazed at my chief in stupefaction greater than the Inspector's.

"The problem for Dr. Cassilis and myself is this," he continued, addressing his explanation to Captain Charles, although I realized that he was speaking at least as much for my benefit. "The corpse shows all the usual symptoms of poisoning by opium. But if the deceased had accustomed his system to opium it is not easy to understand how anyone could have given him enough to produce death. The dose must have been enormous, and he must have detected the taste at once in any ordinary medium such as a cup of coffee."

I just managed to nod my head with assent.

"The inference I am inclined to draw at the moment," the specialist concluded, "is that Wilson was not a taker of the drug and that these pellets were not intended for himself. I think it is more probable that he carried them as weapons of self-defense. Perhaps Salome would have been given one last night if her jealousy had carried her too far, perhaps Zenobia. And perhaps the Leopardess left so early because she had been given one."

My brain seemed to resume its normal clearness as the doctor spoke. There was really nothing very extraordinary in the coincidence, if he was right. After all, opium was the drug which it was natural for anyone to use in such circumstances. It was practically tasteless, its effects were easily mistaken for those of alcohol even by the victim, till it was too late for him to resist them. And the character of the Domino Club was such, and its members came to it in such secrecy, that one of them might be carried home in a narcotic sleep, and die before wakening from it, without his death ever being traced to the place where he had been.

While these reflections were coming to compose my mind Tarleton was renewing his investigation of the dead man's pockets. This time the result was negative, so far as I could see. It gave a start to me and to the Inspector when the doctor suddenly raised himself with a look of triumph and exclaimed, "I see it!"

Charles bent forward with a bewildered gaze. I held my breath. The next sentence was decisive.

"There are no keys—not even a latchkey. Whoever drugged him took his keys, and took them for a purpose." He turned on the startled Inspector, and issued his commands like a general on a battlefield ordering an advance all along the line. "Ring up your people and find out if they have received a report of any house being entered during the night or early this morning. And ask them to send a man round the theatrical costumiers to find out if any of them have supplied costumes lately of a Zenobia and a Salome and an Eastern one with a leopard skin. Though I doubt if you will hear anything about the last. It sounds like one made up privately. Meanwhile we will ask Madame Bonnell to give us some breakfast."

Madame was charmed to give us breakfast. Gerard's report of his examination must have impressed her favourably. It was clear by this time that the great Sir Frank Tarleton could be trusted to conduct the investigation with prudence, and not to bring any unnecessary publicity on the Domino Club. She beamed satisfaction when he informed her that he hoped to learn Wilson's address within the next few minutes, and to have the body removed thither for the inquest. In her absence he added to his instructions to Charles:

"I think, Captain Charles that it will be well if you can go yourself to the Foreign Office and ascertain through them if this Crown Prince actually was present last night. They will feel more confidence in you than in one of the ordinary police."

The Honourable Captain looked pleased. "Do you think it is possible that his life was aimed at, after all, Sir Frank?" he added with deference.

Sir Frank shook his head. "That possibility is disposed of by the abstraction of the keys. The solution of the mystery lies there. But it is just possible that the thief chose his occasion; that he relied on the Prince's presence to screen him from too close an inquiry. At all events I find it difficult to accept too many coincidences in the case."

I thought I might venture to raise a different point.

"Madame Bonnell had ample time to search the body and remove anything she pleased before Captain Charles came."

My chief shook his head good-naturedly.

"I haven't too high an opinion of Madame's ethical code, but I think sufficiently well of her intelligence to feel pretty sure that if she had had any use for her partner's keys they would have been back in his pocket before Captain Charles heard that he was dead."

The remark was unanswerable as far as I was concerned. A moment later the expected message came through from Scotland Yard.

The house of Doctor Weathered, of Warwick Street, Cavendish Square, had been entered during the night, and his safe had been found open, with his bunch of keys in it. And the doctor himself was missing.

CHAPTER 4

THE OPENED SAFE

Inspector Charles, I could see, was deeply impressed by the sagacity with which Tarleton had solved the riddle of the dead man's identity. It was a very simple step, but it is precisely the simple ideas that generally escape the trained mind of the official.

"Doctor Weathered," the Captain pronounced slowly. "I suppose there is no doubt of that being Wilson's real name."

"Very little doubt, I should say," my chief responded. "What do you think, Cassilis?"

I endeavoured to take a judicial tone.

"I don't see much room for hesitation. Here is a man without his keys, and there are the keys without the man. Besides, it all corresponds with what you said, Sir Frank, about the dead man's appearance. A fashionable West End physician is just what I should expect him to be. And no one would be in a better position to introduce people of good position to a club of this kind."

The Inspector's face had become overcast with doubt while I was speaking.

"That's all very well," he demurred, "but we have been hearing a lot about Wilson's being afraid of enemies, and taking precautions about what he drank; and now it turns out to be a simple case of burglary."

Tarleton consulted me by a look. I just lifted my shoulders in answer without speaking. Mine was a difficult part to play just then. On the one hand, I did not wish my chief to think me wanting in brains; on the other, I dreaded above all things betraying any previous knowledge of anything connected with the mystery.

Fortunately he appeared to approve of my reserve. "We may be able to understand that better when we get to Warwick Street," he said to Charles. "The next thing for us to do is to go round there and send some member of the household here to identify the deceased."

To this course there could be no opposition. The plain-clothes man was called in and placed in charge of the corpse with strict instructions to let no one approach it unless he came with a written authority from Sir Frank or the Inspector. Then the three of us entered the doctor's car and drove towards Cavendish Square.

On the way my chief said to me, "It is curious that I can't call to mind ever having heard of a Dr. Weathered. He must have been a man of high standing in the profession, apparently; probably a consultant; and yet his name is quite strange to me. Do you happen to have heard it at any time?"

It was a difficult question for me. I dared not tell a lie which accident might expose at any moment; but still less dared I tell the whole truth.

"I have heard the name," I replied, speaking as slowly as possible to give myself time to frame the least compromising answer. "Perhaps I ought to say that I heard it from one of his patients in the course of a confidential communication, so that I hardly know how far I am justified in making any use of what I heard."

Tarleton promptly raised his hand.

"Not another word," he enjoined to my intense relief. But my relief was qualified when he proceeded. "A confidence made to a medical man is as sacred in my view as a confession made to a priest. You will understand that, Captain Charles, I am sure. We must not ask Dr. Cassilis to tell us anything more."

Captain Charles assented rather reluctantly I thought. His original disapproval of me seemed to revive at the same time. He stole furtive glances at me now and then, as though he were wondering whether it was prudent on his part to keep such doubtful company.

The gold repeater in Tarleton's fingers kept time to his meditations till the car drew up in front of a smart house in a smart street in the region most favoured by Court physicians and the big-wigs of the medical profession, a class for whom I knew that my eccentric chief felt a very moderate respect. The house was brightly painted, and the windows were garnished with boxes of scarlet geraniums and blue lobelias. The brass plate on the door was burnished to shine like glass, and the steps were a dazzling white. Nothing could have been further removed from any suggestion of secret practices or unhallowed consultations.

The man who opened the door to us matched the exterior of the house as far as his own exterior was concerned. He was young and clean-shaven, his hair was beautifully brushed, and his neat clothes were as new and well-fitting as those of the man whom we had left lying in the alcove at the Domino Club. The face itself was that of a simple, harmless young man, incapable of suspecting either his master or his master's patients. It was impossible to think that he had ever been aware of anything strange or doubtful in his environment, so innocent and fresh was his whole aspect.

The very nervousness with which he received us was the nervousness of youth and inexperience finding itself in the presence of unexpected trouble.

Inspector Charles briefly announced his name and official character, and those of my chief, not deeming me worthy of individual mention. Tarleton promptly took the youthful butler in hand.

"Have the police been here before?" was his first question.

Simmons, as he turned out to be named, said that they had. The constable on the beat had noticed that the front door was ajar about five o'clock that morning, and had promptly roused the household. He, Simmons, had been first on the spot, and had begun by supposing that his master had omitted to make the door fast on his return. He knew that the doctor had gone out overnight, though he had no idea where. He went out pretty often, and was generally rather late in coming home. However, the policeman had insisted on his going to see if Dr. Weathered was upstairs; and he had found his room empty and the bed undisturbed.

On that, the officer had come in to search the premises, beginning with the doctor's consulting-room, in which there was a safe. There the first sight that met their eyes was the door of the safe standing wide open. The key was in the keyhole, with the whole bunch, including the latchkey, dangling from it.

"And what had been taken from the safe?" Tarleton asked, calling my attention with a significant glance.

"Nothing," was the surprising answer. "I mean nothing as far as we could see. We opened the drawers in which the doctor used to put his fees till he paid them into the bank, and they were full, one full of notes and the other of silver. The doctor's lowest fee was three guineas," the doctor's man added with some pride.

"Take us to that room," my chief commanded.

Simmons obeyed without hesitation. My heart was beating so loudly in my ears that I could not overcome the childish fear that it might be heard by others, in spite of my medical knowledge to the contrary. I fell back and let my companions go into the room without me while I collected myself before joining them.

Yet there was nothing in Dr. Weathered's professional sanctum to inspire dismay.

The room in which he received his patients was as bright and as well appointed as everything else in the establishment. A handsome walnut writing-table was lightly strewn with medical books and papers, relieved by a handsome china bowl full of roses. The patient's chair was luxuriously cushioned with yellow silk, and the doctor's own chair was a handsome one upholstered in tooled morocco leather. There was only one bookcase, and its appearance was more suited to a drawing-room than a professional man's study. The frame was richly inlaid with ornamental woods, and the glass doors were protected by gilt wires. A small marble group of Eros and Psyche stood on the top, flanked by Chinese dragons. Elsewhere the walls of the room were hung with charming water-colours, most of them of a rather sensuous description, depicting youths and maidens bathing in pools, and scenes of love and jealousy.

Tarleton took in every detail with one of those swift, searching looks of his which seemed to penetrate to some inner meaning beneath the surface of all he saw. Finally, his eye rested on the corner in which a safe about three feet high, painted to look like oxydized silver, was clamped on a supporting stand of ebony.

"You have locked the safe, I see. Where are the keys?"

The sudden demand agitated the nervous butler.

"Miss Sarah has them," he stuttered. "At least she took them away when she locked up the safe. Perhaps she's given them to her mother—to Mrs. Weathered."

Sir Frank opened his eyes. I think we all did. Somehow it seemed incongruous that the founder of the Domino Club should be a married man.

"Is there a Mrs. Weathered then?"

"Why, yes, sir." Simmons showed as much surprise as we had. "Would you like to see her, Sir Frank?" He seemed rather eager to get away and fetch his mistress to deal with us.

The consultant restrained him by an imperative gesture.

"One moment, if you please. You haven't told us what happened after you had found the safe open. Did you go to call Mrs. Weathered?"

"I should have gone, sir, but Miss Sarah came down and found us looking into the safe. So I left it to her."

Again the man made a movement as if to escape, and again the specialist arrested him.

"What brought her down? Did she know what had happened?"

Simmons seemed honestly confused. "I really can't tell you, sir. I suppose one of the servants must have gone upstairs and told her. They were all about."

Tarleton nodded. "Go on. When she came in what did she do?"

"She was rather angry sir, at first. She thought the doctor had come home in a great hurry to fetch something for someone who was ill, and had rushed off again, and forgotten to lock the safe and take his keys. She said we had no business to look inside in his absence. And she locked the safe herself, and sent the policeman away, saying no doubt Dr. Weathered would be back again presently. But that was more than four hours ago, and there's been no sign of him yet, sir."

It was evident that Simmons considered his young mistress had been over-confident. We, who knew it so much better than he did could only sympathize with his feelings. Sir Frank made no further effort to detain him.

"Very well. You can let Mrs. Weathered know we are here, and say that I shall be glad to speak with her as soon as possible."

When the butler had gone he turned to me.

"What do you make of this room, Cassilis? What sort of diseases do you think were treated here?"

I thought it best to glance at the pictures and the marble group before expressing my opinion.

"Not very serious ones I should say," I answered lightly.

My chief frowned.

"And yet one of them has proved pretty serious in its consequences," he observed. "You don't agree with Miss Weathered that it was her father who left that bunch of keys in the door of the open safe?"

I did my best to control myself as I shook my head.

"Rather curious that she should have interfered, though, instead of her mother," Captain Charles put in with an air of sagacity.

Tarleton threw himself into the doctor's own chair, and taking out his watch, began to swing it gently.

"I expect to meet with more than one curious circumstance in the course of this inquiry," he said lazily. "It is just possible that Weathered's daughter knew more about him than his wife did." He sat up suddenly. "But I am wasting your valuable time, Captain Charles. There is nothing here that Cassilis and I cannot deal with. It is simply a question of having the body identified, and brought round here, if the authorities decide to keep the case private. You had better lose no time in communicating with the Foreign Office and the Home Office, and letting me know their decision. And don't forget there are the costumes to be traced."

The Captain was already on the move. I fancied he was not sorry to be released. Tarleton was too big a personality for anyone else to find himself much more than a dummy in his company, and the Inspector's sense of self-importance must have suffered as long as he was in the physician's train.

My chief was good enough to offer me a private explanation as soon as we were alone.

"I have every confidence in Charles's honesty, but very little in his tact. And this is a case that calls for very careful handling. These people won't tell us more than they can help if they are afraid of a public scandal. And, on the other hand, if they know that the whole affair is going to be hushed up they won't tell us anything at all." Tarleton let his eyes rove round the walls of the room as he proceeded. "I don't want Charles to see the direction in which I am feeling my way. You see, he is not my subordinate. He isn't responsible to me for his actions. He is quite at liberty to go to the Chief Commissioner behind my back, and tell him whatever is in his mind, and the Commissioner can go to Sir James Ponsonby in the same way. We must walk warily Cassilis."

I tried in vain to catch the doctor's eye while he was speaking. How much did he mean to convey by that singular warning? Was he referring to my admission that I had heard Dr. Weathered's name before, and cautioning me to make no more such admissions in the Inspector's hearing? I felt a sick apprehension which I dared not show.

Sir Frank seemed quite unconscious of my distress. "You and I," he went on in a confidential way, "know that it wasn't Weathered who crept into this room last night, and crept out again, leaving the keys behind. And we also know that whoever came here didn't come for money. I think we can both guess what he did come for—he or she."

He darted a sudden glance at me as he uttered the last word, and he must have seen me start. But at that instant the door opened, and we both rose to our feet to receive the ladies coming in.

There were two of them. Mrs. Weathered was a woman of about the same age as the man whom we had left lying in the Domino Club, but of a very different social type. She was not vulgar in any offensive sense of the word, but her appearance and manner were those of a woman such as one would expect to meet in the back parlour of a shop in a provincial town, rather than in a West End drawing-room. Her features were plain as well as homely; her gray hair showed no trace of a skilful maid's art, and her fashionable dress only exposed her unfitness to wear it. Such a wife could only be a serious handicap to an ambitious man making his way upward in London society. It was possible to at least understand one of the doctor's temptations to lead a secret life which brought him into more congenial company than his homely wife's. Yet there was something touching in her pale, worn face; and her mild blue eyes searched our faces with a pitiful anxiety that convinced me that her husband still had a hold on her affection.

Her daughter was as little like her as it was possible to be. Young enough in years—I put her down as little more than twenty—her face and figure were those of a ripe woman. Both were queenly. Her sombre crown of hair and flashing eyes made me think of Judith and the tragic heroines of old who were driven to avenge themselves on the men who had done them wrong. She betrayed none of her mother's anxiety. Stern, self-possessed and courageous, she faced Sir Frank and myself with the demeanour of the accuser rather than the accused.

Mrs. Weathered was the first to speak. Although addressing my chief as the elder of us two, I found her turning her eyes towards me as though more hopeful of sympathy from my youth. Her daughter on the contrary kept her intent gaze fixed on Tarleton and seemed barely conscious of my presence in the room.

"Have you any news for me, sir? Dr. Weathered hasn't come back yet—not since he was here in the early morning, and left his keys behind."

The physician shook his head with a grave air.

"I am not sure that you are right in thinking that it was your husband who came here and left those keys. Before I say anything more I should like to look inside the safe."

Mrs. Weathered turned a wondering look on her daughter, who frowned in return.

"Why?" She demanded. "Nothing has been taken. I looked myself, and the money was all there untouched. No burglar would have gone away without helping himself to it, surely?"

"Perhaps it was not a burglar. It was someone who had been in your father's company, or he could not have obtained possession of his bunch of keys."

The girl drew herself up in wrath.

"Dr. Weathered is not my father sir. My mother has only been married to him five years. My name is Neobard."

A glimmering of the true situation came to me. The dead man had married a widow, an unattractive one, with a daughter old enough to resent her mother's action and show it. There could be no reasonable doubt that she must have had money, probably a good deal, and that her daughter's fortune had gone to enrich the step-father. I could pretty well guess the whole story. A provincial doctor with more brains than wealth had courted his rich patient to obtain the means of coming to London and setting up as a consultant in the West End. That was why neither Tarleton nor I had heard of him as a man distinguished in the profession. He had risen, not by scientific merit, but by the possession of money and an imposing manner. There were too many such cases in the medical world.

By this time Mrs. Weathered had sat down and invited us to do the same. But Miss Neobard remained standing, still with the same air of suppressed indignation. Tarleton appeared not to be aware of anything strange in her manner.

"Your step-father, then," he corrected himself amiably. "Dr. Cassilis and I are better acquainted with the usual contents of a doctor's safe than you are, I expect; and perhaps we shall be better able to judge if anything has been taken than you."

"I don't think he kept any drugs in it, if that's what you're thinking of," the girl said obstinately. It was clear that she resented our being there and was disposed to help us as little as possible.

"Indeed!" The specialist turned to Mrs. Weathered, whose face showed some bewilderment at her daughter's attitude. "Perhaps you can tell me, ma'am, if your husband specialized in any particular disease, or class of diseases."

The pale widow glanced at her daughter as though for permission to answer, and was met by a smile of scorn.

"I know that he takes nervous cases," Mrs. Weathered said with a certain hesitation. "He is a psychological expert."

She pronounced the phrase in the tone of a person who had learnt it by heart, and expected us to understand it better than she did herself. Miss Neobard's gall overflowed at the sound.

"He called himself that to begin with," she put in sharply. "Now it is a psychical analyst. Women come and tell him their secrets as if he were a priest."

A quiver in the eyelashes told me that this was the information my chief had been expecting to receive. But his tone showed no animation when he spoke.

"In that case I dare say Miss Neobard may be right about the drugs. However, I must ask you to be good enough to let me have Dr. Weathered's keys."

The mother was evidently divided between fear of us and fear of her daughter to whom she appealed with another helpless look.

"By what right do you ask for them, Sir Frank? My mother is not entitled to give up her husband's keys without his consent. He may be back at any moment—and then you can ask him."

At last it was necessary to speak out. The girl's position was perfectly right if she was ignorant of her step-father's fate.

"I am deeply sorry to be the bearer of bad news," Tarleton said to the widow. "I'm afraid you must prepare yourself to hear the worst." He paused for a moment. The ready tears that began to stream from the poor woman's eyes showed that she had not been altogether unprepared, and the swift flash of silent exultation in her daughter's told plainly who it was that had prepared her. I was pleased to see her throw a caressing arm round her mother's neck before she spoke again.

"You mean that Dr. Weathered is dead?"

"A body has been found on certain premises in Chelsea which there is reason to fear is his. It is part of our business here to find someone to come round and identify him."

A moan from the widow drew her daughter's arm more tightly round her. She thrust her free hand into a pocket and drew out a bunch of keys.

"Take these. And excuse me. I must take my mother to her room. I will come back in a few minutes and go round with you to the Club."

I was quick to open the door as the strange girl supported her mother out of the room. I had no sooner closed it again than my chief repeated her last words.

"The Club!—I fancy that young woman could tell us a good deal about her step-father if she chose. And now!"

He stepped towards the safe, found the right key, and threw open the door.

"What do you say has been taken, Cassilis?"

There could be no doubt as to the answer, although I went through the form of looking carefully inside before I gave it.

It was the doctor's case-book that was missing, the book containing the secrets of the women.

CHAPTER 5

DR. WEATHERED'S PATIENTS

My chief made a swift search through the safe. The cash drawers were empty, and he gave me a significant nod.

"Miss Sarah has been through the safe since the policeman left. A remarkable girl that, Cassilis! How did she come to know of the Domino Club?"

I was as little able to answer the question as he was. Still, I had formed a vague theory in my own mind.

"She rather gave me the impression of hating her step-father on her mother's account," I threw out. "Mightn't she have watched him on her mother's behalf?"

"That is a possible explanation, certainly," my chief was good enough to respond. "We are dealing with one of those family tragedies which so seldom come to light. The ambitious man has married for money, as the girl has seen from the first, and the woman won't see. Then he has found his wife in the way, and begun to neglect her. She, poor thing, has tried to hide the situation from her child, but Sarah has found it out for herself, and resented it. She has tried to open her mother's eyes, and failed; or rather the mother has concealed the fact that she is no longer blind. Then in desperation, perhaps, the girl has gone secretly to work to obtain proof of her step-father's infidelity, proof that will leave her mother no excuse for keeping her eyes shut any longer; that will compel her to leave the man...."

The speech trailed off into a soliloquy, which became a silent one. Suddenly he stood up grasping in his hand a square glass bottle half full of pellets like those we had found on the corpse.

"No need for further evidence of identity than this!" he exclaimed in triumph. "But this must be between you and me, Cassilis; I don't think Charles can have been altogether satisfied with the theory that Weathered only carried these pellets to give to his enemies and this discovery makes it still less probable. He may have administered them for other purposes."

I shuddered at the hint. The Domino Club took on a darker shade in my imagination and I scarcely dared ask myself what horrors might have been concealed by those embroidered curtains that screened its Moorish alcoves.

Tarleton slipped the glass bottle into his coat pocket, and locked the safe. Then he turned to survey the doctor's table.

"Now let us reconstruct the crime provisionally," he said. "A patient of Weathered finds that he is in the doctor's power and finds that Weathered is disposed to take some base advantage of him. He has seen the doctor recording his confession in a book, and he determines to release himself by getting hold of that book and destroying it. He is a member of the Domino Club; most likely he has been tempted or compelled to join it by Weathered. He may or may not know of these pellets and the purpose for which they are used. At all events he conceives the plan of drugging Weathered, obtaining his keys, and coming here to destroy the incriminating record. He carries out his purpose successfully, so far. But in his haste and excitement he overlooks one thing. And it is here."

For the life of me I could not repress a start as the consultant brought his hand down sharply on a small book that lay beside the inkstand on the writing-table. Little need to say what it was! The moment after Weathered's appointment-book was lying open, and my chief's keen eyes were rapidly searching the pages.

I ought not to have felt so intensely anxious as I watched those bushy eyebrows knitting themselves over a meagre list of names and dates. The dead man's patients had been numerous, and most of them no doubt had come and gone without the least suspicion of anything irregular in the doctor's practice, and without compromising themselves by any indiscrete confidences. What evidence could such a book afford against anyone? Still, I was uneasy. My instinct warned me that Tarleton would find some information that he needed in those pages. And my observation told me presently that he had found it.

"Listen, Cassilis. Most of these appointments seem to be perfectly innocent and normal. But there are certain names occurring more than once that have numbers attached to them. What do you make of this?—Sir George Castleton, 17; he has been coming once a fortnight. Mrs. Worboise, 21; about once a month. Miss Julia Sebright, 8; she seems to have dropped off. Colonel Gravelinas, 26; h'm. Mrs. Baker, 35; rather more recent than the others. Lady Violet Bredwardine—what is the matter?"

I jerked myself round towards the door of the room. "I thought I heard someone outside."

By a stroke of good luck someone was. The door opened as I spoke, and Sarah Neobard appeared with a hat on ready to go out.

Tarleton quietly closed the book and placed it in his pocket under her eyes.

"I am taking Dr. Weathered's appointment-book, Miss Neobard. I shall have to make inquiries about some of his patients."

The stately Sarah's eyes flashed vindictively. "You are welcome to any information I can give you about them, Sir Frank. One of them is at the bottom of this crime, you may be sure."

Tarleton lifted his eyebrows. "We don't yet know that it is a crime—in that sense," he said with an air of doubt. "Dr. Weathered seems to have been drugged by someone who wanted to get his keys. But whoever did it may not have meant to give a fatal dose."

I listened anxiously. I was puzzled to understand the specialist's theory. Did he consider that Weathered had succumbed to a dose that would not have killed a man in ordinary health? And if so, was his death due to some organic weakness, as I had myself suggested when we were viewing the corpse? Or was it possible that Weathered was in the habit of taking the pellets found upon him, after all, and that he had just absorbed such a quantity of the poison into his system that the extra dose proved mortal in consequence? My experience was not enough to enable me to form a decided opinion of my own on either of these alternatives.

While these thoughts were passing through my mind Miss Neobard was scrutinizing my companion's face with suspicion.

"You are not saying what you really think, Sir Frank," she pronounced boldly. "He has been murdered, and you know it, but you are afraid of shocking me by saying so outright. You needn't mind. I look on this as a judgment, and I have seen it coming."

The physician gazed at her as steadily as she was gazing at him.

"Have you any objection to telling me why?"

"No. Now that my mother isn't here I don't care what I tell you. Dr. Weathered never loved her, but she loved him. She wouldn't believe anything bad of him while he was alive, and now he's dead I don't want her to hear anything that would grieve her for nothing." She seemed to consider for a moment what to say next. "You mustn't think he was altogether wicked, at all events at first. He was very clever, and he knew that he could do well in London with my mother's money. And he was really interested in science. He had studied psychology for years before he started as a nerve specialist. I believe that he meant to practise quite respectably when he began here. It was the women who led him astray."

A singular statement to be made by the step-daughter who had so much reason to hate him, and who every now and then gave me the impression that she had hated him.

"Half the women who came to consult him, I believe, had nothing the matter with them except a craving for excitement. He told us that himself, though, of course, he didn't say what kind of excitement they craved for. He used to talk about his practice at first, and tell us the names of some of his patients, when they were big people. One was a duchess, another was a famous author. But after a time he stopped talking about them. That was when he began to fall under their influence. They sent him invitations to dinner without inviting my mother. And he accepted them."

One could see, as it were, the rift opening, and this keen-eyed, strong-minded girl taking precocious notice of everything and watching her step-father's downward progress.

"Then he took up with this psycho-analysis, pretending he could cure people of their troubles and change their dispositions by encouraging them to talk to him freely. I knew he didn't really believe in it. He had sneered at it often enough when it first came up. He took to it simply because it was the way to make money. I fancy the other doctors looked down on him because of it. At all events they seemed to boycott him. None of them ever came here, and their wives left off calling on us. I soon saw there was something wrong.

"I tried to get my mother to do something, but she wouldn't or couldn't. She had no influence over him apart from her money, and he was making so much that he was independent of her. And she wouldn't leave him. She had no legal grounds, of course. Whatever went on was carefully concealed from her. He couldn't have afforded an open rupture. That would have frightened off his patients."

Sarah paused for breath, and my chief and I exchanged looks. It was a curious revelation, and the strangest part of it was the manner in which it was being made. The accuser seemed to be also the defender. There was a very thoughtful wrinkle on Tarleton's brow, as though he was listening to more than the words that reached his ear.

All this time there had been no reference to the Domino Club. I think we were both rather eager to learn something about that. But Miss Neobard didn't appear to need prompting. She came to the subject of her own accord.

"At last we almost ceased to see anything of him. He went out night after night, and didn't come home till the early morning. He was a strong man, but his health began to suffer, and I think he was taking to drink latterly. At one time he kept nothing in the house, but lately there was brandy in a cupboard, and I have seen him going to it in the morning as soon as he came down. This was after he had gone to that abominable club."

"The Domino Club?" my chief put in quietly.

"Yes, I dare say you wonder how I came to know of it. Perhaps you think I oughtn't to have taken any notice of what was going on. It was my mother's business, really, but she was determined to see nothing, and I had to protect her."

The explanation was given with a touch of defiance. Was it the true one? Was it solely zeal on her mother's behalf that had inspired the girl of nineteen or twenty to play the part of a detective? Or had other motives mingled with the avowed one? A touch of feminine curiosity, perhaps? A subtle temptation to look down into the gulf in which the man was disappearing? Or else?…

She saw no need to tell us how she had obtained her knowledge, apparently. I didn't think her the kind of girl to employ an agent. She was quite capable, I felt sure, of searching her step-father's papers, or following him secretly. Her object, as far as we were concerned, was evidently to inculpate his patients even more than himself.

"It was the women," she repeated with bitterness, "who dragged him into it. They wanted a place in which they could have all the excitement of a night club without the risk of meeting low-class people. There was a Mrs. Worboise—" I glanced at my chief as I recalled the No. 21 of the appointment-book, but his lips were firmly compressed—"I feel convinced that she provided some of the money. But there were others, too, plenty of them."

I was thankful that she stopped there without mentioning more names. My chief also seemed to think that she had said enough for the present.

"Very well, Miss Neobard. I am sure that you have acted for the best in giving me this information, and I'm very much obliged to you. Now suppose we drive round to the Club for you to identify the body."

The sight of Evans, the doctor's chauffeur, in front dried up the girl's flow of speech, and the drive was a silent one. Arrived at Vincent Studios I noticed that Tarleton stood back to let the young lady go in front, and that she took her way without hesitation towards the door bearing the name of Loftus, A.R.A. The policeman we had left in charge opened the door to us, and my chief again tested Miss Neobard's knowledge by waiting for her to precede us. But this time the test failed.

"Where is the body?" she asked in a whisper, coming to a stand in the narrow passage.

"This way." Sir Frank gravely took the girl's arm in his own and led her straight to the spot. Whether she quivered as they approached the alcove I could not tell, but there was no mistaking her agitation when she caught sight of the stiff form and pallid face. A stifled cry escaped her lips. She leaned forward impulsively, almost as if she had been going to embrace the corpse, and then straightened herself up with a shudder.

"How dreadful he looks!" she gasped.

There was some excuse for the exclamation, out of place as it seemed at such a moment, and from her lips. The leaden tinge that had struck my attention earlier in the day had deepened and spread over the face and neck, and had become noticeable in the hands as well. The roughness was also accentuated, giving the skin the look of crude parchment in need of scraping before it could be written on. My experience was not enough to tell me whether these were unusual symptoms, and remembering the caution my chief had given me, I was careful to make no remark on them. I watched the great expert's face, but I might as well have watched the dead man's for any information it gave me. He had drawn out his golden mascot, as it were unconsciously, and was swinging it with more than usual deliberation as he scanned the ghastly features with an air of the deepest abstraction.

Sarah Neobard was less successful in hiding her emotions. In spite of the constraint she was evidently putting on herself I detected a tear edging its way down her cheek. Perhaps her memories of the dead were not all bitter ones. Perhaps there had been a time when he had treated her with kindness. Perhaps—but my speculations were cut short by a self-assertive step behind us.

All three of us turned round to see Captain Charles striding down the deserted room. By this time the red lights had been put out. The daylight reached everywhere, and gave the whole place an inexpressibly dreary, discomforting look. The gauze curtains showed bare and shabby, and the cushioned divans and couches revealed wine and coffee stains. The floor was dusty and discoloured. A comparison occurred to me between the dismal scene of revelry and the feelings of the revellers themselves as they awoke next day with jaded nerves and scorched palates and guilty recollections of their orgy.

Captain Charles was bursting with self-importance.

"I have just come from the Foreign Office," he began, when Sir Frank pulled him up rather peremptorily.

"Be good enough to wait a moment, Inspector." He turned to the distressed girl. "You identify this as the body of your step-father, Dr. Weathered?"

She bowed faintly. "Yes—though it is fearfully changed!"

"That is sufficient. Do you feel able to go back by yourself, or would you rather have someone to escort you?"

"I would rather be alone," she murmured.

"Very well; then I need not keep you." He looked away towards the outer door of the room, but the girl stood hesitating.

"Will it—shall you—the body?" she inquired in a broken voice.

"The body must be removed to my house first for me to ascertain the cause of death," Tarleton said kindly. "After that I hope to arrange for it to be buried from your house privately. Meanwhile, the less you say to anyone the better."

She bent her head gratefully, and I took her as far as the door of the studios, and saw her walk away. When I got back the Inspector was in the full flood of his report.

"I have never seen the Foreign Office more upset about anything," he was saying. "And the Slavonian Embassy is in a regular turmoil. It appears that the Ambassador had no idea of where His Royal Highness was last night. He slipped out quietly without saying anything, with the Chancellor of Legation, Baron Novara. Baron Novara is a member of the Domino Club; he has always looked on it as a perfectly reputable place, a fashionable resort—in fact, like Hurlingham or the Prince's skating-rink; and he had no idea that he was risking anything in bringing the Crown Prince here. At least so he says. The Ambassador is furious and has ordered him to go home by tonight's express and explain matters to the King, if he can."

My chief listened to the excited Charles with a good deal of indifference, I thought.

"The sum and substance of it all is that they want the affair hushed up, I suppose?"

I listened for the Inspector's answer with an eagerness which I did my very best to hide. I am not sure that I did hide the relief with which I heard it.

"It *must* be hushed up," he cried with positive indignation. "The Chancellor was fool enough to put in the official circular to the Press of the Crown Prince's movements that he was present at a dance at the Domino Club last night."

"That will be good news for Madame Bonnell," the consultant observed dryly. "Is there any idea at the Embassy that the Prince's life was aimed at?"

Captain Charles glanced round cautiously and lowered his voice.

"That's the worst of it. The Bolsheviks are working their hardest to upset the monarchy in Slavonia, and it is believed that one of their agents in this country obtained admission to the club last night disguised as a woman."

"Zenobia!" I could no more keep in the ejaculation than I could still the beating of my heart as I gave it vent.

My two companions turned sharply and looked at me, the Inspector with a certain grudging respect, my chief with a slight frown of something very like disdain. I bit my tongue too late.

"Zenobia seems to have made a bad guess at the Prince's identity," Tarleton said mercilessly. "Unless His Royal Highness wore an Inquisitor's costume, too?"

The Captain's face fell as he responded to the question.

"I didn't inquire about that, Sir Frank," he admitted. "I'll go round again and find out."

"Do, please. It will be time enough to consider Zenobia's part in the mystery when we have heard from the theatrical costumiers. One moment—" Captain Charles had taken a step towards the exit—"I should like you to wait till I have put a question to Madame Bonnell."

He touched the nearest bell-push as he spoke, and the Inspector and I looked at each other with curiosity as to his purpose. The bell was promptly answered by Gerard, and within a few moments the proprietress of the club sailed into the room.

She was decidedly more at ease than she had been when we interviewed her first. Touches of mourning had been added to her elegant dress, and her whole manner had been toned down to that of a dignified lady in distress. Tarleton appeared to meet this assumption by an added roughness in addressing her.

"Will you be good enough to tell me the rules of the Domino Club as to the admission of visitors?"

Madame Bonnell put her head on one side for a moment, giving herself the air of a person who was considering whether to grant a favour.

"I see no objection to that, Sir Frank. You are Sir Frank Tarleton, are you not?"

The question was almost impudent. The physician ignored it with a sharp "Well?"

"Every member was entitled to one card of admission for a friend for each dance. He was required to enter the name of the friend, and the costume he was coming in, in the club register."

"Let me see the register, please."

Madame had evidently expected this demand. She drew herself up.

"The register is confidential. It contains the names of all the members. I keep it for my private information, and I can't show it to anyone else."

Tarleton turned to the Police Inspector with a shrug. "I must ask you to do your duty, after all, I'm afraid."

The Frenchwoman turned red with excitement.

"But what does this mean? Have you seen the papers?" She produced an evening paper from her dress, one of those evening papers that come out early in the forenoon. "Here it is announced that His Royal Highness the Crown Prince of Slavonia honoured me by his presence here last night. My club is under royal patronage, you see, gentlemen. This is not an affair for the police."

My chief had described Captain Charles as thorough. He showed his quality as soon as the angry woman had spoken. First setting a whistle to his lips, he stepped forward and placed a firm hand on her arm.

"I arrest you in the King's name."

CHAPTER 6

THE BOOKS OF THE DOMINO CLUB

It was at once evident that Sir Frank Tarleton had taken the measure of his opponent accurately. As soon as she felt the police officer's touch Madame Bonnell's confidence deserted her, and she collapsed in a state of mingled panic and bewilderment.

"*Mon Dieu!* But what have I done? What is it that I am accused of?" She looked imploringly from Charles to Tarleton and from him to me.

It was the Inspector who answered.

"Obstructing the officers of the law in the course of their duty is the charge at present. There may be others later on. Meanwhile I have to caution you that anything you say will be taken down and may be used in evidence against you."

Madame's reception of the stereotyped warning convinced me that this was the first occasion on which she had come into collision with the English law. It appeared to impress her favourably, and to dispel her first terrors.

"But there is some mistake," she protested. "I did not understand. I have no wish to resist the law. I thought there was an understanding that this misfortune should not be dealt with by the police."

"Nonsense," my chief interjected roughly. "It is being dealt with by the police. They have been in possession of these premises since five o'clock this morning—since you called them in yourself. Do you intend to produce the register, or must we search for it?"

Madame Bonnell gave a last sigh of reluctance. Then she was all submission. She led the way out of the dancing-hall into the adjoining premises. Her private apartment was between the kitchen and the row of dressing-rooms for the accommodation of the dancers who preferred to assume their costumes on the spot. Drawn curtains on one side concealed what was no doubt Madame's bed; the rest of the room having the aspect of a business man's parlour, furnished with a roll-top desk, a typing machine and shelves for books and correspondence. In one corner was a cupboard with a stout door which the proprietress unlocked with a show of eagerness, and threw open for our inspection.

The contents of the cupboard seemed innocent enough. A private ledger, a file of accounts, a cash-box into whose contents Tarleton forbore to pry, and, more important for our purpose, two thin volumes bound in black leather, one of which was labelled "*Members*" and the other "*Visitors*." It would have been unchivalrous to speculate as to the contents of certain little bottles and boxes on a lower shelf which had a look of feminine elegance.

My chief pointed to the two black-bound volumes.

"Will you take charge of these books, Cassilis. We can examine them at our leisure."

The Frenchwoman uttered a faint groan as I stretched out my hand to obey. I could have groaned in sympathy with her. And yet I was not in any fear on my own account. I had no reason to think that my name would be found in the Visitors'-book. I had been too careful for that. But there was another name which I had only too much reason for expecting to see in the other volume. And I cursed the proprietress in my heart for not destroying the dangerous record while it was in her power. She had fancied herself secure, and had cared nothing for the security of her patrons. What did it matter to her who might be incriminated, as long as her livelihood was not threatened? True, she had done her best at the last moment to prevent the authorities from gaining access to these books. But it was easy to see her self-interest in that. Those records were part of her stock-in-trade. They gave her a hold on the members of the club, who might be disposed to forsake it as soon as any hint of the tragedy got abroad. In that case she had only to say to them, "Leave the club, throw me over, and I take my books to the newspaper offices, and sell them for what they will fetch."

Such was the situation, so far as I could see it. Either the reputation of the Domino Club was to be saved, and all was to go on as before; or it would be for Madame's benefit that the scandal should be as widespread as possible, and that every member and visitor should pay heavily for having his or her name kept out of it. In parting with these two volumes she was parting with her most valuable weapons as a blackmailer.

Whether any such considerations as these influenced my chief, I could not tell. Outwardly he seemed to have only one end in view—the tracing of the crime to its perpetrator. As soon as I had possessed myself of the two books he made a sign to Captain Charles.

"It will be as well for you to lock this cupboard and keep the key for the present. Unless there is anything that Madame Bonnell particularly wishes to remove first."

Madame glanced longingly at the row of mysterious little boxes and bottles, but she prudently shook her head.

"*Merci, monsieur.* I will take nothing. I wish to have no secrets from the police. I prefer to replace my perfumes from the shop."

Tarleton smiled with a grudging respect. This was an adversary after his own heart, one who knew every point in the game, and knew when to play for safety. The Inspector locked the door and pocketed the key with the same wooden precision with which he would have taken the number of a taxi or arrested the Crown Prince of Slavonia.

"Is Madame Bonnell still under arrest?" he inquired stolidly.

"Not as far as I am concerned," the physician said lightly. "My business with Madame is over. All I have to do now is to make the medical examination, and to wait for the result of your inquiries elsewhere."

A significant nod conveyed to the Inspector that there was no occasion to let the Frenchwoman know of the search that had been set on foot among the costumiers. It was not unlikely that the proprietress of the club could have thrown some light on the identity of Salome and the mysterious Leopardess, and could have told us whether the Crown Prince had masqueraded as Zenobia, if she had chosen. But it was a good deal more likely that any question put to her on the subject would result in the parties being privately warned.

Inspector Charles formally released his prisoner who affected to take the step as a matter of course. I had remarked, however, a light of intense gratification in her black eyes when Sir Frank announced that he had dismissed her from the case. She impressed me as the sort of woman who could never breathe quite easily in the near neighbourhood of the police.

The arrangements for the removal of the body were soon made. A covered police-van was requisitioned to convey it to the retired house in Montague Street, and the consultant and I drove on in advance, taking the black-covered volumes with us. He talked to me quite cheerfully on the way.

"An interesting woman, that. Her mind would be a curious study for a psychologist—a real one, I mean, not a charlatan like this wretched Weathered. The words right and wrong have no meaning at all for her, I should say. She must find it difficult to understand our point of view. In her opinion, I expect, the only thing that matters is that the name of the Crown Prince should be kept clear of scandal. If he has chosen to commit a murder, all that is necessary is that the King of Slavonia should send me the Order of Saint Somebody or other, and of course the investigation will be dropped."

We reached the house in good time for lunch, and my kindly chief pressed me to make a good meal.

"You are looking fagged," he observed. "If you weren't a teetotaller I should prescribe a half-bottle of Burgundy. Our work is only beginning. As soon as lunch is over I am going through the Members'-book, comparing the names in it with those in Weathered's appointment-book. In that way we may get a key to the mysterious numbers."

I did my best to conceal the apprehension with which I heard of this intention. I could see the search narrowing by degree, and gradually isolating a few names among which I had too much reason to fear that one would be found which I would have given all I possessed to exclude. I made an effort to brighten up and eat the good things before me. The doctor knew how to make the best of life, and an excellent digestion enabled him to enjoy the lobster mayonnaise and the tender cutlets provided by his accomplished cook. He drank nothing stronger than claret, but it was such claret as is not often found in private cellars, and its perfume reached my nostrils across the table like the breath of roses.

As soon as I thought he was sufficiently warmed and cheered to relax a little I ventured to put the question that had been trembling on my lips for hours.

"Is it too soon to ask if you have formed any opinion as to the cause of death, Sir Frank?"

He looked at me rather sharply, and his bushy eyebrows drew together.

"I can form no opinion till I have made an autopsy. If you mean have I made any conjecture, I have made several, any one of which may be right or may be wrong. Up to a certain point I am inclined to agree with your theory."

"With my theory!" I was surprised into repeating.

"Yes. If you recollect, you suggested that whoever administered opium to Weathered had no intention of causing death. The object seems to have been to send him off into a state of unconsciousness so as to obtain possession of his keys; and we know what the keys were wanted for."

"To suppress the evidence against some patient, you mean?" I faltered.

"That is one view. Another possible view is that the person who stole the case-book wanted to obtain evidence for his own purposes. He may have wanted to put pressure on some patient—or patients."

"Oh, no!" The protest escaped from me almost unawares. A slight lifting of Tarleton's brows caused me to qualify it the next moment. "I mean that wasn't my theory." I pulled myself together as I went on. "Putting together everything we learnt from Madame Bonnell and from the waiter and from Miss Neobard, I suspect that Weathered had become a thorough scoundrel. My view is that he was taking advantage of the confessions made to him as a medical man to blackmail his patients, and that one of them was driven to desperation. She thought she could deliver herself by obtaining access to his safe, and destroying the documents. But she never dreamed that she was giving him a fatal dose."

"I needn't tell you that would be no defence in the eye of the law if it actually was fatal," the specialist put in grimly. "So you think it was the work of a woman, do you?"

"The evidence, Gerard's evidence, is to that effect, surely? He described three women in connection with the masked Inquisitor—not one man."

"He described one woman as being rather like a man. He suspected Zenobia of being His Royal Highness."

I hardly knew what to say. If there were any chance of the waiter's theory being adopted by my chief, the relief to me would be as great as to Madame Bonnell herself. But dare I hope anything of the kind? The situation was so critical that I feared to commit myself one way or the other. I fell back on the other point in doubt.

"Do you consider it possible, sir, that an otherwise harmless dose of morphia might prove fatal if the person to whom it was given had already saturated his system with opium?"

Again the specialist's voice had a note of surprise.

"I should have thought your own knowledge was amply sufficient to answer that question, Cassilis. In ordinary circumstances, no; quite the contrary, the dose would fail even to produce the effect intended; it would hardly render the victim insensible. But suppose that he had just taken his maximum dose, and the extra quantity was administered immediately after, then the effect might be very serious, indeed."

Somehow I felt that I was being fenced with. Tarleton must have perceived a lack of candour on my part in discussing the problem, and decided to withhold his confidence for the time being. I had to remind myself of the admissions I had been driven to make in the course of the morning. My chief knew that I had been a visitor to the Domino Club on one occasion. He knew that I had heard something of Dr. Weathered, and heard it in confidence, as he supposed, or affected to believe, from a patient of my own. He must have put two and two together by this time. Some inkling of the truth must be in his mind. It did not call for very much acuteness on his part to see in me the confidential adviser of one of Weathered's patients—perhaps one of his victims—possibly of the very one who had administered the fatal dose, and carried off the incriminating book.

I resolved to hold my tongue for the future. I would make no more attempts to sound Sir Frank, and would trust to his respect for professional secrecy to protect me from any awkward questions from him. The resolution was easier to take than to keep.

As soon as lunch was over the consultant led the way upstairs to his study. It appeared that the autopsy was to be postponed; the first business was to be the examination of the books that Madame Bonnell had been so unwilling to give up.

The physician seated himself at his massive bureau, a combination of desk and cabinet, and drew the volume labelled "*Members*" in front of him, while I placed myself respectfully on a chair at the side.

"The list of members isn't a very large one," was his first observation. "One could hardly expect it to be. The Domino Club has more the character of a secret society than a club; a society for the pursuit of illicit pleasures, let us say. Whom have we here?" He opened the book as he spoke, and ran his eye slowly down the first page. "The Duke of Altringham—I am not surprised at seeing his name; General Sir Francis Uppingham, K.C.B.; the Countess of Eardisley; Honourable Janet Wilbraham; Mrs. Worboise; Sir George Castleton, Bart.—h'm, we are beginning to come across some of the names in the appointment-book, but I don't see anything to account for the numbers attached to them. And I shall be very much surprised if those numbers don't contain the true key to the mystery."

He paused in reflection, and took Weathered's diary from his pocket. "The first thing, it seems to me, is to make out a list of the members who were also patients, and to underline the names of those who had a number as well. It is among them that we may expect to find Zenobia and Salome and possibly the Leopardess as well, though her behaviour suggests that she can hardly have been a patient. She may have been one formerly."

I listened anxiously. Every moment I was expecting the name which I foresaw too surely would be found in the final list of suspects. Suddenly Tarleton turned to me with an unexpected order.

"While I am comparing these two books you can go through the Visitors'-book It may interest you to find the entry of your own name."

I could not tell whether my dismay was visible to the gray eyes that seemed to look at me with such perfect indifference. My dilemma was truly critical. I knew, of course, that my name did not appear in the volume I was required to search. And if I pretended to look for it I should land myself in a series of traps. My chief would want some explanation of its absence; and what explanation could I give? If I said that I had been present under a false name he would naturally expect me to tell him that name. And he would expect me to tell him at once, before I opened the book and began the mock search. I had barely a second in which to make up my mind. If only my own reputation, or even my own life, had been at stake, I think I should have thrown myself on his mercy, and come out with the whole truth. But I was held as in an iron vice. The knowledge that the police were actively engaged in tracing the purchasers of the costumes which had been described to us by Gerard haunted my consciousness. I was driven in despair to tell my first direct falsehood to my chief.

I opened the volume hurriedly as I spoke.

"I don't think I shall find my own name here."

"Why not?" The question came instantly, though it came in a quiet, friendly tone.

"My recollection is that I gave some other name. I am trying to remember what. I was rather doubtful about the character of the place, and didn't want to run the risk of it being known that I had been there. I considered the name didn't matter; I thought it was merely a form." I was glancing feverishly through the pages as I talked, trying to pick out some name too common to be easily identified. "Ah, yes, I remember now—Carter."

I placed my finger on an entry nine months old. A Mr. Robert Carter had been introduced on that date by a Captain Smethwick.

Much to my relief Tarleton accepted the explanation readily.

"I dare say a good many of the names in that book are equally fictitious," he said with good humour. "Look and see what name the Crown Prince took last night."

It was easily found. A Count Donau had been introduced by the Chancellor of the Slavonian Embassy.

"Any other visitors?" the consultant asked lightly.

I read aloud one or two masculine names, but he pulled me up.

"Any ladies?"

There were two lady visitors. I read out both their names without misgiving. One was a Lady Greatorex, the other a Mrs. Antrobus, both of them assumed names for aught I knew.

The specialist paid little attention for the moment. He was busy with his duplicate list. I watched him with increasing anxiety as he ticked off name after name. At the end of half an hour he had completed his task for the time being.

"I have here thirty-eight names of people who were both patients of Weathered and members of the Domino Club. And all of them, without exception, were patients first. It is clear that he started the club for their benefit, at once to keep them under his influence, and to confirm them in the very inclinations he pretended to relieve them from. The man was a moral monster. If ever Satan had an active instrument on earth this Weathered was the man. And I doubt if the law could have touched him."

His words almost invited me to say, "In that case the law can very well afford to shut its eyes to his fate."

The adviser of the Home Office shook his head. "That depends. The law must first know what was his fate. It looks to me as though we were as far off from knowing that as ever. We know neither how he died, nor at whose hands, nor the motive of the assassin at present."

"Doesn't everything point to his death being more or less an accident?" I ventured to plead.

"On the contrary, I should say that everything points to its being a deliberate and deeply-planned murder."

I gave a horrified gasp. Before I could collect myself sufficiently to take in this formidable judgment I was saved from exposing myself by the familiar sound of the telephone bell.

In our hasty departure from the house that morning I had neglected to disconnect the receiver in my bedroom, and connect the one downstairs. I sprang out of the room and upstairs, thankful for the interruption. I was destined to receive a second shock, though a less unnerving one. The call again came from Inspector Charles, who had just received a report from one of his subordinates engaged on the case.

The costumier who had supplied the dress of Salome had just been found. The costume had been delivered two days before to Miss Sarah Neobard, Warwick Street, Cavendish Square.

CHAPTER 7

THE CAUSE OF DEATH

I waited with sickening apprehension for a few instants.

"And the others?—the Zenobia costume, has that been traced?" I was driven to ask.

"Not yet. There are several more places to be visited."

The respite gave me time to breathe. As I slowly descended the stairs, my mind became absorbed in pondering the news I had just received, and the use to which it might be put.

The figure of Salome came before me as I had seen her the night before, pursuing the hooded Inquisitor, luring him to dance with her, and keeping a jealous eye on his movements when he was engaged with other partners. Astounded as I was to learn that the mysterious dancer was no other than the dead man's step-daughter, it did not take me long to reconcile the intelligence with her remarkable character, as revealed in the course of the morning's investigations.

I began to see depths in the strange girl's nature of which she herself had hardly been aware. It was not only indignation on her mother's behalf that had prompted her to trace her step-father's doings. It was not merely curiosity that had brought her to the Domino Club to watch his movements. Her fierce denunciation of the women patients whom she had accused of depraving him had been inspired by a secret feeling of which she was herself unconscious. The man had fascinated her unawares. Without knowing it she had been jealous on her own account as well as her mother's. In a strange ignorance of her own feelings which was yet a natural result of the relationship in which she had been brought up, she had continued to believe herself his enemy. She had imagined that hatred was the passion that inspired her to disguise herself and come to watch him, to dance with him time after time, and to pursue him with restless vigilance when he transferred his attentions to anyone else.

Meanwhile it seemed to me that this discovery offered me a chance of diverting inquiry from myself and from one in whom I was far more deeply interested than in Sarah Neobard. I must try to concentrate Sir Frank Tarleton's suspicions on Salome, and induce him to pass over the other characters to whom his attention had been drawn by the evidence of the waiter Gerard and the entries in the books.

I entered his study again to find him engaged in drawing up a list of names. I let my eye steal towards the paper as I approached and my heart sank as I read the one just written—"*Lady Violet Bredwardine.*"

"The mystery is solved, apparently," I announced in a tone of confidence. "The Salome costume has been traced to Miss Neobard."

To my discomfiture the consultant merely gave the nod of one who hears what he expected.

"Poor girl; I was afraid of it."

He went on writing without further remark, while I dropped into a chair and looked on with sickly apprehension. At last he looked up.

"Listen, Cassilis. I have made a complete list of the names which appear in the members' roll and also in the appointment-book with numbers attached to them. We have still to find out what the numbers mean, of course. Have you formed any theory on that point?"

I shook my head. I was honestly ignorant, and if I had been able to make any guess I should have refrained, for fear of leading Tarleton in the very direction I was anxious to turn him away from.

"All I can conjecture at this stage is that the numbers refer to pages in the book that has been abstracted from the safe," the physician said thoughtfully. "But I confess that that explanation doesn't satisfy myself. My instinct tells me that these names are the names of persons with whom Weathered had some peculiar relation, perhaps financial, perhaps...." He paused and shook his head. "At all events, if Madame Bonnell told us the truth in saying that he went in mortal fear of some of his fellow-members, I am convinced that the names of those whom he feared are in this list."

He passed it over to me. Of the dozen names it contained more than half were those of women. But I had no eyes for more names than one. I was racking my brain for some convincing argument against the course which my chief was evidently bent on following.

"Miss Neobard's name is not in this list," I objected. "And yet we know now that she was present last night, and passed more time in Weathered's company than anyone else. And she had very strong motives for regarding him with hatred."

Again Tarleton exhibited signs of surprise, almost of impatience.

"It seems to me, Cassilis, that you have a good deal to learn in the analysis of human nature, or at all events of feminine nature, if you consider that hatred was the motive that inspired that young woman to follow her step-father to the Domino Club last night. Hatred of the other women who were there, if you like, but certainly not hatred of him."

It was difficult for me to keep up the pretence of believing in a theory which my own judgment had already discarded. I fell back on another point.

"What strikes me, sir, that all the persons whose names appear in your list were old frequenters of the club. They had had many previous opportunities of drugging Weathered. Last night was the first occasion on which his step-daughter was present, and last night was the first time he was attacked."

Tarleton accepted this argument more amicably.

"Now you have made a real point. It might be a good point if there were no other suspicious features in the case. But it is open to this objection that your argument cuts both ways. Sarah Neobard lived in her step-father's house, and had every opportunity of administering drugs to him there. Why should she have chosen the Domino Club for such a purpose? And if her object was to obtain his keys, she might have managed that when he was asleep at home far more easily than anywhere else. That's the one point we mustn't lose sight of in this affair—that the motive was to gain access to Weathered's safe. Revenge was a secondary consideration."

I felt myself fairly cornered. Prudence compelled me to assent to my chief's reasoning.

"I will ask you to make a copy of this final list and send it round to Captain Charles," he went on to say. "The police may be able to find out something about these twelve persons which will narrow the inquiry down to one or two."

I held out a hand that almost trembled for the paper, and hastened to fold it up and slip it into my pocket. The thought had instantly occurred to me that I might omit one name in the copy to be sent to the police without much risk. If the omission were discovered it would be put down to carelessness, and meanwhile time would have been gained.

Tarleton had risen to his feet.

"And now it is time to examine the body," he said gravely.

I followed him out of the room and into the laboratory, where the corpse lay stretched on a marble slab, ready for the surgical knife. The sight distracted me for a time from my other anxiety. I was profoundly puzzled by the symptoms I have described already. The grayness I had remarked had grown deeper, and the whole surface of the skin was corrugated by tiny wrinkles, so that it presented the appearance of a mummy dried by the embalmer. It was impossible to attribute these signs to the action of opium in any quantity of which I had experimental knowledge. My heart sank as I remembered the ominous pronouncement of my chief. If he were right, and another drug, more deadly than opium, had been administered by an unknown hand to the masked Inquisitor during last night's revel, the situation would be terrible indeed. The murder, the deeply-planned murder, as

Sir Frank had termed it in advance, would be attributed to the same hand that had abstracted the keys and carried off the case-book from the safe.

The proceedings in which I had now to play the part of assistant were of too gruesome a nature to be described in anything but a medical report. It is enough to say that the general result was negative as far as my medical knowledge went. There was no sign of any organic injury. There was nothing in the condition of the heart to explain the fatal event. The internal symptoms corresponded closely with the external ones. Everything pointed to death having been brought about by the action of a poison similar in some of its effects to opium, yet having a peculiar influence on the interior membranes as well as on the outer cuticle. But what that poison was I was at a loss to tell.

The specialist seemed to be as completely baffled as myself. He pursued the examination almost in silence, only speaking from time to time to ask me to hand him the different reagents used in testing for poisons. It was quickly evident that none of the common poisons was present. Anything like strychnine or arsenic was out of the question from the first. The rapidity with which death had taken place eliminated the possibility of germs. More subtle agents, such as belladonna and aconite, were tested for in vain. In the midst of my overpowering anxiety I was moved to admiration by the expert's extraordinary skill. All kinds of tests of which I had never heard were brought to bear; drugs unknown to me even by name were called into requisition; minute discolorations were examined by a powerful microscope; a galvanic battery was applied to one organ, and the X-ray to another. And still there was no positive result.

Hours passed away unnoticed in the laborious search. It was nearly dinner-time when Tarleton at length straightened himself up with a look of finality, walked across the room, and began washing his hands.

"I have now tried for every agent known to the British Pharmacopœia that might possibly have produced death with such symptoms as those, and not one is present," he said with extreme gravity.

I felt myself shivering. If anyone else had been speaking I should have thought he was attributing the death to a supernatural cause.

"There are only two possibilities left, so far as I can see," he continued. "One is that I am dealing with a murderer whose knowledge of poisons is more extensive than my own."

I shook my head in protest.

"In that case," Tarleton went on deliberately, "he must be a foreigner. And we must be prepared to find that the life of the Crown Prince was aimed at, after all. The Bolsheviks are in close relation with a party among the Chinese. It may well be that the Chinese possess the secret of treating opium in such a way as to make it produce effects unknown to Western science. I shall have to ask Charles to find out what costume the Prince wore last night, and to learn a little more about the Chancellor of the Slavonian Legation."

He broke off for a few moments, and I breathed more freely than I had done for many hours. He finished drying his hands before he spoke again.

"There is a second possibility. There is one drug known to me which does in fact produce appearances exactly like those we have seen. But it is a drug not mentioned in the Pharmacopœia, and I had every reason to believe that I was the only person in this part of the world who had any of it in his possession. I keep it in a sealed bottle in my private safe, and I am now going to see if that bottle has been tampered with, and any of the poison is missing."

The consultant was facing me as he spoke, and his keen gray eyes were fixed on me with an expression which might have been merely meant to impress me with the gravity of the situation. But my conscience took the alarm. For the first time a sickening conviction seized me that I was being watched. I told myself that my chief had noticed signs of confusion and dread in my behaviour, and had begun to entertain a suspicion that I knew more about the tragedy than I had chosen to reveal.

Now it seemed his suspicion had gone deeper. He was actually asking himself if I had taken advantage of my opportunities as an inmate of his house to search for a more subtle drug than morphia, and had stooped to rob him. And although I knew myself to be innocent of any such action, I trembled at the idea. If the bottle or any of its contents should be missing, how could I possibly hope to exculpate myself?

I dared not to open my lips. Tarleton, with something like a sigh, went towards the cabinet in which his drugs were stored, took out his bunch of keys and applied one of them to a small steel safe on an inner shelf. I held my breath as the door swung open. He put in his hand, took out a square glass bottle of the size known to chemists as four-ounce, and held it up to the light.

The bottle appeared to be full of a gray powder. The glass stopper was covered with black sealing-wax, and he bent his head over it, minutely scrutinizing the edges of the wax, and the impression of a seal on the flat top.

"Thank Heaven!"

I echoed the ejaculation in my thoughts as he raised his head and looked round at me with a smile of unmistakable relief.

"It is exactly as I left it I sealed it with my own signet ring." He extended his little finger for me to see. "The seal is intact. If this was the poison used, it wasn't obtained here."

I had reason to feel satisfied. I knew my chief's generous nature well enough to feel sure that he would feel remorse for his momentary suspicion of me, and would be disposed to atone for it by shutting his eyes to whatever else might point to my being concerned in the case. In fact he now proceeded to give me a short holiday.

"I shan't want you for the rest of the day, Cassilis, if you want to go out. I think we have done all we can till we hear further from the police. I am now going to think quietly over the problem as it stands."

I was thankful to be released. I had certain pressing business to attend to. But first of all I went to my own room and made a copy of the list of names I had been charged to send to Inspector Charles. And although the paper entrusted to me contained twelve names, the one which I posted to Scotland Yard only contained eleven.

My own business took me to a little street within a stone's throw of Piccadilly Circus in which I had rented a room ever since I had taken up my abode with Sir Frank Tarleton. It was my private retreat in which I kept up a few friendships that I did not want my chief to know of; an asylum in which I could resume my independence for a few hours when I was tired of the regular life I was compelled to lead under my senior's eye. I had taken the room under my Christian name of Bertrand for greater security. It was from this room that I had gone in disguise to the Domino Club, and it was here that I had dropped my disguise again, little dreaming that before twelve hours had passed it would have become a precious possession.

Luckily I had taken the precaution to leave it under lock and key in an old suit-case that I kept under the bed. As soon as I had let myself into the room and fastened the door securely, I dragged out the case and opened it with feverish haste. So far all was well. The costume lay exactly as I had left it. And now what was to be done with it?

I thought out the problem carefully. I followed out in imagination the search of the police among the theatrical costumiers. At any moment they might come to a certain little Jew in Wardour Street, and force him to disclose the name and address to which this very costume had been sent more than a year ago. And the next step would surely be for them to inquire what had become of it.

I thought then, and I think now, that I took the most prudent course in the circumstances. I first wrote a letter. Then I locked up the case again, labelled it, and carried it up Shaftesbury Avenue to the post office.

CHAPTER 8

THE LEOPARD'S CLAWS

Inspector Charles presented himself at the house in Montague Street while Sir Frank and I were at breakfast the next morning. My chief ordered him to be shown in to us.

The Inspector's manner struck me as rather more reserved than it had been yesterday. It very quickly appeared that he was acting under instructions not received from the medical adviser of the Home Office.

"The Chief Commissioner is anxious to know if you have any report to make as to the cause of death in this Domino Club affair," he began by saying, as soon as he had sat down.

Tarleton frowned slightly. Then he laid down his knife and fork and faced the Inspector.

"I don't expect to complete my report for some time yet. I have certain inquiries to make which may take anything from a few days to several months."

Captain Charles looked astonished, as he well might.

"Then it isn't a simple case of opium-poisoning?"

"It isn't a simple case, certainly. I don't say that opium was not administered. By the way, I should be glad if you could find out for me what disguise the Crown Prince was wearing when he went to the Club."

The Captain drew himself up.

"I ascertained that yesterday. He wore a plain black domino with a hood."

"Ah! Rather like Weathered's costume, then?"

I could have answered that question better than Charles, I thought. There had been more than one black domino worn at the fatal dance, but none that had any real semblance to Weathered's remarkable costume. The pointed peak with the two eye-slits in the cloth instead of a mask had plainly distinguished the founder of the Club from everyone else present. Of course I dared not offer my testimony as a witness. I did not think it prudent even to make a remark. Tarleton might have an object in putting forward this particular view.

It quickly appeared what his object was.

"I don't think the Commissioner is much inclined to follow up that clue," Captain Charles said coldly. "They seem to think in the Foreign Office that it would do harm to let any idea get abroad that the Crown Prince was aimed at. It would look as if London wasn't a safe place for foreign royalties to visit."

The physician shrugged his shoulders impatiently.

"That has nothing to do with me, Captain Charles. It will be time enough for the Foreign Office to make their view prevail when we have something definite to go upon. At present I am dealing with the cause of death. I want the police, if they can, to find out if the Bolshevik authorities have ever resorted to poison, and if so, what poison they use. I imagine they have no restrictions on opium, and I should be particularly glad to get hold of samples of the opium that is coming into Russia from China just now."

The Inspector pulled a long face.

"I'll tell the Commissioner what you say, Sir Frank, of course. But I'm afraid he won't much like the idea of the inquiry being dragged out. His theory is that death was accidental, the only object being to get hold of the keys of the safe. And if there isn't going to be any public prosecution, he wants to close the Club as soon as possible, and send the woman Bonnell out of the country."

For once I saw Tarleton really angry.

"I trust Sir Hercules will recognize that it is for me to decide whether the death was accidental, and that he will take no such steps until he has received my report through the Home Office. Unless you can undertake that he will hold his hand for the present I must communicate with Sir James Ponsonby at once."

Charles gave way instantly.

"There's no need for that, Sir Frank, I'm sure. Sir Hercules McNaught wouldn't think of acting contrary to your opinion without consulting you first. It doesn't look to him as if the case could be carried much further; that's all."

"We are only at the beginning of the inquiry," was the firm answer. "You haven't yet completed your search among the costumiers."

The Inspector shook his head despondently.

"We have pretty well exhausted the list of costumiers, and there is nothing worth reporting, sir. At least the Commissioner thinks it absurd to attach any importance to Miss Neobard's presence. He says she would have had much better opportunities of getting hold of her step-father's keys at home."

My chief glanced at me. It was the same objection that he had made himself.

"We can't hear anything of a leopard skin," Charles pursued. "You may remember, sir, that you expressed the opinion that the leopardess costume would turn out to be a private one. And the only Zenobia costume we can trace was furnished a year ago."

I stole a glance at the consultant. His keen eyes were no longer on me.

"To whom was it furnished?" he asked quietly.

The Inspector took out a note-book and opened it.

"To the Lady Violet Bredwardine, Grosvenor Place."

At last the name had been pronounced, the name that I had so much dreaded to hear on the lips of the police. Fortunately I had known that it was coming. I had braced my nerves to meet the shock, and I managed to preserve an air of complete indifference while I faced the speaker.

"Well?"

Tarleton spoke a little sharply. Captain Charles looked at him in mild wonder.

"Well?" the specialist repeated impatiently. "What have you ascertained about Lady Violet Bredwardine?"

Charles was plainly put out by the question.

"Her ladyship is the daughter of the Earl of Ledbury. She is quite young—hardly of age. Sir Hercules McNaught has met her in society." His manner conveyed that there was some impropriety in making Lady Violet's name the subject of discussion. The day before I had been inclined to feel some contempt for the worthy Captain, but now I was only grateful for his stolid front.

My chief took a very different view, unfortunately.

"And is that all you have thought it worth while to find out? A peerage would have told us as much as that. I have no doubt that Sir Hercules has met many members of the Domino Club in society. It doesn't follow that they are to be excluded from the investigation."

This time the Inspector did not attempt to conceal his mortification.

"I beg your pardon, Sir Frank. Do you mean that Lady Violet Bredwardine is a member of the Domino Club? I hadn't the slightest reason to suppose so."

It was the consultant's turn to show surprise. He stared at me.

"Surely her name was on the list I asked you to furnish to Captain Charles? I have a distinct recollection of it."

I received the question, for which I had been waiting, with perfect coolness.

"I seem to recollect it too, sir."

The Inspector was already turning over the pages of his note-book. He looked up at us in triumph.

"I made a copy of the list exactly as I received it, Sir Frank, and the name is not here. I am prepared to swear that her ladyship's name was not included."

Tarleton turned to me.

"Will you be good enough to bring me the list I gave you to copy. It looks as though some slip had been made."

I had not ventured to destroy the document. To have done so would have been to expose myself to a serious rebuke, without serving any useful purpose. Tarleton was not the man to forget such a name as Lady Violet's— one of the first that had attracted his attention among those that appeared in Weathered's appointment-book with a number attached to them. All I had hoped to do was to keep the police off her track for a few hours, and that object had now been achieved.

The list was actually in my breast pocket, but I went up to my room as though to fetch it, and returned, carrying it in my hand. I put on an apologetic air as I handed it to my chief.

"The name is certainly here, sir. I can only suppose that I must have left it out of the copy I made for Captain Charles."

Tarleton let me off more lightly than I expected.

"Either you or the Captain left it out, that's clear," he said gruffly. "The point is that Lady Violet was not only a member of the Club; she was also one of Weathered's patients, which means that she may have been in his power, and she was one of those to whom he had given a special number for some reason that we have still to find out. Perhaps she may be able to tell us."

I could scarcely suppress a shiver. This point had never occurred to me. I pictured to myself the question being put to the unhappy girl, and tortured myself with wondering what would be her reply.

The Inspector's attitude had undergone a considerable change as he listened to Tarleton's information. Evidently he realized that the police authorities had been rather hasty in coming to the conclusion that the inquiry was at an end.

"What you tell me makes a great difference, sir," he observed regretfully. "I've no doubt the Commissioner will see the necessity of going further into the case, on this evidence."

"There are many reasons for going into it further," the specialist returned. "You may tell the Commissioner from me that I suspect a book has been taken from Dr. Weathered's safe containing the names and confidential confessions of his patients, and it is of the utmost importance that that book should be traced. Until we know that it is destroyed the reputations of innocent people will be in danger. You may also tell him that there is grave reason to fear that some unscrupulous person in London is in possession of a supply of deadly poison, unknown to science at present; and unless that person can be discovered and the poison taken out of his or her possession, it may be used to commit more murders than one."

Captain Charles's expression was almost humble.

"You may rely on the Commissioner's giving you all the assistance in his power, Sir Frank, I'm certain. I'll follow up Lady Violet Bredwardine without delay, if that will meet your views."

"Thank you. There are two things I should like you to report to me the moment you know them: Lady Violet's present address, and where she was yesterday night."

The Inspector scribbled two lines in his note-book, and hurried off.

Meanwhile my position was becoming more difficult every hour. I had to look on and see the toils closing round one whom I would have given my life to protect, without daring to show the least sign of personal interest in her fate. My own peril, serious as it was, affected me but little in comparison with hers. I can honestly say that I should have been ready to draw suspicion on myself if I could have screened her by so doing. But the very reverse was the case, as I knew too well. The only course open to me was to hold my tongue, to keep a strict guard on myself, and to watch for any chance that might present itself of diverting suspicion from either of us.

I was afraid to commit myself by any expression of opinion on the case as it stood against Lady Violet, but I thought I might venture to remind my chief that she was not the only person implicated. He had dismissed Sarah Neobard altogether from the inquiry, or so it seemed, but the mysterious Leopardess remained to be identified. I ventured on a question.

"Do you think, Sir Frank, there is any chance of the police getting on the trail of the woman who wore the leopard skin? According to the waiter's evidence she was the one who showed most hostility to Weathered. She refused to dance with him, you may remember. Somehow Gerard gave me the impression that she was his only real enemy."

I was gratified by Tarleton's quick response.

"You are perfectly right, Cassilis. That is the very point I was considering before you spoke. In my opinion there is very little likelihood of Charles tracing that woman. I think you and I must try our hand."

I need scarcely say how delighted I was at this prospect. At last I should be able to devote myself to serving my chief without any dread of the result.

"Will it be possible to trace the leopard skin?" I asked. "There are not many taxidermists in London, are there? I have only heard of one. We might go round to them, and find out if any skins have passed through their hands recently. What strikes me is that all the skins I have seen have been mounted as rugs. I shouldn't think that unmounted skins could be very common—skins that could be made part of a costume."

My chief had punctuated these suggestions with a series of approving nods. At the close he spoke.

"Very good indeed, Cassilis. You have the makings of a detective, I can see. And now let me explain to you where I see a chance of success. You may put the taxidermists on one side. Leopard skins are such perishable things, and the climates in which leopards are killed are so treacherous, that the skins have to be roughly cured on the spot if they are to be preserved. And they are too common to be the object of much care afterwards as a rule. The chances are against any particular skin having passed through the hands of a taxidermist in London unless it was to be mounted as a rug."

I felt very small as I listened to this reduction of my ideas to nothing. The specialist had not done.

"I don't think it would be at all hopeful to try to trace the skin, therefore. But I think it quite possible to trace something else. Do you remember what else about the costume the man Gerard described?"

"Do you mean the necklace—of leopard's claws?" I responded in doubt.

"Yes. I see you don't grasp the significance of the claws. I must tell you that the natives of the countries where leopards are found look upon the claws as having a magical virtue. They place a great value on them, and take them from the dead leopard at the first opportunity they find. It is almost impossible for the white man who shoots a leopard to secure the claws. I doubt if more than one entire set of claws comes to England in a year. Now you see that in my opinion we have a very much greater chance of tracing the claws than the skin."

I was fairly puzzled. I could follow Tarleton's reasoning, of course, but I could not imagine how he meant to proceed.

"These claws must have been brought home, according to my idea, by a sportsman and traveller of experience, who knew the ways of the natives, and was able to baffle them. Men of that class are not very numerous, and most of them have published books of their travels. I am going to spend the rest of the morning in going to the libraries and publishers; and I want you to spend it in the Natural History Museum at South Kensington."

There was no occasion for me to express the admiration I sincerely felt for my chief's knowledge and resource. I waited in silent wonder for his instructions.

"I am not an expert in zoölogy," he said modestly. "I know, of course, that leopards, or animals closely resembling leopards, are found along the tropical zone. They are called jaguars in South America, I believe, and panthers elsewhere. At all events their skins are sufficiently like the true leopard's to be called leopard skins by an ignorant man like Gerard. What

I want you to do is to ascertain if such animals occur in the East Indian archipelago, and particularly in the Island of Sumatra."

It was a curious direction. What was there in the circumstances of the case to turn Sir Frank's mind to one part of the tropics rather than another, and to one particular island? Perhaps it showed some dullness on my part; I can only confess that I had not the least idea of his motive.

"Sumatra," he repeated in a meditative tone, "almost the largest island in the world, and yet the least known. Nominally it is a Dutch possession, but the Dutch have never subjugated it. They have never thoroughly penetrated the interior. The natives have been too fierce for them to subdue. They occupy one or two points on the coast, I fancy, but that is all. There was a Sultan of Acheen who fought with them at one time. I don't think he was really conquered. A very interesting field for an explorer willing to take his life in his hand."

And still I failed to grasp the mysterious connection between the vast unknown island lying on the Equator and the tragedy I had all but witnessed in a night club of London.

"You can take my card," the specialist added. "You will find the people at the Museum most obliging. If they have the information they will give it to you willingly."

I took the card, and the Piccadilly Tube from Russell Square soon landed me at South Kensington. As Sir Frank Tarleton had foretold, the staff of the Natural History Museum received it with all respect, and showed themselves ready to give all the information they possessed. The gentleman who took me in hand was confident that there were leopards in Sumatra; nevertheless, when it came to the question of positive evidence he found some difficulty in putting his hand on any.

"You have struck the least-known area in the world, you see," he pointed out. "We know the fauna of the Malay Peninsula, and of Java and all the other East Indian islands as far as the Philippines, and one has always taken it for granted that the fauna of Sumatra corresponded with that of the neighbouring area north of the Wallace line. But if you ask me for an official declaration that leopards are to be found in the island I don't think I can give it off-hand. We might be able to get the information by writing to The Hague. Or you might find it in some book of travels in the British Museum Library."

"Sir Frank Tarleton is searching in the Library at this moment, I believe," I said incautiously.

My guide opened his eyes.

"You surprise me. I had no idea that Sir Frank was so much interested in natural history. I have always associated his name with toxicology."

The light burst on me at last. I understood the true reason for my chief's extreme interest in following up the clue of the leopard's claws, and for his turning his special attention to the region of the earth least known to science. He had perceived a connection overlooked by me between the rare necklace worn by the unknown woman in the Domino Club and the gray powder contained in the small glass bottle in his private safe. He was on the search for some other product of Sumatra besides its leopards. He expected to trace the secret drug whose presence the effects of the opium had concealed.

CHAPTER 9

SARAH NEOBARD SPEAKS OUT

When I returned to Montague Street to lunch, my host was still out, and I had to sit down to the meal without him. No uncommon incident this, in the case of any member of the medical profession, and especially one liable to be summoned at any moment to cases of the most desperate nature. Yet I was uneasy at losing sight of the great man for so long just then. The investigation had reached a point at which I was desperately anxious to follow his every move, in order that I might guard the threatened girl towards whom so many signs already seemed to point.

My lunch was nearly over when I was summoned to the telephone. I answered the call with the expectation that Captain Charles had obtained the information he had been asked for; and I was not disappointed.

"You can tell Sir Frank that Lady Violet Bredwardine is down in Herefordshire at her father's seat, Tyberton Castle. She left London for the Castle the day before yesterday by the noon train, so that she can't have been present at the Domino Club."

I was careful to receive this intelligence as though it were news to me. I even asked the Inspector if he was perfectly sure that his informants were to be trusted.

"I'm perfectly sure as far as this end is concerned," he answered in a tone of surprise. "There is no doubt that she left by that train, and that she hasn't returned. And her letters are being forwarded to Tyberton Castle. But, of course, I can't answer for her being there without sending someone down to make inquiries on the spot. Would Sir Frank like me to do that?"

I hesitated. I had no reason to fear the result of such inquiries, but I distrusted the tact of Charles and his men, and felt afraid lest their proceedings should come to Lady Violet's ears and frighten her. On the whole, I thought it best to apply the brake.

"Sir Frank is out just now. I will let him have your report as soon as he comes in, and let you know what he says. I shouldn't think he would want you to do anything more. It looks as though Lady Violet had a complete alibi."

"Oh, but—" the voice through the wire objected, "but Sir Frank's instructions were that I was to follow up Lady Violet. The police were to follow up everyone on the list you sent me, and find out all they could about them. I have a man detailed for each already. We have ascertained that Julia Sebright is dead. Sir George Castleton is abroad; he was last heard of in Naples, in very queer company...."

This was the sort of thing I had dreaded. At all risks I must try to call the hounds off the trail of Violet Bredwardine's past.

"That's all right, so far," I interrupted. "Of course, Sir Frank wishes you to follow them all up as long as there is any possibility of their being involved in the case. But when they are clearly out of it I feel sure he wouldn't think it right to pry into their private lives for nothing. It would be taking an improper advantage of information obtained from the books of their doctor. Medical etiquette is very strict on that point, I can assure you. Sir Frank Tarleton himself might get into trouble if it were known that he had made use of Dr. Weathered's books for such a purpose."

"What is that about Sir Frank Tarleton getting into trouble?" said a voice in my ear.

The receiver fell from my hand. I looked round to see my chief standing at my elbow. I am a poor dissembler, I fear. I was conscious of a deep flush as I lowered my eyes before the reproachful look in those keen gray ones beneath their frowning brows.

"I beg your pardon, sir," I stammered. "I was trying to explain to Inspector Charles that it wouldn't do to annoy Weathered's patients with inquiries into their private lives unless there were some grounds for suspicion against them."

Tarleton stepped to the telephone.

"You have heard what Dr. Cassilis said? He is perfectly right. We have no concern with any patient of Weathered's who is not implicated in the murder. The moment we can dismiss them from the case they must be let alone."

I hardly know whether I was more astonished or delighted at this handsome endorsement of my words. But I was not yet out of the wood. My chief made the Inspector repeat the information he had just given to me, and Charles naturally took the opportunity to defend himself.

Apparently the Inspector explained to Tarleton that I had not seemed satisfied at first with his report about Lady Violet having gone to Herefordshire before the night of the dance.

It was the physician's turn to show surprise.

"Why did you question Lady Violet Bredwardine's alibi, Cassilis?"

It gratified me to feel that the Inspector had done me a good turn unawares.

"I merely thought it right to ask Captain Charles if he was quite satisfied before I took the responsibility of reporting the alibi to you. He offered to send a man down to make inquiries at Lord Ledbury's seat, and I asked him to take no further steps without your sanction."

My chief smiled with the utmost amiability.

"Dr. Cassilis has exactly understood my views," he said through the telephone. "There is not the least necessity for you to trouble yourself further about Lady Violet for the present. The person in whom I am interested just now is Captain Armstrong, R.A. He is a Fellow of the Royal Geographical Society, and a well-known traveller and explorer. I shall be glad if you can let me have his present address."

There was a brief pause. It was evident that the Inspector had been consulting his note-book, for his reply, which I failed to catch, provoked Tarleton to say testily, "I know, I know. He is not on the books of the Club. I want to get in touch with him for another reason. I think he may be of help in enabling me to decide on the cause of death."

As soon as Captain Charles had been disposed of, the physician came to the luncheon table and made a hasty meal. I reported my failure to obtain any definite proof of the existence of leopards in Sumatra, and found that the point had lost its importance in his eyes.

"I have been to the British Museum Reading Room," he told me. "I met Captain Armstrong about two years ago, after reading his book on Sumatra, but I had forgotten his name, and I had to look through the subject index under the head of Sumatra to find it. Then I got out his book, *Across Sumatra*, and saw from the title-page that he had also written a book on West Africa, where everyone knows there are leopards, so that he had plenty of opportunities of procuring skins and claws."

The situation was becoming clearer and clearer. There was no need for me to ask the specialist where he had procured the contents of the glass bottle. I could see what must have happened. The explorer's narrative must have contained some account of an unknown poison peculiar to the Island of Sumatra; the expert's attention had been drawn to it; he had approached the author, found that he had some of the poison in his possession, and induced him to part with it. His object now must be to find out whether Armstrong had kept any himself, or allowed it to get into other hands.

I was so relieved at the turn the investigation was taking that I had ceased to worry about my own connection with the tragedy. It gave me a disagreeable shock to be reminded that there were other points to be cleared up, when my chief spoke again.

"I think our next step now must be to interview Sarah Neobard. I doubt if she has told us all she knows about Weathered and his woman patients. She may be able to throw some light on the mysterious numbers."

The numbers in the appointment-book were as mysterious to me as they were to him. I had been able to form no theory as to their significance; nevertheless, I felt that danger lay in that direction. I could not forget that a number had been attached to Violet Bredwardine's name, and I dreaded to learn why.

The physician was provided with a good excuse for presenting himself again at the house in Warwick Street. It was necessary to make arrangements for the interment of the body. He had decided, he told me, to give a certificate that would dispense with the necessity for an inquest, and permit of the funeral taking place without delay. For that purpose the body was to be conveyed to the house in the small hours when nobody was likely to be about.

It was a strong thing to do before it had yet been determined whether the murder was to be made the subject of a public prosecution, and the murderer brought to justice. So far as I could see, the authorities both of the Home Office and the Foreign Office were placing entire confidence in my chief, and had given him a free hand. I hoped accordingly that his decision to let the funeral proceed quietly meant that he had made up his mind against any public exposure. But on that point he had been careful not to commit himself, and I was afraid to show too much curiosity.

He took me round with him in the car to Warwick Street, and asked to see Mrs. Weathered. The youthful butler eyed us with the utmost apprehension, and showed us into the patients' waiting-room. There we were joined presently by the widow and her daughter.

Mrs. Weathered was in deep black. Her manner showed that she was resigned to her husband's fate by this time, but she was evidently in a state of extreme nervousness, as she well might be while the mystery was unsolved. Sarah, on the other hand, at the beginning of the interview, was as cold and self-possessed as though her part was over, and she had ceased to feel any personal interest in the sequel.

"I have called on you," Tarleton explained, "to let you know officially that I have examined into the cause of Dr. Weathered's death, and am prepared to certify that it was due to heart failure."

I stared. In one sense, of course, almost every death may be said to be due to heart failure. The question generally is what has caused the heart to fail; and I knew perfectly well that the burial certificate would have to be more explicit. But Mrs. Weathered showed herself quite satisfied.

"Then it was a natural death, after all?" she exclaimed in relief.

"There is no reason why you shouldn't regard it so," was the answer. "I should advise you to accept that view, and refrain from discussing the matter with anyone. I wish to spare you the trouble and unpleasantness of an inquest, if possible. I propose to have the body brought round here some time tonight, or rather in the early morning; and you can then make your own arrangements for the funeral."

The widow clasped her hands in gratification.

"That is good of you, Sir Frank. I don't know how to thank you." She looked up at her daughter, whose face was overcast. "My dear, we couldn't have asked for anything better. I have been dreading the inquest more than I can say."

Sarah's expression was troubled. She tried to return her mother's pleading look with one of sympathy. Then she lifted her head, and let her eyes rest on the consultant with quiet scorn.

"My mother has every reason to be grateful to you, Sir Frank," she said ungraciously. "But you haven't told us what caused the heart to fail."

Tarleton returned her gaze with quiet forbearance. It was in his power to crush her with an allusion to her presence at the Domino Club in the character of Salome, but he generously refrained from doing so in her mother's hearing. Already the poor woman's face was downcast again, and she glanced anxiously from her daughter to us.

"That is a question which Mrs. Weathered is entitled to raise if she pleases," the doctor said gravely. "You have just heard me advise her not to do so. At the same time if you would like to go into the question with me privately I am quite willing."

"Oh, no, no!" The protest broke from the widow's lips. She caught hold of her daughter's hand. "Don't say anything more, dear. I'm sure Sir Frank Tarleton knows best. We must do what he tells us."

The girl compressed her lips with a strong effort. Her eye sought Tarleton's and I thought a signal was exchanged between them. Then he rose to his feet.

"Very well, ma'am. I think you are acting wisely. By the way, there is one question which you may be able to answer. In looking through Dr. Weathered's diary of appointments with his patients I have noticed that some of their names are followed by numbers, and I should like to know what that means."

The widow received the question with an air of complete surprise. It was impossible to doubt her declaration that she had no idea of the existence of the curious ciphers, much less of their use. But Sarah gave the questioner a quick look, and again I thought a secret understanding was established between them.

The first words uttered by my chief, when we were in the car driving away, told me what the understanding was.

"That girl means to come and see me. She isn't satisfied; and she won't be without vengeance on the woman she hates."

The prediction was promptly fulfilled. The girl must have found some excuse for leaving the house within a few minutes after us. We had been back less than half an hour when she was announced. She burst in upon us like a fury.

"Sir Frank Tarleton, what does this mean? My step-father was murdered, and you know it. You are trying to hush up the case, I suppose, because some of the people involved in it are so high up that the police want to let them off. There seems to be one law for the rich and another for the poor. It's the high-up people, the people with titles, who are the worst. I've seen those numbers in the diary, and I can guess pretty well what they mean. They're the guilty patients, the ones who were in his power, and had the greatest motive to murder him. If you want to know more you had better apply to Lady Violet Bredwardine."

It was an appalling shock. Just as I had reached the comforting conclusion that Lady Violet's alibi had put an end to the investigation as far as she was concerned, this passionate girl had launched a denunciation that threatened to drag everything to light. I turned in consternation to my chief.

He had taken out his gold repeater and begun to swing it to and fro at the end of its scrap of ribbon in a way that told me he was pondering deeply on this new development of the case. He made a motion with his hand towards me.

"Dr. Cassilis, here, can tell you that you are mistaken in thinking that the police are trying to hush up the case, or to screen anyone connected with it. Tell Miss Neobard what they reported to you."

The indignant Sarah faced me in some surprise. My own surprise was greater than hers. I was at a loss to understand Tarleton's motive for handing over the vindication of the police to me. Did he expect my word to carry more weight with the excited girl than his own? Or was he simply testing my ability to deal with a critical situation? And if so, how far did he mean me to go? Was I to let the accuser know that the police had been on her track as well as Lady Violet's? I spoke in some confusion.

"The police have made full inquiries about Lady Violet Bredwardine. She was a patient of Dr. Weathered's and a member of the Domino Club, apparently. But they have ascertained that she wasn't in London on the night when he met his death. She was down at her father's place in Herefordshire."

"I don't believe it," was the angry reply. "I don't mean that you are trying to deceive me, but the police haven't told you the truth. I am as certain that she was there that night as I am that I am in this room. She was with him in the very alcove where he was found dead."

In her wrath she had given herself away. Her statement almost amounted to saying that she had seen them together. I looked at my chief in the hope that he would pounce on the admission, but he contented himself with nodding to me to go on.

"You speak very positively, Miss Neobard. May I ask you how you know that?"

The question plainly disconcerted her. It must have opened her eyes to the fact that she was saying too much.

"I don't see what that has to do with it," she answered stubbornly. "You can ask anyone who was there. Ask them if they saw someone wearing a Roman helmet and breastplate with a skirt underneath. That was her disguise."

I was staggered. The girl's persistence irritated me, and I spoke sharply.

"You can't possibly know that, when she was more than a hundred miles away at the time. Did you speak to her—to whoever it was that was wearing that costume?"

It appeared that I had let myself go too far this time. I saw Tarleton frown disapprovingly. Sarah Neobard gazed at me in alarm.

"I speak to her?" she echoed. "What do you mean? I wasn't—I'm not a member of the Club."

A warning glance from my chief stopped the retort that was on my lips. I was longing to tell the accuser that she had been under suspicion herself, but I saw that in Tarleton's opinion I was taking the wrong line. My indignation on Violet Bredwardine's behalf had betrayed me into showing our cards too soon.

The girl herself seemed to feel that some explanation was needed for her confident assertions.

"If you want to know who was wearing that disguise, ask Madame Bonnell. She is the manager of the Club, and she can tell you everything that went on there."

A swift movement of the physician's eyebrows told me that this was the sort of admission he had been watching for. He intervened, I had little doubt, to prevent my drawing attention to it.

"I think Miss Neobard ought to be told that the wearer of the Zenobia costume was not the only one whose movements attracted attention on that night."

I was eager to take the cue. It was time to give Lady Violet's enemy a taste of her own medicine.

"Yes," I said sternly, "the dancer who was seen oftenest in company with Dr. Weathered that night wore the costume of Salome. Can you tell us anything about her?"

For an instant Salome blanched. She was quite intelligent enough to see the red light. She didn't need to be told that if her movements had attracted the notice of the police her identity could hardly fail to come out before very long, if it hadn't come out already. Yet she struggled against what was coming.

"She had nothing to do with the crime. She was a friend of Dr. Weathered's. Her only motive for being there was to protect him from the other women." She spoke almost in a whisper.

"To protect him from being poisoned, do you mean? Or do you mean that she was jealous, and wanted to prevent him from dancing with anyone but herself?"

At last Tarleton had fired the shot which he had had in preparation. Its effect was startling indeed. A dark red flood overspread the girl's face; for a moment she fought with her emotions, and the next she broke down in a flood of tears.

"You know it was I," she sobbed out. "You have been playing with me. You think I am a bad woman, I suppose. But I'm not. I take Heaven to witness that I only meant to do what was right. I never dreamed that I had any feeling for him that—that wasn't—that wasn't right. I was angry with him for the way he treated my mother. When he began to neglect her and go after other women, pretending that they were only his patients, I hated them. I never thought of anything else. I thought I was doing my duty to my mother in watching him. But he found me out. He knew everything about women. He saw that I was jealous on my own account as well; and he set himself to soothe me. He could fascinate any woman if he tried. He pretended to confide in me. He told me about his patients, and complained that they wouldn't leave him alone. Sometimes I believed him, and thought it was their fault, and then I thought it was his. I didn't know what to think at last. I went there that night to see if I could find out...."

The broken utterance ended in a wail of grief.

CHAPTER 10

THE CASE AGAINST LADY VIOLET

I felt honestly sorry for the poor girl in spite of the vindictive attitude she had taken up just before. I had no doubt that she was quite sincere, and that she had unconsciously deceived herself as to her real feelings up to the last moment.

Tarleton remained calm in the face of her outburst; when he spoke again his tone was courteous but businesslike—perhaps the most considerate one to adopt in the circumstances.

"You have told Dr. Cassilis and me very little that we weren't prepared to hear, and nothing that we aren't able to understand and allow for. But now we have to ask you for some information. In the first place I should like to know how you obtained admission to the Domino Club."

Sarah made an effort to collect herself. As far as I could judge she was telling the truth, up to a certain point at all events.

"I bought a ticket of admission from Madame Bonnell."

We both started and exchanged looks of surprise.

"Do you mean to say that anybody could get in by paying?" the consultant asked.

Sarah shook her head.

"I don't know that anybody could. But there didn't seem to be much difficulty. I think it was pretty well known, in Chelsea and in Kensington, that you could buy a ticket from Madame Bonnell. She made a great favour of it, but I expect that was only to keep up the price."

"What was the price?"

"Five pounds. She entered your name in a book, and the name of some member of the Club who was supposed to be introducing you; but whether it was a real name or not I don't know."

Tarleton smiled grimly.

"I'm beginning to understand why Madame made so much fuss over giving up her books. She must have made a good thing out of the Club in one way and another. Did she know who you were?"

"Oh, no! At least, I didn't tell her. I gave my name as Mrs. Antrobus."

"I remember that name in the Visitors'-book," I put in.

My chief nodded. "Did she say anything to you about the disguise you were to come in?"

"Yes. She asked me what I was going to wear. I told her I hadn't made up my mind, and she recommended me to go to a place in Coventry Street where I should be able to see some costumes."

"Another little side line," the shrewd examiner commented. "There's not much doubt she got a commission there. She struck me as a good woman of business." His face became grave once more. "And now, Miss Neobard, I must ask you to tell us what you know about Lady Violet Bredwardine?"

It was the question I had been dreading. I dreaded the answer still more.

The accuser flushed. "I know that she was more than a patient," she said in a low voice. "I know that he met her away from the house, at other places besides the Club."

"I'm afraid I must ask you to tell us more than that. You have practically accused her of poisoning him. I think you must see that I am entitled to know whether you have any grounds for throwing suspicion on her beyond personal ill-will."

The answer came slowly. It was with a painful effort that the girl confessed how far her jealousy had carried her.

"I knew that he was neglecting my mother for other women. I had known that for some time. He was almost always out at night, and he never told us where he had been. I wanted my mother to apply for a separation, and I thought I ought to get evidence. I followed him."

She stopped short, her face burning and her eyes lowered towards the ground.

"Yes? You have told us already that you followed him to the Club that night. But you must have seen them together at other places before?"

The girl nodded. "I have seen them walking in Regent's Park. And I have seen them dining together at...." She whispered the name of a restaurant in a little side street not far from Piccadilly, which is well known to Londoners as a place to which men more often take other people's wives and daughters than their own.

Tarleton prudently refrained from asking his witness anything about her own proceedings. It looked to me as though she must have placed herself in the hands of a private inquiry agent, but if so it was evident that she had insisted on going with him on the trail.

"Didn't that seem as if they were friends?" was the next question.

"No!" The denial was emphatic. "He was making love to her, anyone could see that, but she was resisting him. You could see that she hated him."

"And yet she went about with him."

"It was against her will, I am certain of it. She had the air of a prisoner."

Poor, unhappy Violet! It was hard work to control myself as I listened, and pictured her sitting in that doubtful resort, tormented by the vile wooing of the monster who had her in his power, while her jealous rival, with a hired spy in attendance, gloated over her distress.

The merciless accuser went on.

"That night they dined together. I saw him try to slip a bracelet on to her wrist. She snatched her hand away so fiercely that it fell on the floor, and he dropped his napkin over it so as to pick it up without the waiter seeing."

The scene was as vividly before me as though it was passing on the screen. The eyes of jealousy had been sharper than the waiter's.

"Well, let us come to yesterday night. We knew before you told us that one of the dancers wore the dress you have described. What makes you so confident that she was Lady Violet?"

And now indeed I had reason to listen with all my ears. If this girl convinced my chief that she was right, the position would be one of deadly danger.

Sarah Neobard didn't seem to understand the doubt in his mind.

"Madame Bonnell told me so."

Tarleton gave me a stare which I returned with interest. In my excitement I was rash enough to speak.

"She told you so? Why? How could she know herself?"

"I don't know." Sarah looked a little puzzled. "I suppose she knew everything that went on in the Club. Before selling me the ticket she asked if I knew any member. I thought the question was only put for form's sake, and I gave Lady Violet's name. Afterwards I asked her if Lady Violet was likely to be there, and if she knew what costume she was likely to wear. She told me that she was pretty sure to come, and that she always wore the same costume. She made me give her an extra guinea for telling me. I could see she was the sort of woman who would do anything for money."

There could be no doubt that this last opinion was sound. Unfortunately it was too late for me to act on it. I held my tongue again, and let my chief put the next question.

"You watched her, I suppose, during the night? Did you notice nothing peculiar about her? One of the waiters seems to have thought it was a man."

"A man!" The girl's surprise was unmistakable. Her jealousy had blinded her that time as much as it had sharpened her sight the other. "No, I never thought of noticing anything of that sort. I hadn't any reason for it. I believed what I was told. And she behaved just like Lady Violet. And he certainly believed it was she. I tried to keep them apart, but it was no use. I saw him make her come into the alcove. She went unwillingly, just as I should have expected. I got near, and watched them through the curtain. He ordered coffee for both...."

She seemed to pull herself up. Was she telling a carefully framed story, and hesitating at the last fatal point? Or was she only shrinking from uttering the words that might condemn a fellow creature to death?

"And?" the physician breathed gently.

Sarah braced herself up with a visible effort.

"I saw her drop something into his cup."

I believed it was a lie. To this hour I believe it. Sarah Neobard and I are never likely to meet again on this earth, and I may do her an injustice. Yet on her showing, if she was to be believed, she had looked on at what must have seemed to her an attempt to murder, and had not lifted a finger to save the life of the man she half hated and half loved.

Meanwhile the charge had been made, a charge which the adviser of the Home Office was bound to act upon, as the look he gave me clearly showed. I seized on it as an invitation to speak.

"Did you believe that the person, whoever it was, meant to poison him?" I asked, trying to suppress my indignation.

"What else could I believe?" She gave the answer almost rudely, so as to show that she resented my presuming to question her.

"And you did nothing? You didn't interfere?"

The accuser flushed angrily. She stumbled over her reply.

"What could I do? If I had made a scene she would have denied it, and he would have taken her part. Besides, it was all over in a moment. He had drunk his coffee before I had time to do anything."

"Think again," I said earnestly. "You are not on your oath. Are you certain of what you saw? Remember that you are bringing a charge of murder against a fellow creature, a young woman who has done you no wrong, who, you admit yourself, was your step-father's innocent victim."

"I didn't say that. I said she hated him. She can't be innocent if she poisoned him."

"*If* she poisoned him," I repeated with emphasis. "You have heard that she was more than a hundred miles away, according to the police evidence. But the same evidence shows that you were there, and you have told us as much."

"What?" The girl almost leaped from her seat "Are you suggesting that I had anything to do with it?"

I glanced at my chief for permission to go on. He was lying back on his chair, his timepiece twisting between his fingers, apparently listening with the detachment of an impartial judge.

"You compel me to point out to you the situation you are in, Miss Neobard," I continued. "A death has taken place, the police have inquired into it, and they have found cause for suspicion against certain persons. Lady Violet Bredwardine was one of those persons; you were another. Her innocence has now been proved. Yours only rests on your own assertion—or rather it may rest, because so far you haven't actually asserted it. Therefore, you have the strongest possible motive for trying to throw suspicion on someone else; and you have been doing so all along. Now at last you have made a direct charge, and backed it up by stating what you say you saw through a curtain. I ask you again if you are certain of what you say, and I ask you to be careful."

Sarah Neobard's face underwent a succession of changes while she listened, from amazement to wrath and from wrath to abject fear. Tarleton put the crown on her discomfiture.

"Although we are not policemen, and this is not a formal charge, Dr. Cassilis is right to caution you," he said firmly. "I shall feel at liberty to report whatever you say to the police."

The tables were completely turned. The triumphant accuser found herself all at once standing in the dock. She gave us both a long deep look of despairing hatred and dread. Then, with lips tightly closed, she got up and walked out of the room and out of the house.

My chief gratified me with a nod and smile of approval.

"You did that very well, Cassilis; I congratulate you. I think that young woman's teeth have been drawn pretty effectually. It would never have done for her to be going about accusing the police of trying to hush up the case. She would have got some paper to take up her story, and there would have been the devil to pay."

"Do you think there is any chance that she was mixed up in the business?" I asked with hesitation.

Evidently the specialist was displeased by the question.

"It is not my practice to speculate, as I think I have told you. I prefer to confine myself to reasoning on the evidence before me. At present the evidence points to this death being due to a certain drug, which must have been administered during the dance by some person who was present, and who had a motive for rendering Weathered insensible—the death may have been due to his or her ignorance of the power of the drug. We now have direct evidence, which may be true, that the drug was put into his coffee by the dancer disguised as Zenobia, and we have further evidence that that costume was supplied to Lady Violet Bredwardine about a year ago, and was regularly worn by her in the Domino Club.

"Add to that the appearance of her name in the list of suspects compiled from Weathered's diary and the Club register, and the story we have just heard of her being pursued by Weathered and persecuted with attentions which she resented. It is a case on which very few juries would hesitate to convict.

"Against that we have nothing but an idle suspicion on the part of a waiter that the wearer of the Zenobia costume on this particular night was a man, and the police information that Lady Violet left London by a midday train. Of course she may have got out anywhere, and been back long before night."

What was I to say? What ought I to do? Had the time come for me to make the confession I had held back even more for Violet Bredwardine's sake than for my own? I shuddered at the thought that what I had to tell might not exonerate her—that it might deepen the suspicion against her, if it were believed. And suppose it should not be believed? What excuse could I make for having put it off so long? Would not Sir Frank Tarleton have every right to doubt me, and to think that my story was a false one invented at the eleventh hour to save the true culprit?

There was one slender plank to cling to. I was confident that Lady Violet's alibi was genuine. If the question of her guilt or innocence could be made to depend on that, I had no fear of the result.

"In that case, sir, wouldn't it be best for the police to go down to Herefordshire, and make sure whether she was there or not?"

To my surprise Tarleton raised the objection that had held me back before.

"I think not. Captain Charles isn't a particularly tactful man himself, and we can't trust to his employing a very tactful agent. Whether Lady Violet is innocent or guilty she ought not to be alarmed. It seems to me far the best course for me to go down myself, and call on her openly."

I was startled by the proposal. I hardly knew whether to welcome it or not. Certainly the consultant was less likely to frighten Violet than the police were, but on the other hand he was much more likely to find out whatever was to be found.

"Won't that come to the same thing?" I objected feebly. "If she knows you have come to question her about Weathered's death?"

"I may not have to question her about his death," the specialist put in sharply. "Have you forgotten the numbers in the appointment-book? I propose to ask Lady Violet if she can explain what they signify!"

I was silenced. I could think of no possible objection to such a course. It was clear that the explanation must be obtained from someone, and equally clear that Lady Violet was most likely to be able to give it. My chief's plan was worthy of his shrewdness. He would be killing two birds with one stone—gaining information he needed, and at the same time quietly testing the information of the police.

Tarleton gave me no time for further reflection.

"Just look up the trains for Hereford," he said briskly.

I hastened to obey. "Am I coming with you, sir?"

I put the question almost without hope. I was overjoyed by the answer.

"Why, yes, I think you ought to, in fairness to the poor girl. You have defended her very well from her enemy. I look on you as her advocate. I think you ought to be present and help her if you can."

He spoke with a mixture of seriousness and playfulness that left me in doubt whether he had really noticed anything to suggest that I took a personal interest in Lady Violet's defence. I was glad to feel that in any case he had no animosity against her. Even if he thought her guilty of Weathered's death, it was probable that he saw some excuse for the deed.

Nothing more passed between us on the subject till we were in the train for Hereford. During a great part of the journey the consultant sat silent in his corner seat, with his golden pendulum swinging softly in his hand, to the evident astonishment of the solitary passenger who shared our compartment.

I sat opposite him, filled with bitter-sweet reflections and memories that became more intense as we neared the little city on its rushing river beyond the Malvern Hills. How every feature in the landscape recalled the passionate days of yore, when I had made that journey for the first time! Then I had travelled third-class with a knapsack on my back, and the hopes of youth in my heart, on my way to explore the romantic hills and vales of the borderland, the Golden Valley and the untrodden Beacons that looked down on Breconshire. I recalled every step of the way, from the morning on which I had turned my face to the west and tramped out towards the wooded slopes of Blakemere, to the hour when I had encountered in its romantic setting that figure which became for me all that Queen Guinevere had been for Lancelot.

Less than four years had passed since then, and now I was returning to the scene of my wrecked romance, my unforgotten secret agony; returning in official dignity as a representative of the law charged to examine the partner of my secret on a fearful accusation from which perhaps only I could save her, and only at the cost of my own life.

That night I did not sleep. I passed it in wrestling with the problem, as I tossed from side to side on my bed in the hotel where we had put up. But before retiring for the night I had managed to escape from my chief's observation for a few minutes, just long enough to scribble a brief note and despatch it to Tyberton Castle. It ran:

Be out tomorrow *morning when Sir Frank Tarleton arrives. The barn at twelve if possible. Zenobia.*

CHAPTER 11

WHAT THE CIPHER MEANT

Tyberton Castle was less than an hour's drive from Hereford by motor. I had to conceal my knowledge of the neighbourhood from Tarleton, who left the arrangements in my hands, and question the man who waited on us at breakfast as if I were entirely ignorant of where the Castle lay, and how to reach it.

"No breakfast, no man," was a favourite maxim of the physician's, and he did full justice to the fresh trout, the kidneys and bacon, and the new-laid eggs put before us, while I had to force myself to swallow a few mouthfuls. However, the meal was over at last, and at ten o'clock we were seated in the car provided by the hotel, speeding along the road I had last trodden backward with despair in my heart.

It seemed to me that every tree was eloquent and that every cottage on the way remembered me, and wondered at my coming back. As we came near the village I was tempted to shrink back in my corner of the car and hide my face, lest the villagers should recognize it and greet me. I had to tell myself that the real test would come presently. I had never crossed the threshold of the Castle; I had never ventured into the park in the daytime; but there is no such thing as privacy on the country-side; every hedge has eyes and ears; and it was certain that my comings and goings had been watched, and that every child on the Earl of Ledbury's estate and every servant in his house knew more about me than his lordship did.

Tarleton was delighted with the scenery. What pleased him still more was the absence of all traffic. We did not meet one vehicle in the road, except a farmer's cart.

"This is the least-known beauty spot in England," he cried with enthusiasm. "Those hills yonder must be in Radnorshire, a county whose existence I have always doubted. This is the old Welsh March, where the Britons stayed the Saxon advance at last, and kept their freedom in Wild Wales. What a contrast between this and Tarifa Road, Chelsea!"

The reminder came just in time. I had been on the point of telling him that King Arthur's tomb stood on the crest of one of the hills that overlooked the Golden Valley. I bit my lip, thankful that I hadn't betrayed myself.

We went through the sleepy village, bringing out one or two women with babies in their arms to their garden gates. Then we turned into the park and saw the rabbits scampering to the right and left as we crossed the fern-covered slopes.

"This is a true 'haunt of ancient peace,'" murmured the consultant wistfully. "This is the sort of place I want to end my days in. And we have come to disturb it, perhaps to bring disaster and disgrace. I should be glad if we could turn back now and go away again."

I turned to him expectantly. His words had echoed my own thoughts so closely that I half hoped to find him ready to act upon them. But the frown on his brow and the stern set of his mouth told me that I was deluding myself.

The car drew up at the main entrance to the Castle. The ivy-clad ruins to which the building owed its name were almost screened from view by the huge red-brick front of a dull edifice dating from the reign of George the Second. The mansion had been put up out of ostentation at a cost from which the estate had never recovered, and every Earl of Ledbury since had cursed his ancestor's extravagance. I know that the present Earl found it hard to pay the interest on his mortgages, and that he lived in one corner of the vast house, leaving long corridors and whole suites of rooms to the spiders and rats.

We got out, and Sir Frank Tarleton gave his card and mine to the man who came down the steps to receive us. His suit of black was threadbare, and his coat looked as if it had been thrust on hastily at the sound of our approach.

"Please take our cards to Lady Violet Bredwardine, and ask her ladyship if we can see her in private, on urgent business."

The servant stared at the message. His eyes wandered from Tarleton to me, and I thought there was a vague recognition in them when they met mine. But his manner was respectful and demure.

"I'm sorry, sir, but I believe her ladyship is out. I will inquire if you wish."

He seemed to be hesitating whether to ask us inside. Sir Frank seized on the opening.

"I shall be glad if you will find out when she is likely to be in. Her ladyship is staying in the Castle, I suppose?"

"Oh, yes, sir." The answer was given readily.

"We have come down from London on purpose to see her. They told us at Grosvenor Place that her ladyship had come here—I think it was on Wednesday."

The man bowed. "That is quite right, sir. Her ladyship arrived on Wednesday evening."

I stole an anxious glance at my chief. It was a complete confirmation of the Inspector's report. If Lady Violet had arrived at the Castle in the evening, she could not have been back in town the same night. The alibi stood firm.

Tarleton drew out his watch as though to consult it before deciding what to do next. Suddenly he snapped out, "There is no mistake, I suppose? Her ladyship couldn't have been in London on Wednesday night?"

The man was taken off his guard, and if he had been lying he could hardly have failed to show some confusion. But the only feeling he manifested was one of resentment at the question.

"I'm positive of what I say, sir. But her ladyship hasn't authorized me to answer questions about her movements."

The consultant put on the air of a man who has made a slip.

"No, no; of course not. I meant to ask her ladyship herself." He turned to me. "What do you say, Cassilis? Shall we wait inside, or shall we go for a stroll and come back again?"

I had laid my plans in the expectation that Lady Violet would be out, and I was ready with a suggestion. I made it with my heart in my mouth.

"I think one of us ought to wait here, Sir Frank. The other might walk round the park, and perhaps meet Lady Violet."

Sir Frank seemed to find the proposal quite natural.

"Very good. I shall be glad to stretch my legs for an hour, so I'll leave you here and come back again."

This was an unforeseen check. I had been so sure of being the one to go out into the grounds, if I could effect the separation, that I hadn't thought of the alternative. My only chance now was to slip out as soon as Tarleton's back was turned. I looked at the servant, and fancied that his eye rested on me with a more friendly air than on my companion.

"Would you like to wait inside, sir?" he asked.

I hesitated. But I had to choose between trusting him and trusting the chauffeur who had driven us out from Hereford; and he had impressed me favourably. I followed him into the Castle, while Tarleton moved off down an avenue of beeches in the park.

The servant brought me through a dreary hall full of old suits of armour and ancient high-backed chairs, but lacking in those little touches of modern comfort that are needed to make such a place home-like and attractive to the eye. He opened a door towards the inner end, and ushered me into a gloomy library, fitted up with great bookcases that looked as if they were never opened, stuffed with huge leather-bound volumes of the kind that no human being any longer wants to read. The whole room reminded me of the fairy tale of the Sleeping Beauty in the Wood. It seemed to breathe of the eighteenth century, as though its life had been arrested then, and no one had trodden the faded carpet or taken down one of the dusty tomes for a hundred long years since.

The manservant had taken up a silver plate as we passed through the hall, and laid our cards on it. He now asked, "Shall I take these cards to his lordship, sir?"

He must have seen me start at the question. I put my hand into my pocket, searching his face carefully the while.

"There is no occasion for that," I said. "Our business with her ladyship is private, and she may not wish his lordship to be troubled with it." I took out a note before adding, "Perhaps you remember my face?"

The man looked pleased. His chances of adding to his wages can't have been very many in that lonely mansion. It seemed to me, moreover, that he was genuinely attached to his young mistress.

"Why, yes, sir. I did have a thought as I had seen you here before. You were staying at the Moorfield Farm, if I rec'lect rightly, sir, three years ago or might be four."

I nodded, and the piece of paper passed silently from my hand to his.

"I've come to do a service to Lady Violet, if I can," I told him. "Her ladyship knows I am coming, and she has gone out to meet me. I want you to let me out at the back of the Castle, so that I can join her; and say nothing to the friend who has come with me, or anybody else."

He gave me a quick look of intelligence. "I understand, sir."

He led the way out of the library again, and along a corridor still more deserted and dismal than the hall. It ended at a locked and barred door which he unfastened with some effort.

"This is the way into the ruins," he explained. "You can pass out from them into a path that leads through the home meadows up to the Moorfield Farm. It's a public footpath, and if anyone sees you they'll think you've been exploring the ruins from outside."

Nothing could have suited better with my plans. I knew the path, and knew that at a certain point another diverged from it and led through a well-remembered wood to the barn where I had asked Violet Bredwardine to meet me.

I passed out into the Castle grounds and clambered over the crumbling walls and fallen stones till I found myself on the path. And now every step became tragical. I was treading on the ashes of the fire in which two hearts had been scorched and branded with a mark that could never be effaced.

The grass beside the narrow footway seemed to be stained with blood. I drew my breath in pain as I mounted the slope towards the lonely little farm-house in which I had passed the most glorious and the most miserable hours of my life. When I came to the gate into the wood, I stopped and leant upon it panting, and hardly able to proceed.

The wood was haunted by ghosts more dreadful to me than any spirits of the dead; the ghosts of passion and of pain, the ghosts of love and hatred, of that most terrible of all hatred which is born of love betrayed.

I shuddered as I thrust open the gate and stepped beneath the trees. A sombre fir drooped like a weeping willow over one spot where the way was crossed by a trickling spring that plunged and disappeared down a steep gully choked with brambles and dark ferns. But there was a worse point than that to pass. A tall beech sent out its roots on to the path, and on the smooth rind of its trunk were cut two initial letters entwined—a V and B. The very knife that had scored them there lay in my pocket; I had never parted with it. What madness had tempted me to blazon our secret to the inquisitive country-side? I had used one precaution: I had cut the proclamation of our love on the side of the trunk that was hidden from the public way. Now, when I reached the tree, I forced a passage through the undergrowth to see how time and weather had dealt with that vain memorial. A bitter shock awaited me. Every vestige of the monogram had been destroyed by deep cuts and slashes in the bark. Only a confused web of scars and scratches marked the place. The tree's wounds seemed to reproduce the wounds upon two hearts.

My head drooped as I dragged myself up the rest of the ascent, and came out of the wood on the open hillside. The view was exquisite. The hills of three fair counties stretched away to the horizon, and at their feet the silver Wye clasped the rich cornfields and pastures in its shining arms. But the whole prospect was darkened over for my eyes by an invisible cloud. I turned to the spot where, scarcely a hundred yards away, there rose out of the bracken the high gray walls of the forsaken barn.

Its desolation seemed symbolical. When it was built centuries ago the surrounding land had borne crops worth harvesting instead of the thin grass and waste of bracken that now surrounded it on all sides. Tradition spoke of a time not remote when the hill swarmed with folk engaged in tilling the hard soil. Their ruined cottages still lined the lanes that crept along the crest, and peeped out of the sheltered nooks. The virgin prairies of the New World had tempted some of them away; others had migrated to the mining valleys whose smoke could almost be seen from where I stood.

So the gray ancient barn stood empty, its wooden doors dangling helpless from their rusty staples, and the wind whistling through the narrow slits that showed like the arrow holes of a Norman keep. I made my way across the standing bracken that rose up to my shoulders, and gained the open doorway. But there was no one within. A solitary sheep started up from the litter of chaff that strewed the floor, and bounded out through an opening in the opposite wall, leaving me alone.

And now I began to repent that I had named as the meeting-place the spot where we had parted in such misery those three years ago. I turned with a pang from the scene, and advanced slowly towards the brow of the hill. Just below the crest, seated on a moss-covered stone beside a spring, I found her.

Violet Bredwardine rose and stood where she was, more like a statue than a living woman. Her light ringlets, breaking from beneath a quaint straw helmet, surrounded her face like a halo, and made it seem more than ever like the face of the child angel she had seemed to me when I saw her first. Even then there had been a wistful look in her innocent blue eyes, as though the child angel had lost her way in this troubled earth of ours, and was seeking pitifully for some escape. And I dreamt—in my madness I had dreamt—that I could offer her the help she needed, and change the sadness of her life into joy.

I strode towards her, all the old, passionate impulses of the past flooding my heart like wine, and cried, "Violet!"

She shrank back as if I had struck her and the soft eyes flashed with anger.

"How dare you! How dare you ask me to meet you like this?"

I stopped ashamed. In an instant my sudden emotion was chilled. I felt myself a criminal facing my judge.

"Forgive me," I stammered. "I was obliged to speak to you before you saw Sir Frank Tarleton. I had to explain to you who he was and what he was going to ask you."

She interrupted me with a gesture of scorn. She pointed to the roof of the barn, just visible over the crest of the slope from where we stood.

"How dared you ask me to meet you *there*? Was there no other place?" Her voice shook. "How could you be so brutal? To remind me! To drag me back to the one spot on earth that I was trying to forget!"

The reproach pierced me like a knife. She was right. What was I but a brute? What else is any man in dealing with the mystery of a woman's heart—with those delicate fibres which our rude touch so often bruises and rends unawares?

I could have thrown myself at her feet and begged her to trample the life out of me. But there would have been no reparation in that; there was none in anything that I could think of doing. It was a case of least said soonest mended. I had to leave the wound I had given her to heal itself, and meanwhile try to render her the only service that was in my power.

"You can say nothing to me that I don't deserve, nothing that is severe enough," I answered. "I can only plead that I was distracted by anxiety, on your account."

The indignation in her face turned to terror.

"What do you mean? You wrote to me that I had nothing more to fear."

"I said, nothing more to fear from Dr. Weathered. That was all I thought it safe to put in a letter. And when I wrote it I hoped that I could protect you from any further trouble. But other things have happened since. There are complications in the case that I couldn't explain without seeing you, and Sir Frank Tarleton has come down here to see if you can throw light on them."

"Sir Frank Tarleton? Who is he?"

"He is the principal medical adviser to the Home Office. I am his assistant."

"But I don't understand!" She stared at me in natural wonder. "Why should he be mixed up in it? Have you told him anything?"

"Nothing; you may be assured of that. But I must tell you what has happened. Weathered is dead."

"Dead." The blue eyes expanded for a moment in a gleam of relief, almost of exultation. The instant after they froze dreadfully. "Bertrand! You killed him!" she whispered.

I shook my head earnestly.

"No. I should have killed him, if there had been no other way to save you from him. And I don't believe any honest man or woman would have blamed me if I had. But it wasn't necessary. My only object was to destroy the record of your confession, the statement that had placed you in his power. All I did was to drug him enough to make him insensible, and take his keys. When I left the Club at three o'clock in the morning he was still alive. He was found dead where I left him two hours afterwards."

Violet hardly seemed to be listening. Her eyes were still fixed on me like two blue stones.

"You did it," she repeated dully. "You killed him—for my sake!"

Even in the midst of the intense strain those last three words thrilled me with secret joy. Heaven forgive me for wishing for an instant that they were true. I could have brought myself to accept the terrible possibility which had been haunting me ever since the voice of Inspector Charles had told me through the telephone that Weathered was a corpse, the possibility that I had administered a fatal dose. But I saw that Violet was on the verge of breaking down. For her sake, far more than for my own, I must banish that theory from the field.

"No," I assured her again. "That is out of the question. Sir Frank Tarleton is the greatest living authority on poisons, and he has been engaged for the last three days in trying to ascertain the cause of death. I have been by his side the whole time, assisting him, and I know that his suspicions point in another direction altogether."

I broke off to catch her in my arms as she swayed forward. I was just in time. I laid her gently on the moss and sprinkled her face with water from the spring, the sweet face that I would have given all I possessed to sprinkle with kisses instead. Luckily the collapse was only momentary. While I was still bending over her she opened her lips to say, "Go on. Tell me everything."

I waited till she had recovered strength enough to sit up. It would have done harm to wait longer. It was necessary for her to know exactly how matters stood.

"Dr. Weathered had other victims beside you, and other enemies beside me. The police are on the trail of some of them and Sir Frank has obtained an important clue which may lead us to the true cause of death. But meanwhile notice has been attracted to the costume in which I went to the Domino Club that night."

Violet began to look frightened.

"The one I lent you?—you ought to have destroyed it!" she said excitedly.

"It is very fortunate I didn't," I returned soothingly. "It has come out that it was the costume you generally wore; and you remember that was why you lent it to me, so that Weathered should think I was you. Anyhow, it has been traced to you, and if you couldn't produce it you would be called on to account for its disappearance. Do you see that?"

"Yes, I see that. But surely if they know the costume was mine they must believe that I was there that night. My God, do they suspect me of the murder?"

I was agonized by her terror.

"They know you to be innocent. Your innocence has been proved," I cried out fiercely. "You have what the law calls an alibi; you were more than a hundred miles away when the crime was committed—if there was a crime. Good heavens, Violet, can you believe that I shouldn't have given myself up to justice the very moment it was necessary to clear you?"

Her expression softened more than I could have hoped.

"I know that, Bertrand," she said in a low voice. "Only I don't understand why you are here. What does Sir Frank Tarleton want with me?"

"He wanted two things. One was to make sure that you really were here on Wednesday night. He is now quite satisfied of that. The other is to ask you if you can explain something that has puzzled us in Weathered's appointment-book. Whenever your name appears it is followed by a number, and we don't know why."

Violet lowered her eyes with a frown.

"He gave me that number to sign my letters by when I wrote to him. He told me that it would help me to write more freely if I used a number instead of a name."

I started in alarm. "But why should you need that? What were the letters about?"

The poor girl's eyes still refused to meet mine.

"He made me tell him the whole story in letters. He said that was the only way to get it off my mind."

I clenched my teeth together to keep myself from uttering a word. The doctor's safe had been opened and his case-book destroyed uselessly.

CHAPTER 12

PSYCHO-ANALYSIS

It was one of those moments in which life seems to cast away the mask of convention and spring upon us like a giant fanged and armed for our destruction; one of those moments in which the bravest heart quails and the strongest hope withers to despair.

My crime had been committed for nothing. Whether the death of that despicable villain lay at my door or not, I did not know, and it hardly seemed to matter any longer. Somewhere there was still in existence the weapon with which he had terrorized his unhappy victim, and I could not tell in what hands, nor when it might be employed to ruin her and me together.

Weathered's cunning scheme stood revealed in its full atrocity. His patients had been divided into two classes. Those who had nothing serious on their consciences, and those whom it was not worth his while to blackmail received the ordinary treatment given to nervous patients by respectable physicians. Those who came to him to be cured of vicious propensities, on the other hand, were encouraged to indulge them under his eye, under the pretence that they would thus be gradually overcome; and those who sought relief from evil memories were bidden to rid their mind of its secret burden in correspondence which could be preserved for future use.

So far as I could judge he had fallen into those evil courses by degrees. Sarah Neobard's defence of her step-father might not be far from the truth. I thought it likely that such a man as Weathered, with no strong principle to keep him straight, might naturally have deteriorated under the influence of his patients. All the precautions with which the confessional is surrounded in Catholic churches were wanting in this case. The doctor was probably a man without any religious feeling, and without any real scruples on the subject of morality. Instead of curing his patients he had let himself become infected with their disease. The confessions he had listened to had inflamed his own imagination, and made evil familiar to his thoughts. In the end he had come to take a fiendish pleasure in gloating over tales of guilty indulgence and innocence betrayed. He had delighted in the analysis of women's hearts; he had learned to play upon their sensitive natures like instruments, and draw the notes of passion and pain. The devils in hell must soothe their own torments with such music.

It was torture enough for me to think of my own tragedy, as well as Violet's, profaned by the coarse curiosity of a blackmailer. If I had sinned—and I never could admit that she had sinned at all—if I had sinned, at least I had not done so wilfully and basely, but swept away on the overpowering flood of that tremendous impulse by which all the planets move in heaven, and all the earth is wrapped in her green garment, and all the birds burst into song, and all the race of man is renewed forever.

Our sad romance began in the purest innocence. I did not know of her existence on that morning when I set out with a knapsack on my back to explore the old borderland of England and Wales. I had formed no fixed plans; I meant to walk where fancy took me, and stop when I felt inclined; and the last thing I expected was that I should pass all my holiday on one spot. It was not till I reached the village that I heard of the ruins that lay hidden at the back of the Earl of Ledbury's stately seat, and was persuaded to turn aside and see them.

I was told that a footpath leading from the churchyard up the hill would bring me past them, and, as far as I could make out, his lordship had laid down no absolute rule against strangers going over them. I was young and irresponsible enough to take the risk of being turned out as a trespasser. I climbed over a gate padlocked and fortified with barbed wire, crossed a meadow, and passed through a gap in the outer wall. I had spent half an hour in scrambling over heaps of fallen masonry, and was just beginning to descend a broken stairway up which I had climbed for the sake of the view, when I saw standing on the grass near its foot the loveliest girl I had ever seen.

She was watching me with the shy wonder of a child, and I came down slowly, scarcely daring to breathe, lest she should turn and run away. But no such thought was in her head. I seemed to her a boy, very little older than herself, and it turned out that she had come to take me under her protection.

When I lifted my cap, and expressed a hope that I wasn't trespassing, she gave me a cordial smile of a comrade in mischief.

"Yes, you are trespassing," she said frankly, "but they won't take any notice if they see me speaking to you. I saw you from my window and I came to prevent any of the servants driving you away."

I hardly knew which was more delicious, the simplicity or the friendliness of the child angel, as she was named already in my thoughts. That night I heard her story from the good mistress of the farm. She had lost her mother as soon as she was born, and, as sometimes happens, she had lost her place in her father's heart in consequence. He was then a middle-aged man, his wife had been the only woman he had ever cared for, and she had borne him no other child. Life for him was closed. He resigned himself to let the earldom and the encumbered estate pass to his brother, and shut himself up with his grief in the one habitable corner of his desolate house.

Of Violet he took no more notice than he could help. His sense of duty bade him engage a strict governess, and direct that his daughter should be brought up to marry money, since he could leave her none. The governess conceived that the way to attain this end was to keep the girl in absolute seclusion till a suitable bridegroom was found, and then to thrust her into his arms. The result was that her life had actually been very much like that of a princess in a fairy tale who is immured in a tower and kept from the sight of men. And I had been cast unconsciously for the part of the fairy hero who scales the tower and wins the maiden's heart.

In the first confusion of the meeting I was far more tongue-tied than she. I guessed, of course, that she must be the daughter of Lord Ledbury, and this was the first time I had ever spoken to anyone of her rank. I was in doubt whether to address her with the word ladyship. I think the awe with which her rank inspired me had a great deal to do with what followed. It lifted her so far above me in my own mind, that I was blind to her growing love, and at first mistook my own love for the devotion of a vassal to his queen.

She talked to me about the ruins, holding me there spell-bound till neither of us could find more to say. At last, when I felt obliged to come away, she asked me wistfully where I was going. And I, who had made up my mind already not to go, if I could find any excuse for staying in the neighbourhood, with any chance of meeting her again, answered vaguely that I didn't know. I was looking, I told her, for some place where I could put up.

Her whole face brightened when I said that, and she cried eagerly, "There is a farm-house on the hill where they take visitors in the summer, and I don't think they have anyone yet. I often go past it in my walks, and I haven't seen any strangers about."

My heart exulted within me. There was to be no walking tour for me that summer. When one has come within the gates of Paradise how can he want to wander more?

And so I took off my knapsack in the honeysuckle porch of the little farm-house, and stayed on. It chanced for our undoing that the strict governess had gone away for her own holiday a day or two before I came, and did not return till it was time for me to exile myself from Eden. Violet was left alone. No callers had come to the Castle for many years. There were no neighbours in her own station of life within many miles. The clergyman was an old bachelor interested only in butterflies and moths, of which he had a wonderful collection, and blind to everything that went on in his parish. If our romance was watched, and I have no doubt that it was watched by many curious eyes unknown to us, none of the watchers dared to carry tales of his daughter to the Earl of Ledbury. Violet saw her father twice a day at meals, and he never dreamed of asking her how she spent her time between.

The golden month rolled by. The first few days each of us made believe that our meetings were accidental. But soon we ceased to pretend that it was chance that had led her steps up the hill and led mine down them to the wood in which we came together. We explored the hills in company, rousing the partridges from the corn and rabbits from the fern. The wood-pigeons cooed and wheeled above our heads; the robins peeped at us from the hedges and the squirrels from the trees. We stood beside the lonely cromlech named after the mythical hero who held the Saxon hosts at bay, and we looked down into the Golden Valley and saw the peaks of the Welsh mountains far away. And we were happy....

Lightly, O lightly, broke upon me the knowledge that she loved me. What I had never hoped for had come to pass. I had been content to worship her in silence. Endymion might so have worshipped Artemis if he had been the first to see her. Bottom, the weaver, might so have worshipped Titania if the magic juice had touched his eyelids before hers. She had been as unapproachable in my eyes as any inhabitant of the moonlit world of sleep. It was with almost a pang, with a strange shrinking of the heart, that I first perceived that she was mortal like myself, and that I had awakened her. I seemed to have broken into a temple and profaned the shrine.

I do not recollect that we said anything. One day when we were walking side by side along a sunken lane that led to a little waterfall I stooped suddenly and kissed her.

From that day we were sweethearts as openly as any rustic pair. To her it was all as natural as the romances she had read, and she can never have had the least suspicion of the misgivings that had vexed my soul. She seemed surprised even when I touched on the social gulf that separated us. She owned sorrowfully that her father would never hear of such a match, but she evidently took it for granted that I should not heed his opposition. I was her knight, and it was for me to overcome every obstacle in the way. Her faith in me was perfect. All affection for her father had been crushed out of her in childhood. She had loved me more easily, and she loved me more passionately, because she had no one else to love.

And what were we to do? I was barely of age. I was not qualified; I had no means of support except a dwindling legacy that would be exhausted by the time I was able to earn my first fee. The knights of old seem never to have been troubled by such hindrances as these; the dragons they vanquished were creatures who could be subdued by strength of arm; they never had to ride into anything worse than an ogre's castle or a wizard's cave. The terrors of the bank parlour and the house-agent's office were unknown to them; and they never had to face a baker or a butcher armed with his weekly bill.

I put off as long as I could the pain of confessing to Violet that these dragons in the way must take years to vanquish. And at first she hardly grasped what it would mean to her. The mere waiting, I could see, would cost her less than me. After all, courtship is the supreme time of womanhood. Then she is queen indeed, and marriage is for her dethronement. Her bridal is like the glorious pyre on which the Hindu widow once expired in religious ecstasy. It was not until she realized that I was going that Violet broke down.

There the burden was shifted to the other side. Delay is the suffering of man, separation the suffering of woman. I had my work to go back to; I had my friends and all the distractions of life in London. She had nothing before her but her remote and solitary prison.

We had fallen into the way of meeting most often in the deserted barn. Its situation assured us of a privacy more secure than that of the lanes and woods. No one could approach us without being seen, and no one ever did approach. No one could see through the openings—a bare two inches wide in the thick wall; and no one could overhear. A pile of bracken made our seat, and there we rested many a long summer afternoon, the battered door thrown wide to let us count the windings of the river far below, while we talked of all the coming years might bring.

So it was there we met on that last afternoon to say good-bye. We had put off till the last moment any consideration of what was to happen next. We had made no plans to meet again. I did not even know that Lord Ledbury had a house in London, to which Violet was taken at rare intervals, when it happened to be without a tenant, but always under strict guard and more for business than for pleasure. We had not even discussed any plans for correspondence, though it was evident that I could not write to her at her father's house without everything coming out. It was understood between us that my very existence must be kept secret if it were possible. Beyond that we had not found courage to face the situation.

And now we had to face it at last, and it was too much for us to bear. It seemed to both of us like death. It was idle to think that we could part like that, uncertain if ever we should meet again. It was a waste of breath to pronounce the word good-bye when we were clinging to each other in the desperation of young life in travail with its destiny. I dare not try to recall that agony…. I stole across with the footstep of a felon and closed the battered door.

When I had slain my love I understood too late what I had done. Her anguish was a revelation to me of what her utter purity had been. We passed out from that brief frenzy into a strange world. The sun had fallen from our sky, and Joshua could not have called it back again. We were two spectres in each other's sight. I did not ask her to forgive me—I could not forgive myself. Rather would I have begged her to reproach me. But no such thought was in her mind. Her whole feeling was one of horror at what she had destroyed in herself; and I was only hateful to her as the mirror in which she had seen her unknown self. She moved her lips to implore me never to let her see me again. She shuddered past me, and went down the hill with the stumbling gait of a wounded bird.

I know there are some men, and there may be some women, who will think that I was a fool to let her go. They will tell me that I ought not to have taken her at her word; that if I had waited, in a short time she would have recovered, and the breach might have been patched up, and the wound healed. I cannot tell if they are right; I only know that I obeyed her, and fled from her neighbourhood with no hope of ever coming back.

And so the lonely girl, left to herself with no one to confide in, brooded over her secret till it became like a viper gnawing at her heart. How she came to hear of the charlatan she had not told me. Somehow or other during one of her stays in her father's house in town, the news reached her of the new science of psycho-analysis, and of the practitioner who undertook to do what Macbeth longed for in vain, to pluck from memory a rooted sorrow, and erase the writing from the tablets of the brain.

She went to him, of course, without consulting those about her, and from that moment she became his helpless prey. What arts he used to beguile her it is easy to guess. At first she believed in him, and when her suspicion began to be aroused she was already in his power, and dared not break with him.

By this time the Earl of Ledbury and the duenna had put their heads together and decided that Lady Violet must pass a season in London, and be seen in the great world. In consequence she had much more liberty. She made some girl friends whom she was allowed to go about with, and among them were not a few who held modern notions on the rights of girlhood, and were ready to encourage and to screen her in the courses into which she was compelled by her taskmaster. Her most intimate comrade willingly became a member of the Domino Club.

But not even to her most intimate friend dared Violet disclose the true situation. While she still trusted in Weathered and believed in his power to heal her soul of sin, she had written the whole story of our love in letters which the scoundrel now refused to give up, except as the price of a far worse surrender. There was only one being in the world whom she could appeal to without the risk of further shame. And thus we met again.

The medical directory gave her my address, and she wrote to me at Sir Frank Tarleton's. But her letter begged for a strictly private interview in such urgent language that I thought it safer not to let her come there. I asked her to meet me at the corner of Shaftesbury Avenue, as though by accident, and I took her to the little room which I could call my own.

Nearly four years had gone by since our tragic parting, but when we stood face to face again they did not seem four hours. Violet's face changed from red to white and back again as she half held out a trembling hand and dropped it woefully; and my hand trembled too as I raised it to my hat. I thought it best to say nothing except the few words necessary to explain where we were going, and she seemed glad to keep silent till we were safely there.

The story she had to tell was so appalling, and the effort of telling it cost her so much, that naturally a good deal was left out. Certainly I quite failed to gather from her that Weathered had induced her to make her confession to him in letters. I supposed that he had taken it down from her lips. It is the familiar practice of West End consultants, who see their patients at long intervals, to make a careful entry of all the particulars of the case for future reference; and I supposed that Weathered had taken advantage of this to make a damning record in his case-book, which would be quite sufficient to enable him to blast his victims' reputation, although it might not be evidence in a lawyer's eyes.

The truth is that I was myself too agitated to go into the matter carefully even if Violet had been in a state to be cross-examined. The whole interview resolved itself into a series of wild outbreaks on her part, and attempts to assure her on mine. Indeed, I hardly know that we arrived at any clear understanding of what she was asking of me, or what I was promising her. The one thing clear to me was that the only way to save her would be for me to get at the doctor's case-book and destroy it. And to do that I must obtain his keys.

What Violet had told me about the Domino Club and their meetings in that accursed place gave me my plan. I would do what I could not ask her to do. All that was necessary was that I should be able to approach Weathered without putting him on his guard. I must disguise myself in a costume with which he was familiar, one which would allure him, and in which I could play the part of the sought rather than the seeker. And so the fatally easy plot took shape.

There was barely an inch between Violet and me in height, and that inch would be concealed by the Zenobia helmet. It would not be too difficult for me to imitate for an hour or two the lighter movements of a woman. Weathered would be quite unsuspicious; the dress, the artificial light, the noise and excitement of the revel would all be in my favour. The doctor, I gathered, drank freely on these occasions; I had only to wait till the night was advanced and the wine had done its work.

I told the distressed girl as little as possible of what I meant to do, or to attempt. I said merely that I must meet Weathered, and that it would be the best way for me to impersonate her for one night. She consented readily enough—what else could she do? She told me the date of the next dance, and undertook to send the mask and costume to my room some days beforehand, so that I should have time to see that it fitted, and to practice moving about with it on.

We did not bid each other any formal farewell. Nothing was said about our next meeting, indeed I felt no confidence that there would be another. She had been driven to appeal to me in her extremity, but she showed no sign of having forgiven me. Rather she seemed to find every moment painful that she passed with me. All the time she was struggling with herself, trying to speak to me as if I were a stranger whom she found herself obliged to trust, but continually faltering and letting her voice die down to a broken whisper.

When I had let her out at the street door she hurried away blindly like an escaping prisoner. And as soon as she was out of sight I hastened round to Montague Street, and locked myself up in Tarleton's arsenal of poisons.

CHAPTER 13

THE EARL OF LEDBURY INTERVENES

My first thought, when I knew that Violet's confession was still undestroyed, was to hide the fact from her. I must spare her the torturing apprehensions that I felt myself. Fortunately she did not seem to be thinking of her own danger; at all events, she put no questions to me about the letters. Perhaps she took it for granted that I had secured them, or that they were no longer in existence. At all events, the possibility that they might be in other hands as dangerous as Weathered's did not seem to strike her at the moment. The idea that I had murdered Weathered overpowered all her faculties.

Again and again I went over with her all that had happened.

"I don't believe that I killed him," I told her with the utmost earnestness. "Surely you can trust me to know what I was doing. I am not an ordinary doctor. I have made a special study of poisons, as the pupil, I may say the favourite pupil, of the greatest expert alive. I am prepared to swear to you or in any court of justice that the dose I gave him would not have killed any man in a normal condition of health. Sir Frank Tarleton and I both observed symptoms that point to some other drug having been administered to Weathered. Remember that you were not his only patient, and you are not likely to have been the only one whose confidence he abused. The Domino Club probably swarmed with his enemies, in fact the manageress as good as told us so. His own step-daughter asserts that there were other women with whom he had mysterious relations—"

"Other women!" She interrupted me with a cry of dismay. "Do you mean—does she know anything about me?"

I recollected Sarah Neobard's fierce denunciation, and the scene she had described, when she sat with her hired spy in the restaurant watching the persecuted girl. I tried to explain away my unlucky slip.

"No, no; I didn't mean that for a moment. She told us that her step-father had dealings with some of his women patients, and one of the waiters in the Club described some women who were there that night. He described me among others; that is to say, he described the costume I was wearing. But he suspected that it was worn by a man. He must have keen eyes."

"Then you are under suspicion!" Her anxiety was instantly diverted from herself to me again.

"Not at all," I answered. "No one has the least suspicion who the wearer of the costume really was. The police made inquiries, and all they learned was that a similar costume had been supplied to you a year ago. They followed up the clue, and found that you were down here on the night, so that it must have been someone else in the Club. Now you see why I sent it back to you. If Sir Frank Tarleton says anything about it, all you have to do is to say that you remember having such a costume, and offer to find it and show it to him. He and the police will naturally believe that the one worn at the Club that night was a duplicate."

Violet looked a little uncertain, as she had some excuse for being. I thought I might venture now to ask her to come back to the house to meet my formidable chief.

"Sir Frank will be there by the time that we get down," I said. "He has gone for an hour's stroll in the park."

She put her hand to her head as she stood up and prepared to come with me.

"Will he ask me anything else? What were you going to tell me just now?"

"The numbers," I reminded her. "He will ask you if you know what they meant."

"Ah! Must I tell him that? Must he know about the letters? Will everything come out?—O Bertrand!"

Her gasp of anguish wrung my very heart-strings.

"No!" I cried. "Don't give way to such thoughts. You don't know Tarleton. He is the soul of honour. He is delicacy itself. He won't ask you one word more than he can help. You need tell him nothing more than that Weathered gave you a number to use in writing to him. You can trust Sir Frank not to ask you what the letters were about."

"But he will know—he will know!" she sighed despairingly. And I could say little in reply.

We found the door unlocked that led from the house into the ruins, and we parted in the corridor, Violet going upstairs to her room while I made my way back to the library into which I had been shown at first. Waiting for me outside the door I found my friendly manservant.

"You'll find the other gentleman inside," he whispered. "He's been back about five minutes."

I went in trying to look unconcerned, and found Tarleton comfortably seated in an armchair engaged in the familiar rite of waving his mascot to and fro as if it were a censer with which he was offering invisible incense to the Sphinx.

"I hope I haven't kept you waiting, sir. I have been taking a look at the ruins of the old Castle."

"I have had a look at them, too," was the enigmatic answer. "Twelfth century, I should think. One of the first castles put up by the Normans when they began penetrating South Wales."

I could only hope that that was the extent of his observations. I could not bring myself to ask.

There was silence between us till Violet came into the room. The change in her amazed me. She was rather pale but perfectly composed. Her manner was full of courteous dignity. It was the first time that I had seen her as the Lady Violet Bredwardine, the daughter of a noble house, conscious of her claims to deference from strangers.

The consultant rose from his seat with every mark of respect and consideration, and I clumsily imitated him. She was the first to speak.

"Sir Frank Tarleton?—I am told that you wish to see me on urgent business. I am sorry that you have been kept waiting, but I had gone out for a walk. Won't you sit down?"

She included me in the invitation by a slight, distant bow, as she seated herself facing us.

"It is very good of you to see me, Lady Violet.—Dr. Cassilis is my assistant." Another distant bow. "I have been called in as a physician in the case of another medical man who had the honour to include you among his patients, I believe—Dr. Weathered."

A bow in the affirmative, still colder, if possible.

"I regret to have to inform you that Dr. Weathered has died—of heart failure."

A little gasp, natural enough in the circumstances. A gasp of relief in my ears, relief at hearing the death described as natural. A gasp of surprise, I could only hope, in the keen ears of my chief.

"Dr. Weathered's death was rather sudden. It is desirable for the sake of his family to dispense with an inquest if possible, but it has been necessary to make some inquiries into his affairs, and I have had to go through his appointment-book, the book in which he entered the names of his patients who came to see him, you understand."

"I understand." Just a tremor, immediately subdued.

"Naturally your name appears in the book among others. And it happens to be one of several that have numbers attached to them, as if for purposes of identification. If you know, or can suggest, the reason for that, I shall be very much obliged by your telling me."

Violet straightened herself up and spoke very distinctly. It was clear to me that she had prepared her answer carefully.

"I can tell you exactly. When Dr. Weathered's patients had to write to him about whatever he was treating them for, he gave them a number to use instead of their own names. The letters were confidential."

Tarleton's face told me that he had grasped the full situation, as I had grasped it half an hour before. He looked at me instead of her, but he failed to hide his consternation altogether.

"What is the matter? Why do you look like that?" the startled girl exclaimed.

The specialist pulled himself together.

"There is nothing the matter, Lady Violet. I was staggered for a moment at the thought of what might have happened if I hadn't taken the precaution of coming here and questioning you. I will see that this correspondence is destroyed unread as soon as I get back to town. Unless, that is, it has been destroyed already. Dr. Weathered may have burnt the letters as soon as he had read them."

The explanation was not very happy. Poor Violet's dignity forsook her as she realized for the first time that the outpouring of her heart, the record of her secret shame, were at the mercy of whatever stranger first gained access to the dead man's repository. She did her best to keep her eyes from straying in my direction, but the half turn of her head towards me before she spoke to Tarleton was enough to tell me what she felt.

"Do you mean," she faltered, "that there is a danger of someone finding these letters?—someone who might make use of them?"

I had not often seen my chief at a loss, but he was plainly put out now.

"My dear young lady, there isn't the least fear of that. It may ease your mind if I tell you more than I intended. Dr. Weathered's death occurred in a club in Chelsea, and the proprietress or manager, whichever she really is, sent for the police. They thought the death might be due to foul play, and they have been making some inquiries. Meanwhile, they have had their eyes on everyone who would be at all likely to have anything to do with the case, and you may be sure that if the doctor left any secret correspondence it will be secured and burnt immediately."

Violet had glanced at my face while he was speaking, and had read in it, no doubt, that it would be her best course to appear satisfied. She murmured a "Thank you."

"There is one other question I should like to ask you, but I hope you won't think it concerns you personally. The doctor's death took place on Wednesday night, and as you were more than a hundred miles away, no one supposes that you can throw any light on what took place in the Club that night."

He paused for a moment, as if to give her a chance of asking how he came to know that she was so far away. But of course I had already given her the information, and she was afraid to speak.

"But it seems that you have a double, or rather that someone was impersonating you that night. The attention of the police was drawn to the presence of a dancer wearing a fancy dress which the costumiers consider to represent Zenobia, the famous Queen of Palmyra who fought against the Romans in the third century. They made inquiries, and heard that a similar costume had been supplied to you about a year ago.—Can you tell me what has become of it?"

The final question was put abruptly. It was well that Violet had been prepared for it. She kept perfectly cool; if anything, too cool. I should have liked her to show a little more disturbance.

"I have no idea. I suppose my maid has put it away somewhere among my things. But I will ring for her, and ask."

"Permit me, Lady Violet." Tarleton sprang to the bell before she was out of her chair. It was answered by the manservant, whom her ladyship dispatched in quest of her maid.

I watched my chief while we were waiting. I flattered myself that I had outmanœuvred him in this direction. His lowered brows told me that he was puzzled. He must have come down to Tyberton expecting to find the costume missing, and to receive some made-up story to account for its disappearance.

A woman came into the room, an elderly person, of very plain appearance, whom I put down as Lord Ledbury's housekeeper. I didn't think his lordship's means were sufficient to provide his daughter with a lady's maid.

"Oh, Henderson, do you know what has become of that fancy dress of mine with the helmet and breastplate? Can you put your hands on it?"

Henderson showed no surprise.

"Certainly, my lady. It is in the drawer at the bottom of your ladyship's wardrobe."

"Just go and fetch it, will you?"

"Yes, my lady."

She went out with the movement of a well-drilled actor, leaving me with the uncomfortable impression that the scene had been rehearsed, and that Tarleton could hardly miss coming to the same conclusion. He muttered some vague expression of regret for the trouble he was giving to Lady Violet, and then sat with his lips pursed up in rather ominous fashion, and his eyes fixed on the door.

Henderson reappeared rather too quickly. She carried all the articles that made up the much-talked-of costume, the paste-board armour coated with silver paint, the flowing shirt, even the sandals which the Wardour Street Israelite had deemed appropriate footwear for a desert queen.

Tarleton gave them the barest glance, as they were spread out on the table, and bowed to Violet.

"I have to thank your ladyship."

He was in the act of rising when the door of the room was thrown open abruptly.

The figure on the threshold presented the appearance of a man just roused from sleep and inclined to resent the interruption of his dreams. He was tall and thin, and seemed to hold himself upright with an effort. His gray hairs straggled over his head in unbrushed disorder, and his clothes hung on him as though they had been dropped where they were in a fit of absence of mind. In spite of these signs of neglect there was an air of dignity about him that left me in no doubt as to his identity.

The Earl of Ledbury advanced into the room, turning a glance of disapproval from Sir Frank Tarleton to myself, and addressed his daughter.

"Violet, what business have you with these gentlemen?"

What excuse she would have made if it had been left to her to answer, I don't know. Tarleton instantly took the burden on himself.

"My business with Lady Violet is official, my lord. I am right, no doubt, in thinking that you are the Earl of Ledbury?"

"Official?" The word sounded like a snarl. "Who are you, sir?"

"I am the principal medical adviser to the Home Office. My name is Sir Frank Tarleton, and this gentleman is my assistant, Dr. Cassilis."

I was already on my feet. I gave the Earl a deferential bow which only seemed to increase his irritation.

"And may I ask what you mean, gentlemen, by coming into my house and interviewing my daughter behind my back?"

Tarleton was not the man to let himself be addressed in that fashion.

"I think you forget yourself, my lord. The Lady Violet is of age, I believe. We are here in the discharge of our duty, and I need not remind your lordship that the law is not a respecter of persons."

Lord Ledbury's look of anger changed to one of amazement and alarm.

"Good heavens, what do you mean, sir? What has the law to do with Lady Violet Bredwardine?"

"Very little, I hope, but it was necessary for us to see her ladyship and put a few questions to her, for her own sake."

The Earl turned suddenly. "Henderson, leave the room."

"One moment, please." The physician detained the woman by a gesture. "Can you tell me if this costume has been where you just found it during the whole of last week? Would it have been possible for anyone to take it without your knowledge, send it away, and put it back again afterwards?"

It was a fatal question, the one question I ought to have anticipated and prepared for. Violet's face must have betrayed her to a duller eye than my shrewd chief's. As for Henderson, she gazed stupidly at her mistress in the evident need of prompting.

The irascible father could see this as plainly as ourselves.

"The truth, woman!" he thundered. "Tell the truth this instant."

Henderson turned very red.

"I had no wish to tell anything else, my lord. The drawer wasn't locked, that's all I can say. I can't tell whether anyone might have taken the costume out and put it back again, I'm sure."

"Thank you. That is all I have to ask of you at present." Nothing in Tarleton's tone or look showed what amount of importance he attached to the answer he had received; and the woman, after gazing uneasily round at us all in turn, went out of the room with a subdued mien.

What the effect was on me, I need scarcely say. The whole question of Violet's connection with the case had been reopened. If the astute investigator chose to follow up the clue he would not find it difficult to obtain evidence through the post office that a parcel large enough to contain the incriminating costume had been received by Lady Violet since the discovery of the crime. It might not be possible to trace it to me as the sender, but she might be placed in such a position that only a full confession on my part could clear her. That confession, of course, I had been ready to make all along, the moment it could do her the least service. My difficulty had been to make it without involving her as what the law calls an accessory before the fact. How could my chief, how could Inspector Charles, fail to draw the inference that we had acted in collusion, and that she had lent me her disguise knowing the use I meant to make of it?

The torturing problem racked my brain the whole time that Sir Frank was explaining the situation to Lord Ledbury. The explanation was a painful one. He did his best to soften the ugliest features, but it could not be concealed that Lady Violet had consulted a doctor without the knowledge of her father or her chaperon, that the doctor had died in suspicious circumstances, and that some suspicion had attached to the wearer of a fancy dress similar to the one spread out before us.

The shock would have been a terrible one for any father. It must have been doubly so for a man who had lived for so many years out of the world, ignoring the changes that had come about since his youth. The whole story must have taken him out of his bearings. The society in which night clubs flourish, and girls as young as Violet are found in them, was as strange to him as it would have been to any parent of the Victorian age.

I could see his mood turning from surprise and bewilderment into growing fury as he listened. And his anger was no longer directed against Tarleton and myself.

"It comes to this, that my daughter's name is mixed up with a murder case," he exploded at last. "If she is not actually under suspicion her clothes are. Violet!" The stricken girl turned beseeching eyes on him. "Unless you can assure me that you had no more to do with this business than I had, you shan't pass another night under this roof."

The injustice of it nearly stung me into speech. The Earl had done nothing to deserve his daughter's confidence. He had let her grow up a stranger to him. He had handed her over to a mercenary with no qualifications beyond those of a drill-sergeant or a prison warder. And he was ablaze with wrath because she had grown into a living creature with blood in her veins, instead of a wooden doll.

Violet's eyes filled with tears.

"What do you want me to say?" she implored. "I didn't even know that Dr. Weathered was dead till these gentlemen told me."

"You knew him, it seems. What did you go to him for? You haven't been ill."

I began to feel anxious for myself as well as her. But she replied with unexpected spirit.

"I went to him as a doctor. He was a nerve specialist, and I went to him about my nerves."

"Nerves!" His lordship spat out the word in scorn. "A girl of your age has no business with nerves. Did you tell Miss Pollexfen that you were suffering from nerves?"

"No." Violet flared up with a touch of her father. "Why should I? Miss Pollexfen is no friend of mine. I didn't choose her for a companion. I am old enough to decide for myself whether I want to see a doctor, without consulting her."

Lord Ledbury was clearly taken aback. He can have had no real suspicion that his daughter had done anything seriously wrong, or he would hardly have cross-examined her before us. Little as he loved her, regard for his own good name would have made him refrain from going on.

"So you consider yourself independent, do you?" He pointed to the clothes. "Have you lent these things—to anyone?"

I held my breath. I dared not make the least sign to Violet. And if I had, she would not have seen it. She kept her eyes steadily fixed on her father's.

"Yes." It was the wisest answer to give now that so much had come out. A falsehood must have been detected in a few hours.

"Tell me her name."

My heart seemed to stop beating. There was a tense pause in which the air of the room vibrated with suspense. Then the girl slowly shook her head.

"I cannot."

"You mean you won't. I command you, Violet. Do you hear?"

Her head sunk obstinately on her breast.

"I shall never tell."

CHAPTER 14

THE UNKNOWN POISON

I sat fascinated. This was not the Violet Bredwardine I had known. The girl had sprung up into a woman, and the woman was making a brave fight for me more than herself. If my name came out she would be no worse off than she was already, as far as her connection with the death in the Domino Club was concerned. Her father would have to know that she and I had been friends in the past, but he need know nothing more. It was I who stood in danger. It would be useless for me to deny that I had drugged Weathered, and had carried off the case-book. His death would lie at my door unless it could be proved that something had been given to him that night in addition to opium. And it would take very strong evidence to convince a jury that there had been anyone else concerned in that night's business besides me.

Whether her refusal to betray me was due only to loyalty, or to a faint survival or revival of the love I had forfeited, I could not tell. I only knew that my own heart was touched anew, and I longed more than ever to redeem myself in her eyes and wipe out the past.

The Earl of Ledbury controlled his wrath with an effort. He may have seen that it would be useless to persist just then. He may have feared to press his daughter too far in our presence lest she should make some admission that would bring her within reach of the law.

"Very well; if that is your attitude, you have ceased to be my daughter. You will pack up your things and go to London by the afternoon train. I shall wire to Miss Pollexfen to meet you, and you can stay in my house till she has found you a home with some respectable family; and I shall pay for your board as long as you choose to remain with them. Beyond that I have done with you. Now go."

Violet got up, shivering all over, to obey. Her misery was too acute for me to indulge in selfish thoughts of what her forced emancipation might mean for me.

The Earl turned to Sir Frank as if by an afterthought.

"Have you gentlemen anything else to ask Lady Violet before she goes?"

My chief passed on the question to me by a nod. His own expression was one of pity. I caught at the opportunity.

"Nothing for the moment, but I presume your lordship will be willing to let us have Lady Violet's new address if we should want it later on."

It was the first time I had spoken since Lord Ledbury came into the room, and he glared at me as though resenting my presumption.

"Lady Violet is of age," he said shortly. "I have just been reminded of that. She is her own mistress; you had better ask her."

Violet slowly turned and faced me. I threw all I dared of longing and pleading for forgiveness into the look I gave her. The despair in her eyes found a dull echo in her tone.

"I will send you my address as soon as I know it. But it will make no difference. I...."

Her voice choked. The next moment the door had closed on her.

And now Tarleton proceeded to astonish me. I think he astonished the Earl of Ledbury as well.

"My lord," he said in a tone of deep gravity, "it is clear to me that you have no idea of the danger in which your daughter stands."

"Danger!" The Earl fairly started.

"Danger," the consultant repeated firmly. "The man whose death has brought us down here was an unscrupulous scoundrel. He laid traps for women. Under the pretence of soothing their nerves he induced them to tell him their secrets, and to write him letters containing their inmost thoughts. There is every likelihood that he met his death at the hands of some woman whom he had entrapped in that way, and whom he was attempting to blackmail."

"But what has that to do with my daughter?" his lordship burst out. "You don't suppose that she knew he was going to be murdered?"

"I haven't suggested it. The evidence is to the contrary, I am glad to see. But your daughter has been beguiled into writing to this man, and in her innocence she has very likely written a good many things that you would not care to see published. Those letters are still in existence, probably, and we don't know in whose hands. Until they are found and destroyed Lady Violet will be at the mercy of the holder."

"Wretched girl!" Even now the selfish father could find nothing better to do than to blame his child.

"Who made her wretched?" Tarleton's face wore the stern look of a judge passing sentence. "Who drove her to confide in a stranger and a charlatan? Who handed her over to a hired companion whom she seems to have disliked and distrusted? Who taught her to look for sympathy anywhere except from her own parent and in her own home?"

Never have I witnessed a rebuke better administered or with better effect. Lord Ledbury was utterly subdued. If the condemnation had come from a young man like myself, or from a professed preacher, he might have tried to defend himself. But from a man of his own age, and a man in authority, the representative of law and public opinion, it was an unanswerable charge.

For the best part of a minute he sat silent. His face worked. Memories of the past must have come back to him; perhaps he asked himself what account he could give to Violet's mother of her only child. His voice was altered and broken when he spoke again.

"You have been very plain with me, Sir Frank. I recognize that you have spoken as a friend—as my daughter's friend at least, if not mine. It may be that my treatment of her has been mistaken, although I meant it for the best; at all events, it has turned out unfortunately. But her good name is the first consideration now. These letters—what do you advise me to do?"

The physician considered for a time before he spoke.

"I didn't know of the existence of these letters when I came down here, and the problem is one that requires thinking out. It may be that they will give us a clue to the whole mystery. As far as I can see at present, three things may have happened to them."

He turned from Lord Ledbury to me as he went on.

"Weathered may have kept them in the same safe with his case-book. In that case the person who opened the safe and carried off the book ought to have found the letters as well. But according to my present theory the person who took the book was the wearer of this costume—" he pointed to the dress in front of us. "In other words, he or she was Lady Violet's friend. And if her friend had found any such documents he would have destroyed them and let her know at once. In my opinion, therefore, either he overlooked them, or they were kept in some more secret receptacle."

As Tarleton seemed to expect my opinion I nodded in confirmation. I could have sworn that the safe contained no such correspondence, but that, of course, I dared not tell him.

"The next person who seems to have had access to the safe," said the consultant, "was Weathered's step-daughter. And if he had some other hiding-place in the house she is the most likely person to have known of it, and to have opened it since his death. Her mother, no doubt, would have a better right to examine her husband's papers, but she impressed me as a weak woman, very much in her daughter's hands. We have to face the possibility that Lady Violet's letters have been found by a young woman of very determined character who has actually denounced her ladyship to Dr. Cassilis and myself as guilty of this man's death."

The Earl showed himself greatly shaken.

"But this is terrible. You, sir, and you"—he appealed to each of us in turn—"don't believe anything so hideous."

"Not for one moment." It was my chief who answered. "Our presence here is the best proof of that. We found ourselves accused by this young woman of hushing up the case and screening the criminal, and we came down to obtain proof of Lady Violet's absence from the scene of the crime. You have nothing to fear on that score, I hope and believe. You can trust us both not to let anyone know of the admission Lady Violet has just made to you that she lent her costume to someone else."

"To the actual murderer, do you mean?" the father gasped.

"Not necessarily. That point is still in doubt. As I have said, the crime may have been committed by a woman—or a man—who had been driven to desperation. I should be glad to think so, and to think that he or she had seized the secret correspondence."

"Why?" It was Lord Ledbury who put the question, but I waited for the answer with equal curiosity.

"Because in that case we might have every hope that it would be promptly destroyed. Such a victim would have no motive to injure her fellow victims, and we might credit her with a sense of honour. Whereas the step-daughter has shown a strong animus against Lady Violet, and we know that she is not too scrupulous when her feelings are aroused. If Miss Neobard has found these letters it may take some pressure to make her give them up."

The Earl wrung his hands. "My means are not large, but if any sum within my power—" he began.

Tarleton cut him short with decision.

"That is one means which must not be resorted to, my lord. I must make that an absolute condition. The one thing I have to ask of you is that you will protect your daughter from any attempt that may be made to blackmail her. Try, if you can, to win her confidence. I strongly advise you to come up to town with her yourself. Her chaperon has shown herself to be incompetent, and I shouldn't let her into your house again. Look out for some bright, sympathetic woman of the world, and don't engage her unless Lady Violet takes to her as a friend. And let it be seen that your daughter is under your personal protection. A blackmailer who would find a solitary girl an easy prey will think twice before he threatens one who is guarded by a father in your position. Take her with you to the theatres and picture galleries. Believe me, as a doctor, she is in need of distraction just now. I won't answer for her sanity unless she can be cheered up and taken out of herself. I will call on her, with your permission, and keep an eye on her for a time."

The change in the Earl of Ledbury was great indeed by now. He thanked the consultant with emotion, and undertook to carry out all his recommendations. He pressed us both to stay and lunch with him, but my chief decided that we could not spare the time.

"We must get back to town as soon as possible," he declared. "The sooner we get on the track of the missing letters the better chance there will be of our recovering them."

He shook hands with the Earl very cordially at parting and his lordship seemed to include me in his expressions of gratitude and good-will.

When we were seated in the car going back to Hereford my chief summed up the situation for my benefit.

"There was a possibility that Lady Violet had lent her old disguise to a friend as a blind and come to the dance in a new one. I thought it was on the cards that she might prove to be the Leopardess. Now I think we may rule that out, and I am very glad of it. She is a dear girl, and I confess she has won my heart."

I glanced at him a little uneasily. In spite of his age, Tarleton was a fascinating man. I had seen enough of him to know that he was popular with women of all ages. Young women seemed to regard him as an uncle, and became familiar with him at very short notice; and I could not be sure that he always regarded them strictly as nieces. Glad as I was that my chief had acquitted Violet in his mind, I was not altogether pleased by the warmth with which he spoke.

"We may take it that she lent her dress to a friend who meant to impersonate her. We don't know whether the friend had a grievance of her own against Weathered, or whether she was acting as Lady Violet's champion. And in the second case we can't say whether Lady Violet knew or guessed what her champion intended to do. You see, there is still a serious case against the poor girl. If the police knew that she was in Weathered's power, and that she had lent her costume to his murderer, they might come to a very ugly conclusion."

"I am certain she had no idea that any crime was going to be committed," I spoke earnestly.

"Quite so; you feel certain of that, but Captain Charles might feel certain of the opposite. You see now why I thought it better for us to come down here instead of one of his men."

I did indeed see it, and inwardly I thanked Sir Frank with all my heart.

"I think we will tell Charles that we obtained satisfactory proof that Lady Violet was at Tyberton Castle on Wednesday night, and that her maid found the Zenobia costume for us in her wardrobe. That ought to make him dismiss her from the case."

I could have asked for nothing better, so far. "And the letters?" I put in anxiously.

"Ah! I didn't care to tell Lord Ledbury all I feared about them. I shouldn't be surprised if Weathered had stored them in the Domino Club."

I could not restrain a cry of alarm.

"Yes," Tarleton went on, "that would be the worst case of all. Because by this time they must be in the hands of Madame Bonnell."

The smooth, smiling face of the Frenchwoman with its shrewd black eyes and thin lips rose before me. As my chief had said, this was the worst case of all.

"If that woman has them it may be some time before we hear of them," the specialist pursued in a meditative tone. "She may wait till the inquiry into the death is over, and the case disposed of as far as the police are concerned. Then the victims will each receive a discreet letter, probably from an agent, informing them that certain letters which appear to be in their handwriting have been found, and asking if they wish to have them returned. There won't be a word about money in the first communication, you may be sure. The victims will simply be invited to call on the agents and inspect the letters. That woman knows her business, I fancy."

It was horrible to think of Violet being slowly drawn into the serpent's coils. There would be less mercy to look for in such a woman than in Weathered himself.

The physician moved his shoulders as if to shake off an unpleasant burden.

"We will put that aside for the moment, and consider the question of the murder. Everything now depends on the information I expect to find waiting for me when we get back. If my diagnosis is correct, Weathered died from a poison described in the book I have told you of, *Across Sumatra*, by Captain Armstrong. The natives have some name for it which I forget, but I have called it *Upasine*."

"Upasine!" I repeated the name in stupefaction.

"Yes. You have heard, no doubt—everybody has heard—of the famous upas tree. According to the tales of the old explorers, it was a tree that exhaled a deadly vapour, so that the traveller who went to sleep beneath its shelter never woke again. The bones of animals were found scattered round the trunk, and they were supposed to have perished in the same way, by going to sleep within the deadly radius."

"But surely," I said in astonishment, "surely no one believes that any longer? I thought it had been proved to be a fable."

The great expert shook his head.

"There are not many fables that haven't some truth in them," he pronounced. "The legendary glories of Timbuktu were dismissed at one time as travellers' tales, but it turned out there was a city called Timbuktu on the southern edge of the desert of Sahara; that it was the great market to which the caravans from the Mediterranean coast made their way, and even that it once possessed something like a university, when it became a refuge for the Moors who were driven out of Spain. The accounts of the upas tree and its fatal shadow were dismissed in the same shallow way without any inquiry as to how they originated. Armstrong happened to be an intelligent man, and he told me that one of the objects of his exploration of Sumatra had been to find out the truth about the upas."

My incredulity began to give way before my chief's sober words.

"He started out with the conviction that bones and corpses had been found under some trees by some explorers, who had accepted the native theory that the tree cast a deadly spell on all within its range. Other travellers had tested the theory and found that it was possible to sleep under the tree in perfect safety. And so they had treated the whole thing as a pure fancy, without inquiring further. Armstrong did inquire further, and perhaps you can guess what he found?"

For some moments I was hopelessly puzzled. "The leaves are poisonous, perhaps, and the sleepers die because they have eaten them?"

"Not a bad guess. No; Armstrong discovered a minute fungus that grows in the soil round the root of the upas tree, and apparently nowhere else. The animals that browse on this fungus are overcome by sleep, and die without waking. It contains a soporific poison which acts rather like opium at first, but has a peculiar effect on the skin, which it dries up like parchment. You were the first to draw my attention to the parchment-like appearance of Weathered's face, you may remember."

I did remember. A burden was lifted from my heart by the recollection. Whatever peril I might stand in from the law, I could assure myself at last that I was not a murderer. The drug I had administered to Violet's persecutor had contained no grain of any other poison than opium. And now I need not fear that I had given him an overdose of that. He had died, he must have died, from the poison discovered by the explorer of Sumatra. And that meant that he had died by some other hand than mine.

The specialist continued his explanation.

"You see now why I asked you to make no more remarks on what you saw. Whoever used this poison probably believes that he is the only person who possesses any, or even knows of its existence. Armstrong's book attracted very little notice. It was badly written, for one thing, and there were no illustrations, a fatal omission in a book of travels nowadays. I don't think there was a word about this discovery in any of the reviews. Naturally the murderer thinks that he is safe from detection."

"How did you come to hear of the poison?" I ventured to ask.

"In the simplest way. Captain Armstrong himself brought me a sample to analyse."

Of course! I could have kicked myself. Tarleton was the one man to whom any such discoverer would be certain to come for an opinion.

"He had picked and dried a handful or two of the toadstools, as he called them, but they had crumbled on the voyage home, and what he brought me was dust. I detected the presence of an agent not yet known to science, and I gave it the name of upasine. It seemed to me so dangerous that an unknown poison should be in the hands of anyone but a man like myself, that I asked Armstrong to sell me all he had brought home, and he agreed to do it."

"But in that case—your bottle was untouched?" I objected.

"True. It is clear that he deceived me. Either he had parted with some of the poison before coming to me, and didn't like to admit it, or else he kept some for himself as a curiosity. If it isn't in his possession, I expect to hear of it in the same quarter as the leopard skin and claws."

CHAPTER 15

THE LADY OF THE LEOPARD SKIN

I got little more out of my chief during the rest of the journey to town. The gold repeater came into action as soon as we were seated in the train, and I could only wonder what was the problem that was still baffling that keen intelligence.

To me, I confess, the solution of the mystery seemed now to be well in sight. On our return to town I expected to find that Inspector Charles had ascertained the present whereabouts of the explorer of Sumatra. From him it should not be difficult to learn the identity of the Leopardess, as I called her in my own mind; and I took it for granted that she was a victim of Weathered's who had delivered herself out of his power by the use of the deadly fungus of the upas.

My one anxiety at present was the thought of the missing letters. I wearied myself with speculating as to whose hands they had passed into since the murder, and by what means they could be recovered and destroyed without their contents becoming known. I was as far as ever from seeing my way clearly when we arrived in Montague Street that evening.

A serious disappointment waited for us there. An official envelope stamped with the seal of New Scotland Yard lay on the table in the hall. Before I had closed the front door Tarleton had pounced upon it, torn it open, and scanned the note inside with an impatient scowl.

"Fool!"

He almost flung the Inspector's communication in my face. It stated briefly that Captain Armstrong had met his death by malarial fever in Yucatan six months ago; and that was all. I hardly know what more Charles could have said, since he was quite ignorant why the explorer's address was wanted. Tarleton sometimes failed to allow for the fact that his assistants were not all gifted with his own quickness of apprehension. However, I didn't venture to defend the delinquent.

My chief's irritation soon subsided, and as soon as we were seated at a well-spread table he acquitted the Inspector handsomely.

"After all, I didn't take Charles into my confidence, as I have taken you, Cassilis. But now we must set to work in earnest. What do you suggest as the next step?"

The question was too much for me, as I had to confess. Perhaps I was too much worried about the letters to be able to give my mind to anything else.

The consultant smiled good-naturedly.

"Our only clue to Captain Armstrong's friend is his book. Books are produced by publishers, and publishers pay royalties. By this time the publisher of *Across Sumatra* ought to have heard from Armstrong's executor. And the executor should be able to put us on the track of the person who has come into possession of his effects."

He paused to let this reasoning sink into my mind before he added, "I think this greatly simplifies matters. It is much more likely that Armstrong kept some of the upasine himself among his trophies than that he gave it away, to a woman, above all. Depend upon it, we shall find that it passed on his death to the lady of the leopard's claws."

He seemed about to say more but broke off abruptly, as though a new thought had struck him. "She will have to be handled carefully," was all he said after a short silence.

It was impossible for me to listen any longer without reminding him of the other task before us.

"Have you made any plans yet for the recovery of the letters?" I asked anxiously.

"Ah!" He gave me a shrewd look. "You are quite right to interest yourself in that business, my boy. It is more important to protect Lady Violet than even to detect Weathered's murderer. The living come before the dead, eh? I am inclined to trust that part of the work to you."

I suppose I must have shown some dismay. My kindly chief proceeded to explain himself.

"We must begin with the assumption that everything that Weathered left behind him, including his correspondence, has become the property of his widow. If he kept these letters in his house they must be now in her possession, unless her daughter has annexed them. I think you should go round to Warwick Street tomorrow morning, and ask to see Mrs. Weathered."

I thought of the rather commonplace widow, who had appeared to be completely dominated by her daughter, and I did not hope much from the interview.

"I doubt if she will part with them without Miss Neobard's consent," I said with hesitation. "Even if she has them."

"Try," the physician urged. "I should not be surprised if that woman, quiet as she looked, was deeper in her husband's secrets than Sarah Neobard was, in spite of her jealousy. Still waters run deep, remember. See her alone, if you can, and put the matter to her as a woman and a mother. Ask her how she would feel if her own daughter had been enticed to writing very confidential letters to a doctor, and those letters were now in a stranger's hands. I fancy you will get something out of Mrs. Weathered."

"And if I fail?"

Tarleton compressed his lips rather grimly. "In that case, one of us may have to show her that her own daughter is not yet out of the wood. We have both heard a confession from Sarah Neobard, and it was not made under any pledge of secrecy."

There the matter rested that night. The next day soon after breakfast my chief set off to make inquiries at the publishers of *Across Sumatra*, and I started on my difficult errand to Warwick Street.

Only my knowledge of the desperate position in which Violet had placed herself could have nerved me to the task in front of me. It was painful enough to have to plead for mercy from a stranger; the prospect of having to threaten the mother with her daughter's prosecution for a crime of which I did not believe her guilty was so repugnant to me that I made up my mind beforehand not to act on Tarleton's hint. My confidence in his sense of justice was very strong, but I felt that I was too much in the dark myself to accept such a responsibility.

The blinds of the house were down, a circumstance which I attributed to the presence of a corpse inside. But there was a long delay in answering my ring, and when the youthful butler opened the door to me his untidy dress and rough hair suggested that he did not consider himself on duty.

"Mrs. Weathered isn't here," he told me, without ceremony, as soon as I asked to see her. "The funeral took place yesterday and the ladies have gone out of town."

"Where have they gone?" I demanded in dismay.

The youth put on a stolid look.

"My instructions are to say that letters will be forwarded," he answered, with a touch of sullenness.

And I could get no more out of him. To all appearances Sarah Neobard and her mother had fled.

As soon as I had got over my first surprise, I felt more relief than disappointment. Tarleton himself would now have to take the matter in hand, and I had more confidence in his power to deal with it than in my own. When we met again at lunch time I reported my failure to him, and he heard me with a tightening of the jaws that boded no good to the fugitives.

"Our friend Sarah has made a mistake," he commented. "She ought to have known that she could not hide herself very long if the police really wanted her. I think we can trust Captain Charles to let us know where she is before many days have passed. I wonder what she told her mother to persuade her to run away like that."

Again some thought seemed to strike him which he did not see fit to disclose to me. He shook his head doubtfully, and then sprang to his feet and hurried to the telephone.

When he came back it was to tell me that the police had been put on the trail of the two women. "I have told them nothing about the letters," he added for my consolation. "We don't want them to get on the files of Scotland Yard if we can help it. I have given them a hint that I have something up my sleeve."

He poured himself out a glass of wine and sipped it with a relish.

"I have been more fortunate than you this morning," he resumed. "It appears that Armstrong had another book in the press when he died, so that his publishers have been in active communication with his executor—or rather his executrix."

The correction startled me. Tarleton had laid some emphasis on the feminine termination.

"She is Armstrong's sister, his only one. He had no other near relations, so far as the publishers could tell me, and with his solitary, wandering life he is not likely to have had any intimate friends. At all events, he left everything he possessed to his sister. I have made sure of that by looking up the will at Somerset House."

The atmosphere seemed to become heavier as he spoke. At last the quarry was almost in sight. If the explorer had kept any of the mysterious poison it must have passed into his sister's possession on his death.

"The publisher couldn't tell me whether she was a married woman or a widow," the specialist continued, "but he gave me her name and address: Mrs. Amelia Baker, Carlyle Square, Chelsea."

"Carlyle Square!" I ejaculated. "That is within a stone's throw of the Domino Club."

My chief gave me a look of mild disappointment.

"Is that the only thing that strikes you? What about the name?"

"Amelia Baker." I repeated the name to myself. "Baker"—surely one of the commonest of English surnames. There must be hundreds of Bakers in the London Directory. And yet I had a dim consciousness of some association with it that I couldn't quite fix. Tarleton's patience gave out before my helplessness.

"Think? Where did you come across that name last?" He snatched out a slip of paper from his breast pocket and passed it across the table.

It was the list of names he had given me to copy three days before, the list of Weathered's patients who had given numbers under which, as we had learned since from Violet, they could write to him. And at the bottom of the list there stood, "Mrs. Baker, 35."

To me it looked like proof conclusive. This was Weathered's latest victim, to all appearance, and in making her his enemy he had at last met his match. I remembered the waiter's description of her at the dance in her savage dress and savage ornaments, as though she meant by her attire to signify that she was bent on vengeance. And now we knew that she was in possession of a deadly drug which could be given without fear of detection, as she might well suppose if her brother had not told her of his dealings with the great expert. Gerard had testified to her showing a repugnance for Weathered that looked like hatred. The case appeared to be complete.

Something like this I said to Tarleton, carried away by my delight at the thought that I had now no more to dread. But he did not show himself altogether satisfied.

"There is such a thing as having too complete a case," he remarked in a meditative voice. "Even if we are right in believing that we have found the Leopardess, as Gerard called her, we have still to prove that she murdered Weathered. The waiter himself told us that she left early, hours before he showed any symptoms of being poisoned. My instinct tells me that there is something in this business that I don't yet know. There is no crime so difficult to detect as one in which a woman is concerned. In this case I find myself surrounded by women, and every woman is an enigma to the wisest man.—Now listen to this."

He took out another paper from his pocket, and read aloud from it.

"This is the report of the Inspector. He has had men engaged in looking up all the names on that list, and the moment it struck me that Armstrong's executrix might be the Mrs. Baker who figures there, I asked Charles to let me know what his man had found out. Here is what he writes: 'Widow with independent means. Perfectly respectable. Favourably known to local tradesmen. Keeps two servants. Interested in scientific movements. Sister of well-known traveller. Visits freely in Chelsea. Has friends among literary men and artists. Also fond of animals, cats and birds. Not known to suffer from any serious form of illness. Has been attended by local doctor for small ailments. No connection can be traced with Weathered.'—That is the police report."

It was a deeply disappointing one to me. My vision of the enraged woman in her leopard costume engaged in a murderous plot against a sinister blackmailer faded as I listened. This harmless, middle-aged woman, living quietly on her income in a good neighbourhood, and amusing herself with animal pets and such artistic and intellectual society as was within her reach, failed altogether to come up to the portrait my imagination had drawn.

Tarleton folded up the report and replaced it in his pocket. "You and I will call on this lady presently, and see if we can find out something more."

I wondered what we should find. I was wondering still when the physician's car drew up before a house in the pleasant little square named after Chelsea's most famous resident since the time of Sir Thomas More. The house was only distinguished from its neighbours by an air of dinginess which seemed due to neglect. In spite of the two servants kept by the owner or tenant, there was a lack of neatness both outside and inside. The steps looked in need of scrubbing, and the paint on the door was disfigured with blisters. The door was opened to Tarleton's vigorous knock and ring by a housemaid who had evidently not changed her dress since her morning's work was done, and the hall into which we passed was more like an ill-kept lumber-room than the ordinary entrance to a lady's house.

The explorer had evidently left many treasures picked up on his travels which his sister had taken no great pains to arrange to the best advantage. Savage weapons of various kinds were nailed up anyhow on the walls, one hiding another. Horns of different strange animals, either deer or oxen, surmounted such doors as we could see. Our feet were entangled in a draggled buffalo skin spread on the floor. The maiden who let us in took no notice of our trouble in following her, and offered no apology for the untidiness of the surroundings. She led the way upstairs to the first landing and threw open the door of a front room which was no doubt dignified with the title of drawing-room.

"I'll tell the missus you're here."

With this ungracious promise, and without suggesting that we should sit down, she shut us in and left us. Tarleton glanced round him with a humorous expression.

"I am reminded of what someone said of a famous explorer—'Sir —— is admirably qualified to deal with savages because he is just as savage as they are.' Captain Armstrong seems to have shared the same qualification with his sister, judging from her household."

The drawing-room resembled a museum as ill-arranged as the hall. Cases of stuffed birds met the eye in every corner. A badly preserved fish of enormous size, lacking an eye, monopolized one wall; I inclined to think it was a tarpon. The space was choked with rickety small tables, and those pieces of furniture dear to the past generation as chiffoniers and what-nots, every one laden with curiosities in the way of shells, savage ornaments, beads and rude knives in sheaths of coloured leather. But what naturally drew our attention most were the skins that strewed the floor and made all movement well-nigh impossible, unless by way of skips and jumps. Every known species of Africa, I should think, was represented, except perhaps the elephant. Two of those in sight were leopards, and my chief gave me a quick look of triumph as he pointed them out. Neither of them, none of the skins in fact, were mounted on cloth in the common fashion. The owner of this weird collection could have picked one up and fastened it across her shoulders without the least difficulty.

Mrs. Baker took some time to appear. Although we had postponed our call till four o'clock, it is probable that her siesta had been interrupted. Certainly she had the air of having only been roused from sleep long enough to make a rather imperfect toilet. Her hair could best be described as touzled, but it was of that light straw colour that lends itself to a pleasing disorder. The face beneath was bright and birdlike, animated by an expression of lively interest amounting to perkiness. The dress, I can only suppose, was intended to rank as a tea-gown, although it was strongly suggestive of a dressing-gown. But whatever impressions of slovenliness and neglect were produced by Mrs. Baker's appearance and surroundings, they were almost instantly dissipated by her manner, which was the perfection of genuine cordiality and ease.

"I'm ashamed to have kept you waiting, Sir Frank!" she exclaimed, grasping me warmly by the hand. "But dear me," she proceeded before I could speak, "if I haven't mistaken the son for the father! How are *you*, Sir Frank! I declare the likeness would deceive anybody."

My chief extricated his hand from her friendly clutch with a smile.

"You flatter me, madam. Dr. Cassilis, I regret to say, is no relation to me, though he is good enough to assist me."

Mrs. Baker was not in the least embarrassed. Her smile at the mistake was heartier than either of ours.

"Just like me," she avowed good-naturedly. "If there's a chance for me to put my foot in it, I'm sure to do it. And I know you so well, by name, of course. To think of all our diseases being due just to tiny weeny insects! I'm sure everybody ought to be grateful to you."

It was apparent that there was some slight confusion in the mind of our hostess between Tarleton and some other scientist of equal if not greater eminence—possibly the immortal Pasteur. Meanwhile, one thought possessed my mind to an extent that made me indifferent to everything else. This chatty, blundering, good-natured creature could by no conceivable possibility be connected with the tragedy in the Domino Club. Whatever part she had played and whether she had or had not been present on the fateful night, it was no less than absurd to credit her with any responsibility for Weathered's death.

With an agility which I could only envy she skipped lightly over the many pitfalls that bestrewed the floor, and stage-managed us both into comfortable chairs, while she took up an attitude on a couch smothered in cushions, which faintly recalled Thorwaldsen's statue of Ariadne.

"I hope you will accept my condolences on Captain Armstrong's death, if it's not too late," the consultant contrived to slip in presently.

The bereaved sister brightened up. Doubtless this was the clue she had wanted to our reason for calling on her.

"To be sure!" she exclaimed. "You knew my brother, of course. Everybody knew him. What a man he was! The greatest explorer who ever lived, so I think. He would have discovered America, and Livingstone, and the North Pole, if only those other people hadn't done it first." Her face fell for a moment, as she added, "He was careless in money matters, I know. It was his open, generous nature. Did he borrow from either of you gentlemen?"

The question was put in a tone of resignation which I understood as soon as we had both disclaimed any such transaction with the late Captain Armstrong.

"I am so thankful," the loyal sister sighed. "So many of his friends have come to me since his death was announced in the papers, and they all brought I O U's for money that he owed them. I have paid them all, of course, but I had to do it out of my own money. Poor Edgar left nothing."

I glanced at my chief in some surprise. But he knew the world better than I did, as his answer showed.

"I was afraid that his books hadn't brought him in very much, valuable as they were to science."

Mrs. Baker shook her head. "Not one of them paid its expenses. I had to advance the money to publish them, and I don't suppose I shall ever get it back."

"You have some things to remember him by, at all events," Tarleton suggested. "Those leopard skins are very fine."

"Ah, yes." The sister brightened up again. "Everything he brought home he gave to me. It's a wonderful collection, isn't it? People tell me I ought to give it to the nation. I think I shall leave this house and its contents to trustees as a memorial, like Carlyle's house in Cheyne Row, you know."

We could only express approval of this pious intention. My chief now came to the object of our visit.

"Captain Armstrong did me the honour to come to me some time ago, after his return from Sumatra. He had heard of me as a student of poisons, and he brought me a sample of one he had discovered."

"I know the one you mean, the toadstool that grows round the upas tree. Wasn't that a wonderful discovery? I can tell you—" She checked herself rather sharply, and said no more.

"I persuaded him to sell me all he had brought to England," the specialist remarked, without appearing to notice anything. "But it has occurred to me since that he might have kept a little as a specimen, and if that is so, and you are disposed to part with it, I shall be glad."

Mrs. Baker eyed us with a touch of uneasiness, I thought.

"I know I can trust you, Sir Frederick; and if Dr. Castle is your assistant I suppose I can trust him too. Dear Edgar did leave me a little bottleful, but he told me not to part with it to anyone, and not even to let anyone know I had it."

This was disconcerting news. I saw Tarleton's thick eyebrows go up and down.

"That was very sound advice," he responded quietly. "However, your brother trusted me, as I have said, and I hope you can do the same. I shall be very greatly obliged if you will let me see the bottle."

The little woman got nimbly off the couch. "After all, it will be a relief to me to get rid of it," she murmured. "I have always taken care to keep it under lock and key."

She produced a bunch of about two dozen keys from her pocket, all of them of that common design that will open each other's locks with ease, and advanced to a chiffonier. "It is in here," she informed us as she threw back the flimsy door and thrust her head inside.

The next moment we heard a startled cry.

"The bottle is gone!"

CHAPTER 16

THE RED LIGHT

Sir Frank and I both sprang to our feet to go to the chiffonier. But it was useless to turn over the rubbish it contained. The bottle of upasine was not there. And either the sister of the explorer was a very perfect actress or she was as much surprised as I was by its disappearance.

"Whoever can have taken it?" she cried, gazing at us as if not quite certain that we were beyond suspicion of the theft. "Both my maids have been with me for years, and I have never missed anything before."

It was at moments like these that I most admired my chief. The encounter with a new perplexity seemed to afford him the keenest pleasure. He was like an angler who finds that he has hooked a trout where he only expected a chub. I could see from the knitting of his brows that he was already readjusting his ideas to this new factor in the case, and working out a different solution.

His first step was to soothe the mistress of the house.

"If you will allow me to help you I think we may be able to get on the track of the thief. Shall we sit down and talk it over quietly?"

Mrs. Baker, still rather distrustful, let herself be led back to her couch. But this time she did not attempt a statuesque pose. She sat bolt upright, turning her head from one to the other of us like a nervous robin.

"You haven't missed anything else, you say," Tarleton began, "so that it looks as though the thief must have been someone who knew what he was taking. The question is how many of your friends knew about this poison?"

"Not one of them," was the positive answer. "I have never mentioned it to a soul."

"Think," the doctor persisted courteously. "Remember that Captain Armstrong mentions his discovery of it in his book, *Across Sumatra*. Surely some of your acquaintances must have read the book and talked to you about it?"

The little woman began to show signs of misgiving.

"I can't remember," she confessed.

She had shown us both already that memory was not her strong point. The consultant prompted her gently.

"The person most likely to be interested in such a thing as a new poison would be a scientist or a medical man."

Mrs. Baker's eyes sought the floor. "I am positive that my doctor knew nothing about it. Besides, I haven't seen him for the last six months—not since my brother's death." The disclaimer was made in a rather shaken voice, however.

"But a lady like you must have some acquaintances in the scientific world," the examiner insinuated. "I was under the impression that I had heard of you as a patroness of science."

The flattery did its work. Mrs. Baker lifted her head again and repaid it with a gracious smile.

"I am interested in science," she admitted. "When my poor brother was alive I used to give At Homes for him to show his curiosities to people. I have had as many as six Fellows of the Royal Geographical Society at one time before now."

"I felt sure of it. And you see your brother may easily have mentioned this bottle, or shown it, to someone without your knowledge."

The birdlike head wavered. "But I am certain that it hadn't been taken when he died. I had to make a list of everything he left for probate, and I should have missed it if it hadn't been there. And I have had no At Homes since."

It struck me that this was said rather unwillingly, under the stress of conscience. Tarleton seemed to think the same. The look he gave to the little woman showed me that he believed she was keeping something back.

His next question was a bombshell.

"May I ask if you have taken any interest in the science of psychoanalysis?"

Mrs. Baker's collapse was pitiful. If the specialist had suddenly changed into a cobra before her eyes she could not have looked at him with greater terror.

"What do you mean, Sir Roderick?" she faltered.

Tarleton slowly shook his head.

"My dear madam, it is time for us to leave off fencing with one another. Dr. Cassilis and I are both incapable of betraying your confidence and neither of us has the slightest desire to injure you. This dangerous poison has been stolen from you, and you cannot feel easy in your mind till you know that it has been recovered, and is in safe hands. All we ask is your help in tracing it, and that help I am sure you feel that you ought to give."

He had struck the right note this time. The poor little woman took out her handkerchief and dabbed her forehead in a distracted manner as she nerved herself to speak.

"You are quite right, Sir Robert. I know I ought to tell you everything, but it isn't at all pleasant. Have you ever heard of a Dr. Wycherley?"

The situation was too grave for these erratic names to provoke a smile. "I have heard of Dr. Weathered," the specialist said gravely.

"Weathered, of course! How could I have forgotten it. But I never can remember names, Sir Herbert. He isn't a friend of yours, I hope?"

"He never was." Evidently she hadn't heard of the death in the Domino Club, and my chief didn't think the time had yet come to tell her of it.

Mrs. Baker gave a sigh of relief before plunging into her tale.

"It all began with my going to hear him give a lecture on psycho-analysis at the Caxton Hall. He looked quite a distinguished man, and he lectured beautifully. I was fascinated by the things he said. He told us that he could look inside our minds, and see things there that we had never dreamt of—in our subconscience, he called it."

"Subconsciousness, yes," Tarleton put in with the least touch of impatience.

"I dare say that was it. He said we might have murderous propensities without knowing it. Think of that! I might be secretly longing to kill my dear brother, and if the propensity wasn't found out and removed in time, I might end by doing it. I was horrified."

I confess I was horrified, too, as I grasped the methods by which Weathered had drawn this harmless little creature into his toils.

"I couldn't sleep for thinking of all the dreadful things that my subconscience might be planning and plotting behind my back. I felt I must know the worst, so as to be on my guard against it. I went to consult Dr. Weathered at his house, and it was a dreadful experience. He found out that I had a murderous propensity. And he told me that the only way for me to rid myself of it was to write letters to him telling him every evil thought that came into my mind."

My chief and I looked at each other. There was no need of words to express the idea we had in common. There could be little doubt as to Weathered's line of action. He had found himself dealing with a credulous weak-minded simpleton, and he had proceeded to use the power of suggestion. He had simply put into the poor woman's mind the thoughts he pretended to be driving out. The only question that remained was whether he had gone so far as to instigate her to the commission of a crime.

"I wrote him letter after letter," Mrs. Baker continued. "Every time I felt angry with one of the maids I had to let him know. Sometimes he answered the letters, and sometimes he didn't. When he did write he generally asked me questions about how I was tempted to commit the murder. That was how he found out about the poison."

Even I had seen this coming. Tarleton no doubt had seen it some time before, and worked up to it deliberately; but he let no sign of satisfaction appear.

"Did he ever ask you to let him have it?" he asked. The answer surprised me.

"No, never. He told me to be very careful never to part with it."

"Ah, I understand. He told you to take the greatest care of it, and you told him exactly where you kept it?"

"Yes, yes." The explorer's sister gazed at him in admiration. "How did you guess that?"

"I think it is quite plain, ma'am. He didn't want you or anyone else to be in a position to say that he had obtained the poison from you. With the information you gave him he could walk into the house at any time, and take it—secretly."

This was a development I hadn't foreseen. Was the mystery going to resolve itself into a case of suicide, after all? After failing to put an end to himself by means of opium, had Weathered finally resorted to a more certain drug? But then, in that case, why shouldn't he have demanded it openly from his deceived patient? Truly the riddle was becoming more insoluble as we advanced.

Mrs. Baker was rather indignant at the suggestion that her precautions for the security of the dangerous bottle had not been sufficient; but the consultant brushed aside her objections almost irritably.

"Nonsense, my dear woman, that lock of yours could be picked by a clever child of twelve. All that the thief had to do was to come to the house when he knew you were out, give a false name to the servant, and ask to be allowed to wait. As soon as he found himself alone in this room he could help himself to what he wanted, and then remember an engagement, and come away. Very likely the maid who would let him in wouldn't even trouble to tell you a visitor had called."

The mistress of the house was reluctantly obliged to admit this possibility. Tarleton folded his arms, a sign that the interview was over as far as his interest in it was concerned, but he was good enough to give me a chance of satisfying my curiosity.

"What do you say, Cassilis? Do you think we ought to ask Mrs. Baker to tell us anything more?"

I thought our hostess looked as little willing as I was to leave her story unfinished.

"Oh, but you must hear the end," she protested. "And you mustn't go away without so much as a cup of tea." She hopped lightly to the electric bell. "I want you to know that I'm not a patient of Dr. Weathered any longer; and I think I ought to tell you why—when the maid is gone."

The saving clause was prompted by a rough bang at the door, followed by the entrance of the untidy servant. She had anticipated her mistress's orders, and brought in a huge tray laden with food sufficient to satisfy a large party of hungry people. The variety of sandwiches was amazing. Mrs. Baker's popularity with the local tradesmen and the success of her At Homes seemed to be fully explained.

"You will hardly believe it," she resumed as soon as we had settled down to a serious attack on this provender, "but Dr. Willoughby ended by actually tempting me to commit a crime."

It was easier for us to believe than she supposed, but I did my best to look incredulous.

"Yes, Dr. Carstairs, he told me that the only way to get rid of my murderous propensities was to give way to them. He advised me to kill Samuel."

This really was beyond my power to believe. "Samuel?" I repeated.

"Yes, my beautiful black cat, the one that slept at the foot of my bed every night."

Tarleton raised his head quickly.

"Did he suggest that you should give him the poison from Sumatra?" he put in.

The explorer's sister nodded.

The object of the advice she had received was plain enough. The scoundrel wanted to test the effect of the poison; perhaps he felt some doubt if it was still active. Beyond that his intentions were dark. Such a man was quite capable of committing a murder by deputy, and he might have designed to make an instrument of this deluded patient of his. But, if so, there was nothing to tell us whose life he had been aiming at. He had felt himself to be surrounded by enemies, according to Madame Bonnell's statement. He may have wished to provide himself with a weapon for use in case of need.

The worthy owner of Samuel told us that she had refused to slay her pet.

"I sent him away for fear I should be tempted to kill him," she said with tears in her eyes. "I found him a happy home with a former maid of mine who is married and living in the country. She writes me about him once a month, when I send her a postal order. I shall never dare to have him back again."

My youthful indignation became too much for me.

"There is not the slightest reason why you shouldn't have your cat back tomorrow," I said bluntly. "You are no more likely to kill it than I am. The man was telling you a pack of lies from the beginning. Sir Frank Tarleton will tell you the same. We have been finding out a good deal about this man during the last few days; and you were not his only victim."

Mrs. Baker opened her eyes in a way that showed more offence than gratitude. I had gone the wrong way to work to disabuse her.

"I am much obliged to you, Dr. Cassidy," she said stiffly, "but I much prefer to be on the safe side. We none of us know the secrets of our own hearts, it seems to me. I consider Dr. Witheredge a cruel man, and I have done with him; but he was extremely clever; and I am satisfied that there is something in the science of psycho-analysis."

Tarleton came to my rescue. "The more there is in it the more dangerous it may be in the hands of a clever man without scruples. If you'll allow me to say so, I think you acted very wisely in deciding to have nothing more to do with Dr. Weathered."

The lady accepted this graciously, and smoothed down her ruffled feathers. I thought I might venture on a fresh question.

"Did you know that he was the real proprietor of the Domino Club?"

"Never! You don't say so? I understood it was run by a Frenchwoman—Madame Bonnet."

"You have been there, I suppose?"

"Only once. I heard so much about it that I thought I must go and see what it was like. I was there only last Wednesday. But I didn't stay more than an hour. Dr. Weathell was there, disguised as an Inquisitor, and I was so afraid of his recognizing me that I came away."

There could be no doubt, as far as I could see, that this was the truth. And if it was the truth the lady of the leopard skin and claws was now ruled out of the case. Her part in it had been confined to supplying the poison, or rather in innocently letting it be known where it could be found. To clinch the matter I said:

"I wasn't there, but we heard that a lady had been present who left early. She wore the skin of a leopard, and a necklace of leopard's claws."

"Yes, that was me; I went as a Leopardess," our amiable hostess responded with a frankness which put an end to the last doubt. She added in a tone of quiet triumph, "I can see now that that was where my murderous propensities came out. Why else should I have gone as a beast of prey?"

I had to admit that she had scored off me. Anything less like a beast of prey or a potential murderess than the bright and birdlike little woman I have never seen.

My chief picked out one point that I had overlooked.

"Did Weathered mention the Club to you, ma'am? Or did you know this Madame Bonnell?"

Mrs. Baker drew herself up.

"I didn't *know* her," she said with emphasis. "Such a person is not in my social circle. I knew of her. A friend of mine in Chelsea gave me her card when I went to buy a ticket for the dance, but she was a friend of Madame Bunner's. It was only a form."

The answer was equally decisive. It seemed clear to me that the only person who could have known of the existence of the poison, and abstracted it, was the man who had perished by it. I saw Tarleton's watch come out of his pocket, and its slow, steady motion told me that his brain was already at work on the last winding of the mystery.

When we had done full justice to the refreshments put before us we came away pledged to attend the first At Home given by our hostess, which she explained would be as soon as she was out of mourning for her brother. I think she had won both our hearts in spite of her eccentricities, and we entertained no serious dread that her murderous propensities would be indulged at our expense.

Tarleton was very silent till we were back at Montague Street. Even when we were in his study again he did not seem much disposed to discuss the new situation with me. For the first time since the beginning of the investigation I had the impression that I was not entirely in his confidence.

When I expressed my curiosity as to Weathered's motive for stealing the bottle of upasine he lifted his bushy eyebrows and looked at me almost as if he were annoyed.

"We don't know that he did steal it," he growled. "Everyone who read Armstrong's book knew of his discovery, and would expect to find some of the new poison among his belongings. And as for that little woman, she has probably babbled about it to a dozen persons whom she has forgotten. Her memory is like a sieve."

The judgment struck me as harsh. Mrs. Baker certainly had a genius for forgetting names, but so have many people whose memories are good enough in other respects. It seemed to me that she had shown a pretty fair recollection of her dealings with Weathered at all events; and I said so.

Tarleton hunched himself up in his favourite armchair and growled again.

"You ask me to believe that a doctor who had stolen what he knew to be a deadly drug, and who was actually taking precautions to prevent himself being poisoned at the time, was careless enough to let it be taken from him?—Well, I don't."

I had never known him to speak so irritably before. I sat dumb, asking myself what was in his mind. And all at once the explanation flashed upon me.

If he didn't believe that Weathered had taken the fatal bottle he must have been searching for the probable thief among Weathered's enemies.

The last question he had put to Mrs. Baker showed that his thoughts had turned for a moment in the direction of the Frenchwoman, who of all others had the best opportunity to administer the poison. Who else was left?

The one enemy of Weathered's whom we both knew of, the one person who had not only a reason but, it might be said, a moral right to take his life in self-defence was Violet Bredwardine. And she had confessed to having lent the disguise worn on the night of the murder by one who must have been her friend, and probable champion. A dozen trifling incidents rushed back into my mind; the specialist's anxiety lest his own bottle should have been tampered with; the way he had contrived—it looked like contrivance to me now—to give me a chance of meeting Violet alone. There could be only one meaning in it all.

My chief suspected me, had suspected me from the very first, of being the murderer. The red light was in my eyes at last.

CHAPTER 17

A SINGULAR DISMISSAL

Perhaps it may be wondered why I didn't at once make a frank statement of my part in the mystery to my kind-hearted chief and throw myself on his mercy.

I was withheld by more than one reason. In the first place I couldn't feel sure that I should be believed. I had no means of proving my innocence. The circumstantial evidence against me was as strong as it could be. I had the strongest motive to kill the monster who was trying to put my secret to the basest use; I had been on the spot, and been there in disguise; and I had given him a drug which was only less dangerous than the one that had caused his death. Who would believe that I had stopped short there? And Sir Frank Tarleton had shown by this time that he did not believe me. To him, as to everyone else, it must appear evident that the man who was prepared to commit a crime in defence of a woman would be prepared to tell a lie as well.

Then, again, the relations between my chief and me were not merely private ones. Both of us were Government officials, and I owed my own post to his recommendation. His official conscience might well be different from his private one. He might be willing to make excuses for me personally, and yet feel it his duty to report to the Department we both served that I was no longer worthy of its confidence.

And, lastly, there was the consideration that had controlled my action all along. My secret was Violet's secret. To no living being had I a right to tell it without her consent. That consent I need not say no peril to myself would have tempted me to ask. The only question I now put to myself was whether I ought not to put her on her guard by letting her know what I had come to fear.

I slept, or tried to sleep, that night without coming to my decision. In the morning Sir Frank extracted from the pile of letters beside his plate on the breakfast-table one with an earl's coronet on the flap of the envelope.

He did not show me the contents, but said carelessly, "I shall be out to lunch. Lord Ledbury is anxious to see me in John Street."

The news decided me. Before Violet was exposed to any further questioning from my shrewd chief she must be warned how things stood. I couldn't complain of not being included in the invitation. In Lord Ledbury's eyes naturally I was a mere subordinate, only acting under Tarleton's orders.

There was another letter that interested the consultant more than the Earl's. It came from New Scotland Yard.

"Sarah Neobard and her mother have gone abroad," he remarked with something like satisfaction. "Charles has sent a man after them. They seem to have gone to Paris. You must have frightened that young woman rather badly."

I forced my wandering mind back to the subject of the letters. Had they come into Sarah's hands, and, if so, had she taken them with her? After all, this was a more pressing matter than any danger of mine.

"Will it be possible for them to hide in Paris?" I asked anxiously.

The specialist shook his head.

"Charles knows his business—up to a certain point. Depend on it a smart officer will have been there to meet them at the Gare du Nord, if the French police were notified in time. I don't think there is much chance of two Englishwomen slipping between the fingers of the Paris detective force."

"Then what will be the next step?" I inquired vaguely.

"I shall leave for Paris by tonight's mail."

The announcement was made curtly. The day before it was I who had been charged with this part of the case. I was to have interviewed Mrs. Weathered and appealed to her womanly feelings on behalf of her husband's victims. Now it seemed that my chief had changed his mind, and intended to see her himself. I dared not even ask if I was to go with him. A shadow had fallen between us which it was not for me to pierce.

I held my tongue, and went on quietly with my breakfast. The consultant went through his mail, passing on to me such letters as I was accustomed to deal with on his behalf—requests for appointments and consultations with other doctors, and so forth. There was no sign that he had withdrawn his confidence in me except when the mystery of the Domino Club was concerned.

The meal was just over when a loud summons at the front door was followed by the entrance of Tarleton's man showing in Inspector Charles.

The Inspector was in a state of excitement. In his hand he carried a newspaper which he waved at us both.

"Have you seen this morning's paper?" he called out before the door was closed. "The advertisement in the Agony Column?"

Tarleton glanced at me before answering, and I remembered his prediction to Lord Ledbury as he spoke.

"What, have they got to work already? What does it say?"

Captain Charles read out from the paper in a round, commanding voice:

"Dr. Weathered, deceased. Any patients of the late Dr. Weathered desiring to have their letters to him returned are requested to apply, mentioning number, to Messrs. James, Halliday and James, Solicitors, Carmichael House, Chancery Lane, E.C.4." He did not spare us even the 4.

Sir Frank nodded approvingly. "Very well worded, very well worded, indeed. It sounds like a perfectly respectable offer."

It sounded so to me. But the Inspector was puzzled.

"What does it mean?" he exclaimed. "Why should they advertise? Why not return the letters at once, or write to the patients? And why should they want to know the exact numbers?"

"Ah, that is part of the case that I haven't had an opportunity of going into with you yet, Charles. Won't you sit down. The fact is, I have been rather expecting some approach of this kind. Dr. Cassilis and I have ascertained that Weathered induced some of his patients to write him letters of a rather compromising kind. The arrangement was that the letters should be signed with a number instead of a name, probably they bore no address. The object of this advertisement is to find out who the writers are. The demand for money will come later."

"Blackmail!" the Inspector gasped in horror.

"I'm afraid so. An honest person who had found such a correspondence would have burnt it. You see now one of my reasons for not dropping the case to oblige that Crown Prince of Slavonia."

One of the reasons only. I had little doubt as to another. Captain Charles looked extremely subdued.

"I had no idea of anything like this in the background, I needn't say, Sir Frank. I will look up these solicitors at once. Chancery Lane—there are better addresses than that, and there are worse. Unless you have anything else to advise."

"I should advise you to find out what you can about the solicitors, certainly. But I doubt if they are in possession of the letters. I shouldn't be surprised if the letters were in Paris by this time."

Captain Charles struck his forehead.

"Of course! The widow has carried them abroad to be out of reach in case of trouble. It was fortunate that we heard of their flight so soon. We know where they are already. They have some smart men in the Rue Jerusalem."

"I shall be glad if you will write me a line of introduction to the French police," Tarleton responded. "By the way, have you secured me that finger-print yet?"

"I have it here, Sir Frank." The Inspector took out a substantial pocket-book and extracted a mounted photograph, which my chief slipped into his own pocket without giving it a glance. Charles looked as if he were as much in the dark as I was as to the meaning of this proceeding.

"It may come in useful," was all the consultant said. "But you were going to tell us where Mrs. Weathered and her daughter were hiding."

"They don't seem to be hiding, that's the curious part of it. Perhaps they don't understand the law about extradition. They've put up at a respectable hotel on Cook's list, a hotel swarming with English tourists, the Hotel St. Catherine in the Rue Tivoli."

Tarleton knitted his brows at this intelligence. "We don't know yet the reason for their flight, if it is a flight," he observed thoughtfully. "We have nothing against either of them so far, remember."

He drew out his mascot and played with it gently for a minute while Charles and I watched him in keen suspense. Suddenly he looked up and spoke to the Inspector in a brisk voice.

"We mustn't lose time. Some unfortunate victim may be answering that advertisement already. Luckily, I have come across one of Weathered's correspondents whose letters to him were quite innocent—that Mrs. Baker your man reported on for me. I want you to see her at once, using my name if necessary, and get her authority to deal with these solicitors on her behalf. Ask for the letters first, and if they make some excuse for not parting with them, ask who is instructing them. If they refuse to give you their client's name we shall know the worst."

It seemed to me that we knew the worst already, if my chief was right. As he had said, an honest woman, finding such letters after her husband's death, would have put them in the fire. It was more than ever imperative that I should see Violet at once. She might have read the advertisement by now, and taken it in good faith.

Directly after Captain Charles had left us I made some excuse for going out on business, and hailed the first taxi I saw. It was still early when I got to John Street, Mayfair, where the Earl of Ledbury's modest town house stood. The door was opened by the same man whom I had made a friend of down at Tyberton, and I was careful to confirm the friendship in the surest way. He was much more smartly dressed on this occasion, and everything about the house indicated that Lord Ledbury had taken Tarleton's advice to heart, and was preparing to give his daughter her proper position in the fashionable world.

Violet, too, was changed. Her dress was still a little lacking in those touches which only the most expensive houses can impart, but she bore herself quite differently. Her father's new-born care for her had given her confidence, and done something to banish the look of hopelessness and resignation I had last seen on her face. I hate to confess it, but glad as I was on her account I felt a little sorry on my own. The old gulf between us I was beginning to hope had shrunk, but now a new one seemed to have opened. Who was I, what was plain Bertrand Cassilis, M.D., that he should venture to go on loving the bright star set high above him in the social firmament?

"I think I know why you have come," was her greeting. She did not offer me her white hand. "They are offering to return those letters. I can't tell you how thankful I shall be."

It was what I had feared. I would have given anything to leave her in ignorance, but the risk was too great.

"Have you answered the advertisement yet?" I asked.

"Not yet. I was tempted to go there at once, but I thought I had better consult you first. Why, is there anything wrong?"

She must have seen there was by this time from my air. Yet at that very moment the knowledge that she had thought of me, that she had put her trust in me and no one else, made my courage rise; and I answered her with a boldness that surprised myself.

"Thank Heaven for that! I came here the first moment I could to warn you to take no notice of that advertisement. It shows that they don't know whom the letters are from, or they would have written to you direct. Trust me; the matter is in good hands; those letters shall either be returned to you or destroyed unread, I swear it."

"Thank you, Bertrand. I do trust you. I know it isn't your fault if they haven't been destroyed already."

The words rolled a great burden from my heart. I was on the point of murmuring that I hadn't deserved her trust, but some instinct bade me refrain from the least reference to the past. I believed that the sad old wound was beginning to heal, and that the best chance for both of us was to bury the past in silence, and never to conjure up its ghost by one single word.

Already Violet was forgetting her own trouble to think of mine. She went on before I had found anything to say.

"But what about yourself? Has anything more been discovered about the murder?"

It was necessary for me to tell her what I feared. "We have found what caused Weathered's death," I answered. "It was a poison that only Sir Frank Tarleton knew of. He recognized the symptoms from the first, and now he has found out where it was obtained from." And I briefly related the story of the stolen bottle.

Violet looked relieved when she had heard it.

"Then he must have stolen the bottle himself. Did he commit suicide, do you think?"

"I'm afraid that's not what Sir Frank thinks. Unless I am mistaken he suspects me of having taken the bottle from Mrs. Baker. His manner towards me has quite changed. He is going to Paris tonight on the track of the letters, but he isn't taking me with him."

I had alarmed her more than I meant. She uttered a cry of despair.

"Bertrand! It isn't true! Will he have you arrested? Shall you be—" She began to sob.

"No, no; it isn't as bad as that. There's not going to be any arrest if the police can help it. Any way, I don't believe Sir Frank would let them arrest me. But I shall have to resign my post, I expect, and I may have to leave the country."

She looked at me through her tears. "That will be almost as bad, won't it?"

It was all I could do to keep from answering, "Not if you come with me." But I could not take advantage of her like that.

"I shall always have my profession," I said. "Sir Frank has confidence in me as a doctor, I know. But I didn't mean to distress you like this. I shouldn't have said anything to you about it, but Sir Frank is coming here to lunch today, and I was afraid he might find out something from you."

"Surely you didn't think that," she protested. "You don't think I should betray you. If you had killed that villain it would have been for my sake. And he deserved to be killed."

My heart glowed within me. I spoke out.

"And I would have killed him if I had seen no other way. No, I didn't think for a moment that you would give me away knowingly; but Tarleton is a past master in the art of sounding people and extracting information from them unawares. I only wanted to put you on your guard, lest you should think that you could trust him as a friend of mine."

"I certainly thought he was. He looked so kind and good," Violet said thoughtfully.

Perhaps I was a little irritated. "He impresses all women in that way," I said with a touch of jealousy. "I could see that he admired you."

Violet's eyes brightened. "I must try to make a friend of him. If I let him see that—that I should be sorry if any harm came to anyone through me, perhaps that may influence him."

I ought to have been very grateful, but I'm afraid my response was lacking in warmth.

"Don't tell him I have been here," I said as I rose to go. And she smiled at me rather pathetically as she promised.

I had a rather dismal lunch by myself, wondering what was passing at Lord Ledbury's. When I saw Tarleton again I was staggered by his gay appearance. He had blossomed out in a new coat and a white waistcoat and a fancy tie. Most wonderful of all, the shabby black ribbon by which he was so fond of swinging his watch had been replaced by a brilliant gold chain that I had never seen before. It was evident that he had decked himself to make an impression in John Street.

He had not long been back when we had another call from Captain Charles. He came in looking grave, and greeted my chief with increased respect.

"I have been to Chancery Lane, as you advised, Sir Frank, and seen the principal. There is only one. The names in the advertisement are bogus ones, unless he bought the good-will of some old firm going out of business. The man's real name is Stillman. I saw it on his notepaper. And he strikes me as hot stuff."

"What did he say?"

"It was just what you expected. Made an excuse for not giving me Mrs. Baker's letters. Said he was only authorized to hand them over to the writer in person. And when I asked who was instructing him, said he wasn't authorized to give his client's name."

Tarleton shrugged his shoulders.

"Clever, very clever," he repeated. "There's nothing for you to take hold of, so far. If you go back again with Mrs. Baker you will put him in a corner, and very likely her letters will be given up, as they contain nothing serious. It's a nasty business."

"What had we better do?"

"Do nothing till you hear from me again. I am off to Paris tonight, and when I come back I shall know where the letters are, if I don't bring them back with me."

The Inspector bowed himself out quite meekly. My curiosity prompted me to venture on a rash question.

"Do you think it possible that Miss Neobard has the letters?"

My chief swung himself slowly round in his chair and gave me a steady look, under which I quailed inwardly.

"I don't think I ought to tell you, Cassilis. It seems to me that you are an interested party."

So my fear had been well grounded. I listened breathlessly for more.

"From the beginning of this investigation you have shown a bias that is fatal in one who is playing the part of a detective, or aspiring to play it. A man in your position should be absolutely impartial. He should not let himself be swayed for a moment by personal prejudices or personal preferences. Now you have all along showed a disposition to screen Lady Violet

Bredwardine. You have made excuses for her to me, and you have defended her to others. At the same time you have shown an inclination to think the worst of Sarah Neobard. And your animus against her came out most strongly when she showed herself Lady Violet's enemy."

What could I say? I was only too thankful that he had spared me any reference to the omission of Violet's name from the list I had copied for Inspector Charles. That was a clear breach of duty, as I had to admit to myself.

Sir Frank's voice was perfectly bland as he continued:

"Lady Violet is worthy of any man's admiration, and I am quite as determined as you are to protect her from any dastardly use of her correspondence. I should not have blamed you severely for anything you might have done for her protection if you had been acting in a private capacity. But you are here in a responsible position. You owe it to the Home Office and to me to conduct the inquiry into this murder without fear or favour, whatever may be the consequences, and whoever may be guilty. You must ask yourself if you have done so."

I am afraid I asked myself instead how much he really knew. So far he had made no definite accusation. He had charged me with nothing but a display of personal sympathy and antipathy, a charge which it would have been foolish to deny.

"It is a question of temperament, it seems to me," pursued the consultant in the same even tones. "Sympathy is a valuable quality in a doctor, but it is fatal in a criminal investigator. I think I made a mistake in inviting you to enter the Government service. You would get on better in private practice."

The blow had fallen and I had only to make the best of it. "Of course, I am in your hands, sir. If that is your opinion I will send in my resignation."

Australia, Canada, South Africa passed before my mind's eye as I spoke, as possible refuges for a penniless medico. I could not hope for anything in England after being practically dismissed from the Home Office.

My prompt offer, however, seemed to have greatly softened my judge.

"We will talk of that after I have come back from Paris," he said kindly. "For your own sake I don't advise any sudden step. And there is Lady Violet to consider. As I said before, you have acted as her champion. Anything like a public slur on you, or an admission on your part that you were to blame, would be certain to give her pain, even if it didn't reflect on her. She spoke of you to me this morning in a very friendly way."

Poor Violet. So she had done the very worst thing she could have done in my interest. To praise a young man to an elderly admirer—what other result could it have but to ensure his being driven from the field?

I was too much cast down to make any response to Sir Frank's well-meant advice, beyond a silent bow. He was as friendly as ever the next minute, invited me to come to Charing Cross to see him off, and shook my hand cordially at parting. I preferred to walk home afterwards, dreading the dull hours till bedtime. So miserable was I that, when I came in, I should have gone straight upstairs without looking to see if there were any letters for me if I had not been arrested by a faint fragrance that had many memories for me.

I looked down, and there was a delicate blue envelope beckoning me by name.

Dear Bertrand,

I write at once to tell you that you have nothing to fear from dear Sir Frank. He spoke of you most highly to my father, said you had a distinguished career before you, and that he would not take £3,000 a year for your practice in a few years' time.

Yours,
Violet.

CHAPTER 18

MOTHER AND DAUGHTER

Sir Frank Tarleton had not given me all his reasons for not taking me with him to Paris. One of them, as he told me afterwards, was that I had made an enemy of Sarah Neobard, or, to put it the other way, I had made her regard me as an enemy. My chief believed that my presence would prevent him from obtaining any information from her or her mother. They would think he had come on a hostile errand, and they would obstinately hold their tongues, for fear lest anything they said might be used by me against her.

Tarleton's intention was to appear in the character of a friend of Sarah's, who did not share my suspicions and only wanted to be able to clear her from them. He was quite frank with me about the way in which he had spoken of me in my absence, and about everything else in which I was interested.

He put up at his favourite hotel, the Saint Lazare, on his arrival, one that suited him because it was near the centre of everything without being overrun by English and Americans. He liked to be among French people when he was in France. After the "little breakfast," that first delicious taste of French coffee and French bread which atones for the stuffiness of the French railway carriage, he made his way round to the Rue Jerusalem, where he was received with high distinction by the head of the French police to whom his name and official standing were well known.

The Chief presented to him Brigadier Samson, the detective who had the two fugitives under supervision, and he undertook, at the doctor's request, that a formidable-looking gendarme in the showy uniform of the French police should be stationed opposite the Hotel Saint Catherine, in full sight from the windows, till further notice.

Another small piece of business was transacted. Tarleton laid before the Chief the photograph he had obtained from Inspector Charles, and invited him to find out if it corresponded with anything in his register of finger-prints.

The hour now being reached at which the ladies might be expected to show themselves, the visitor next went on to their hotel in the Rue Tivoli.

In the hall he found the English detective who had followed them from London, and who had taken a room on the same floor, in the unsuspicious character of a tourist who found himself in Paris for the first time and was unwilling to venture far from his hotel.

"The birds are in their cage, Sir Frank," he reported as soon as he recognized the specialist. "I've been hanging about here since the early morning and I've arranged with the management that they shan't be allowed to go out by any other way."

Tarleton, in reply, explained why he had asked for a gendarme to be posted across the way. "I don't want them to know that you're a police officer, of course; but I may want them to know that they are being watched by the police."

He had hardly finished speaking when the representative of French law appeared on the scene, a truly imposing figure with a huge moustache, who began pacing the pavement opposite like a man who was not to be trifled with.

The consultant asked if Mrs. Weathered had taken a private sitting-room and finding that she had, sent up his card, on which he had scribbled the words "*Official Confidential*." When he was handing it into the office, however, the detective followed him to make a correction.

"She's not staying here under her own name. She has taken the name of Neobard."

He had to wait some minutes for a response. When at length he was taken upstairs and shown into the room he found, as he had expected, Miss Neobard alone.

"My mother asks you to excuse her, Sir Frank. She is not yet well enough to see anyone on business. May I ask the meaning of those words on your card?"

Sarah spoke with the utmost coolness. If she was frightened she had evidently resolved to hide her fright under a mask of defiance. Tarleton's manner was one of entire friendliness.

"They mean that although I have come to see Mrs. Weathered as a Government official, on official business, our interview will be strictly confidential. I shall not make use of any information she may give me, without her consent."

The daughter looked at him doubtfully.

"Does that apply to me as well?"

Sir Frank purposely hesitated before answering.

"There is no reason why I shouldn't have a confidential talk with you as well, if you desire it. But at present I have only asked to see Mrs. Weathered."

The name seemed to irritate the girl.

"My mother has dropped the name of Weathered," she said sharply. "In future she desires to be known as Mrs. Neobard."

Tarleton was struck by her tone. It conveyed to him that the change of name had not been made with a view to concealment, but was due to some deeper cause.

Up to now Miss Neobard had made no reference to the whereabouts of the travellers having been so soon discovered. She now threw out the question scornfully.

"I suppose the police are on our track, as we came here without giving anyone our address. Is that confidential?"

"Certainly not." The doctor was getting a little irritated by this time. "Your leaving London while the mystery of Dr. Weathered's death was still unsolved was enough to provoke the suspicion of the police. They were bound to keep you in sight."

Sarah couldn't very well contradict this. She lifted her head more defiantly than ever.

"My mother can't see you," she repeated. "Anything you want to say to her can be said to me."

Sir Frank admired her courage. He tried to soften her.

"My dear Miss Neobard, I wish you would let me speak to you as a friend. You can't think I have come here as an enemy. If I had I should have brought Dr. Cassilis with me. Or rather I should have sent him instead of coming myself."

This shot told as he had expected. It was evident that Sarah cherished a strong resentment against me. It was a new light to her that my chief might take a different view of the case. For the first time she looked at him as if she thought it possible that he might be sincere.

"Dr. Cassilis has practically accused me of murder," she said.

"Dr. Cassilis is a young man without much experience. He has let himself become interested in the young lady you seemed to suspect. He spoke in her defence; I don't believe that he really thinks you had anything to do with Dr. Weathered's death. He went too far, of course, and I have told him so. In fact, I have now taken him off the case."

The defiance began to die out of Miss Neobard's eyes. They were fine eyes and she knew how to use them with effect.

"Does that mean that I am not under suspicion any longer?" she inquired in a more gracious voice.

"You never have been under suspicion as far as I am concerned," the doctor answered a little evasively. "I feel sure you are a truthful woman, and whatever you choose to tell me in confidence I shall believe."

Sarah was fairly conquered. Her voice broke down as she replied.

"I am a wicked girl, Sir Frank. I did have thoughts at one time that he ought to die. But I never went farther than that. I swear to you on my oath that I have no more idea how he was murdered, or who murdered him, than you have—I mean, I have no idea at all."

The consultant thanked her with a grave bow. "The evidence I have obtained so far points to suicide," he said quietly. "But I only tell you that in confidence, to relieve your mind. Dr. Weathered carried poison about with him."

The step-daughter looked even more relieved than Tarleton had expected, but a good deal surprised as well.

"I knew that he took opium sometimes," she whispered back, "but I never guessed that he meant to take his own life. I was afraid...." She stopped short and shuddered.

The specialist took no notice of the suppressed hint.

"You will see now, I hope, that I haven't come here to try and get your mother to tell me anything about you. As a matter of fact, my business with her has nothing to do with the murder, or whatever it was, except indirectly. I have come in the interest of some of Dr. Weathered's patients and I think Mrs. Neobard may be able to help me to obtain certain information on their behalf. I am sure you won't wish any evil he has done to go on after his death."

This way of putting it appealed to what was best in Sarah Neobard. She looked puzzled but not disposed to resist. She made another half-hearted attempt to extract from the visitor what it was that he had to ask her mother, but when she found him firm in insisting that he must see Mrs. Neobard herself, she gave way, and went to fetch her.

A quarter of an hour, half an hour, passed. There must have been a severe struggle going on in the next room, although no sounds reached the consultant through the wall. He had laid his hand on the bell to summon a waiter and send a peremptory message when the door at last opened and the widow came in.

Tarleton felt convinced from the first moment that she had guessed his business with her. Her eyes were red and her naturally pale cheeks showed a feverish flush. She was hardly able to walk and her daughter supported her tenderly till she was in a chair. Sarah herself was clearly ignorant of the cause of her mother's emotion. She glanced wonderingly from her to Sir Frank and back again, and seemed to be holding herself in readiness to defend her parent or to back up Tarleton's demand, according to her judgment of what was the right course.

The examiner came to the point quickly.

"Miss Neobard has explained to you that this is a confidential interview, I hope. Whatever you say to me will be a secret between ourselves, unless you authorize me to make use of it. It is for you to decide whether your daughter is to remain in the room, of course."

The mother stretched out a hand and took hold of one of her protector's, who answered for her. "I have promised my mother to remain."

"Very good. I had better begin by reading you this advertisement. It appeared in the paper yesterday."

He read out the invitation from Messrs. James, Halliday and James to the patients of the late Dr. Weathered to apply for the return of their correspondence and continued:

"The solicitor who put in this advertisement refused to give the name of the client who is instructing him. Will you tell me if it is you?"

Mrs. Neobard shook her head faintly without speaking.

"Can you tell me if your late husband left a will, and who is his executor?"

"I can answer that question," Sarah put in. "My mother is sole executor and he has left everything to her. She wanted to renounce execution; but the lawyer told her that it would be no use, as the law would make her administrator. She is not going to take a farthing of his money, if there is any."

"Quite so; then Mrs. Neobard is the only person who is lawfully entitled to deal with any papers Dr. Weathered left behind him. Can you explain to me how these letters came to be in the possession of this solicitor, or the person for whom he is acting?"

The flush had faded from the widow's cheeks, leaving her very pale.

"I can't explain," she said in a whisper.

"Does it matter?" her daughter asked. "As long as these people get their letters back again, what does it matter who they got them from?"

"They won't get them; that is what matters," the physician said gravely. "There is a criminal behind this advertisement. I must explain to you and to Mrs. Neobard, if she doesn't know already, what these letters were about."

Very deliberately and keeping his eyes fixed on the agitated woman all the time, Tarleton outlined the story of his discoveries. He was careful not to mention names. He explained why the doctor's case-book had been taken from the safe, and why that precaution had proved useless. The dead man's real hold over his victims had been through the letters he had persuaded them to write to him; those letters had been signed with a cipher, and the object of the advertisement was to make the writers disclose their identity so that they might be blackmailed by the holder of their secret confessions.

The widow's distress became pitiable as the explanation proceeded. There could be no doubt that she was no party to the plot and hardly a doubt that its revelation had come to her as a complete shock. As for Sarah Neobard, her fine eyes fairly blazed with indignation.

"I never knew that such things were possible," she exclaimed. "I don't believe—I can't believe—that my step-father ever meant to use the letters in such a way."

At this point the consultant saw Mrs. Neobard open her eyes and look at him wistfully, as if to ask him to take no notice of her daughter's tenderness for the scoundrel who had passed to his account.

"Surely you can't think," the girl pursued, "that my mother knew anything about this? Mother!"—she turned to the shrinking woman—"do you hear? You must do everything you can to help Sir Frank Tarleton to stop this iniquity."

Now Sir Frank knew perfectly well that it could be stopped pretty easily by the simple step of Mrs. Neobard's solicitors taking proceedings in her name for the recovery of the letters. The legal property in them, of course was vested in the writers, but until they claimed them the executrix was entitled to their possession; and if the Chancery Lane sharper refused to give them up or to disclose their whereabouts he was pretty sure to be struck off the Rolls and stood a good chance of being indicted for conspiracy. All this the adviser of the Home Office had known from the first, but he took care to keep the knowledge up his sleeve. For him the question of the letters was a secondary one and he was only using it as a means of opening the widow's lips.

Miss Neobard suddenly stopped pleading with her mother to say to the specialist, "I think I can guess who has those letters—Madame Bonnell!"

This was another thing about which Tarleton had entertained no doubt since seeing the advertisement. But he received the suggestion with every sign of disbelief.

"Madame Bonnell is the last person to whom I should think Dr. Weathered would have trusted them," he answered.

"She may have stolen them," the girl persisted. "Perhaps he kept them at the Club and she has found them since his death."

"He kept nothing whatever at the Club except the disguise he wore at the Club dances. I have had the premises searched carefully by the police, and they have questioned the staff. The letters are not there now, and there is no receptacle in which they could have been stored."

Mrs. Neobard had been listening anxiously to this discussion. Now she spoke.

"Who else do you think can have them?"

"That is what I want you to tell me. And I think you can."

The widow shivered again. Her daughter looked at her with a dawning comprehension that something was wrong.

"Mother, you must tell if you know."

"Your husband kept these letters in a concealed cupboard of his dressing-room," Tarleton told her. "Your house has been searched for a secret hiding-place and the cupboard has been found." It was a bold shot, but the widow's face showed that it had hit the mark. "That cupboard is empty now. The law presumes that you opened it, as you were entitled and bound to do, after his death, and that you took possession of its contents as executrix. I am here to ask you in the name of the law what you have done with them."

He watched Dr. Weathered's relict very closely while he was speaking. She seemed to be wrenched by conflicting fears. At one moment her lips parted as if to speak, at the next they closed again more tightly than before.

"Tell him, mother!" pleaded the girl.

The mother turned to her despairingly.

"I can't! I daren't! Don't ask me to," she cried hopelessly.

The representative of the law looked at his watch.

"If that is your last answer you must be prepared to take the consequences, Mrs. Weathered." He pointed dramatically to a window of the room. "Look out of that window, Miss Neobard, and tell your mother what you see."

Sarah rushed to the window and gave a sharp cry. "Mother, there is a gendarme watching the hotel!" She looked reproachfully at the physician. "And you told me you came here as a friend!"

"I am trying to act as one. Your mother has only to tell me the truth and I will open the window and send that man away."

"Do you hear, mother? You won't let me be arrested?"

Mrs. Weathered—Tarleton had meant to remind her that she was passing under a name not legally hers—had merely shivered again when she heard who was outside. Now she sprang out of her chair, a different woman.

"You! Arrest you! What do you mean, Sarah? What have you to do with it? The police have come for me."

Sarah was not less amazed and horrified than her mother.

"Nonsense; they can't touch you," she exclaimed. "You weren't at the dance that night!"

"And you were? My girl, my poor girl, what have you been doing?"

"Sir Frank Tarleton knows. I have told him everything. I think he means to be friendly, but he can't save me unless you speak out. She can speak safely, can't she?" the daughter asked imploringly. "My mother isn't in any danger?"

It was a question difficult to answer either way. Tarleton felt the eyes of both women searching his face, each with the same anxiety, though each on the other's behalf.

"It is only right that I should let you know that Mrs. Weathered may be in danger. The letters which ought to be in her possession may contain the clue to your step-father's murder."

And now the scene became painful indeed to witness, as the mother and daughter stood facing each other with the questions in their eyes that they were too terrified to put. Both of them at some time had loved the murdered man; both of them, perhaps, had come to hate him. And now each had been shaken by a sudden revelation of the other's hidden side. The mother had just caught an appalling glimpse into her daughter's unknown relations with her step-father; the daughter had been staggered by the suggestion that her mother might have been his mortal enemy. And all the time, beneath these mutual dreads and suspicions it might be, these unconscious jealousies, there prevailed, stronger than any other feeling, that blind, unselfish love between mother and child which made both of them eager to thrust themselves into danger in the other's place.

The parts had been reversed. It was Sarah who was now anxious to close her mother's mouth and Mrs. Weathered who showed herself determined to speak. The skilful manipulator of human nature who had wrought up this dramatic situation knew that he had only to wait for the *dénouement* at which he had aimed.

He had not to wait long.

"If you have trusted Sir Frank Tarleton I can do the same," the elder woman said at last. "I have more to tell him than he knows. He thinks that I only found those letters in the cupboard after my husband's death. I have been reading every one of them for more than a year."

If the consultant had not quite expected to hear this he had been expecting something more than he thought it wise to indicate just then. He let no sign of his thoughts appear outwardly. The two women, exhausted by the tempest of emotion they had passed through, sat down side by side; but they kept their eyes averted from one another, and only raised them from time to time to watch the effect of Mrs. Weathered's narrative on him.

"You mustn't think that I am an inquisitive woman, Sir Frank. I didn't discover my husband's secrets by prying. I never knew the existence of the cupboard or the letters till one of the women who had been led into writing to him came to me."

This was news to the doctor. He pricked up his ears for the name.

"She was a Miss Sebright—Miss Julia Sebright."

"Ah! She is dead." Tarleton thought it sound policy to show that he was able to check the statements made to him.

"Yes. She died soon afterwards, of a broken heart, I think. She came to me in despair and appealed to me as Dr. Weathered's wife to protect her from him."

Sir Frank got up, walked to the window, opened it and waved his hand. The gendarme outside saluted respectfully and marched away.

CHAPTER 19

THE MEANS TO DO ILL DEEDS

The pale, weak woman had suddenly been transformed in Tarleton's eyes into a heroine. He saw in her someone greater than himself. He was the official, salaried guardian of society, called upon to run no risks that a brave man ought to fear. But this forlorn woman, without a friend in whom she could confide, without support from public opinion or from the law, had taken into her trembling hands the task of delivering her sister women from a wretch whom neither opinion nor the law could reach.

Mrs. Neobard—she had surely earned her right to be called that now—thanked the doctor for his impulsive action with a look. But it was not a look of triumph. She proceeded with her story in the tone of a loser rather than a victor.

"Miss Sebright told me that she had felt a longing to become a mother, which she had no hope of satisfying because she suffered from a depravity, a club foot. She had been told as a child that no man would ever want to marry her, except for her money, and the result had been to make her distrust every man who came near her. It was a sad story and I'm afraid it is true of other women. Their self-distrust robs them of the happiness within their reach, if they only knew it."

The speaker sighed as though contrasting their fate with her own opposite mistake.

"She told me she had come to my husband to have the longing driven out of her mind; instead of which he had persuaded her to become the mother of an illegitimate child, by a man whose name was not told her. The child was never born, happily—or unhappily; I daren't say which. But she had written letters that disclosed what she had done, and now the doctor was holding them over her. He hadn't gone so far as to demand money, but he was compelling her to come or write to him every week and charging her high fees. She would rather have paid a lump sum to end it. The persecution was driving her out of her mind. The poor thing actually offered me a thousand pounds."

It was a sickening story. Hardened as he was to the ways of criminals, Tarleton listened to it with nausea.

"I promised to find the letters and return them to her if I could. I had to go to work secretly. If I had said anything to my husband it would have put him on his guard, and he would have placed the letters somewhere out of my reach. I spied on him till I saw him one day through the keyhole going to a cupboard in the wall of his dressing-room—the one you found."

The consultant forbore to correct her by saying that the discovery had been made by Inspector Charles.

"Of course, it was locked and I had no key that would open it. So I went to an ironmonger's one day when the doctor was away for the week-end, and asked him to send a confidential man to open it. I pretended that my husband had lost the key while he was away on a holiday, and wanted something in the cupboard to be sent to him. I don't know if they believed me, but they said nothing, and they made me a new key."

In the same quiet way she went on, seeming to see nothing extraordinary in the patient contrivance by which she had outwitted the schemer who most probably looked down upon her as a simple piece of domestic furniture.

In the cupboard she had found a mass of correspondence, by no means all of it from women, but in almost every case containing painful and sometimes hideous revelations of depraved and distorted natures. The horrified woman had been obliged to leave a good deal unread. The letters from each correspondent were neatly kept on a separate file, marked with the number under which he or she wrote. These numbers puzzled her at first, as they puzzled Tarleton himself, but she had only to ask Miss Sebright for the explanation. Several numbers were missing from the series. Either the writers must have redeemed their rash confessions, or else they had gone abroad or died, and the papers had become valueless.

The real difficulty before Mrs. Neobard had been to keep her promise to Miss Sebright without the doctor's knowing that his cupboard had been opened. Now she saw her way. If the poor victim defied him and he went to look for her file and found it gone, he would probably think he had destroyed it himself by mistake.

"He wasn't always sober when he came in at night," the unfortunate wife said in a tone that breathed of her past sufferings. "I felt sure he couldn't suspect me or anyone of taking one set of letters and leaving all the rest. Anyhow, I decided to risk it. I took Miss Sebright's letters and sent them to her by registered post. She wrote thanking me very gratefully, but telling me that she was dying and asking me to go and see her. I went more than once. It was the sight of her sinking into her grave under my husband's cruelty that nerved me to go on."

"I should have returned all the other letters now, without caring what happened, if I had known where to send them. But I had no key to whom the numbers stood for."

"You would have found that if you had looked in Dr. Weathered's appointment-book," Sir Frank told her.

The widow opened her eyes.

"I never thought of that! I see you know how to find out everything, Sir Frank. Stop me if I am telling you anything you know already."

The consultant waved his hand courteously for her to go on. Her story had held one surprise for him already, and he foresaw that others were to come.

"I waited. I now went to the cupboard every day when I knew I was safe from interruption, to read any fresh letters that had arrived, in the hope of finding something in them that would give me a clue to the writer's identity. At last I found one in which the writer had put her address at the head in the usual way. I suppose she did it in forgetfulness."

Tarleton breathed softly while he waited for the name he was pretty certain of hearing.

"The address was Carlyle Square, Chelsea. I looked it up in the Directory and found she was a Mrs. Baker. Have you heard of her before?" Mrs. Neobard gave him an imploring look.

"I knew her brother, the late Captain Armstrong," the specialist said, without answering the question directly. "Please tell me everything."

Mrs. Neobard made an effort and went on.

"I was disappointed, in a sense, to find that her letters weren't worth returning to her. There was nothing in them that anyone could make use of to harm her, as far as I could see. She was simply a very foolish woman with fads. She had come to my husband out of mere curiosity, I should think, and he had played on her weakness. He had pretended that she was secretly longing to commit a murder; and the silly woman believed him. She seemed rather proud of it than otherwise. I suppose it gave her a feeling of self-importance to think of herself as a possible Mrs. Maybrick. In one of her letters she compared herself with Miladi in *The Three Musketeers*."

It was so exactly in keeping with his own impression of the odd little woman in Carlyle Square that Tarleton gave a nod of satisfaction.

"Ah! I see you do know her. But I suppose you won't tell me how much you know?"

The physician was obliged to shake his head. "You could not trust me yourself, ma'am, if I did."

"I suppose you are right," she admitted regretfully. "Well, I went on reading this Mrs. Baker's letters on the chance of finding something serious in them; and at last there was. He had prompted her to think out plans for committing a murder, and she was actually sending them to him."

A gasp drew Tarleton's attention to Sarah Neobard, who had sat hitherto listening in silence. Now she seemed roused to a sense of impending tragedy, and gazed at her mother with dilated eyes.

The widow directed a swift glance at her, and withdrew it instantly.

"You can understand my terrible position, Sir Frank. My eyes had been opened to my husband's character. I don't say that he had always been a bad man, but he had become one by now. I had the proof under my eyes that he was a criminal, and a danger to society. And here he was discussing plots of murder with a weak, silly woman who seemed to be under his thumb. Judging from her letters she was quite capable of committing a murder out of vanity, just to give herself the feeling that she was an extraordinary person."

The consultant did not credit this. But he was not there to defend Mrs. Baker, and he did not want to interrupt.

"I felt that if she did commit a crime she would be doing it as my husband's instrument, as much as if he had hypnotized her, and that I must find some way to prevent it. Then, while I was wondering how to interfere, a letter came in which she said she had a bottle of poison in her possession, a poison unknown to the medical profession, that her brother had brought with him from Sumatra. But I expect you know about that?"

"I know the poison you speak of, certainly. The brother sold me a quantity of it. He professed it was all he had brought to England."

"He deceived you, then. In the next letter she described exactly where she kept the poison, in a chiffonier in her drawing-room within reach of the first caller. She boasted that she kept it under lock and key, but almost anyone could pick a lock like that, as even I could see. Of course, I knew from that moment that the poison was within my husband's reach, and I felt sure he meant to take it. Why else should he have asked about it so particularly? What did it matter to him where it was kept, unless he wanted it himself?"

"I quite agree with you," said the specialist, seeing that he was expected to reply.

"Now you see where I stood. I knew that my husband was capable of committing a murder, if he had anything to gain by it, and now I knew that he was actually scheming to obtain a poison that couldn't be detected. I don't think Mrs. Baker had an idea that her brother had parted with some to you. She wrote as though her bottle held all there was. And who was it that he was thinking of murdering? I couldn't see anyone but myself."

"Mother!" The word burst from Sarah's agonized lips. If she had retained any lingering softness for the dead man it must have expired in that cry. Her mother did not turn her head.

"I had to defend myself. I couldn't prevent him from taking the poison in any other way that I could think of. I went to Mrs. Baker's house and stole the bottle."

"You were quite right," the physician agreed again.

"I had no difficulty. I took a bunch of all the keys I could find in the house, keys of wardrobes and drawers and boxes of different sizes, and went round to the Square. I walked up and down till I had seen a woman who looked like the mistress of the house come out, and then I knocked, and asked to be allowed to wait upstairs. I gave some common name." She put her hand to her forehead. "That's strange! I can't remember the name. Well, almost the first key I tried opened the chiffonier and there stood the bottle just as she had described it I put it into my pocket and came away."

Whatever theory Sir Frank had formed as to the case, it had certainly not included this incident. He had thought it possible that after Weathered had carried off the bottle his wife had found it and taken it in turn from him. He had never conjectured that the feeble-looking woman had been brave and cool enough to checkmate her husband in advance like this.

"For the moment I felt safe," Mrs. Neobard went on steadily. "But how long could I expect to be from such a husband as mine? He was a doctor, and it was easy for him to obtain other poisons. He would have had to do that in any case, I think, as it turned out. Mrs. Baker quarrelled with him soon after, because he had advised her to kill a favourite cat. She refused to have anything more to do with him, and as her letters were more damaging to him than to her he had no hold on her. I soon found that he had destroyed them."

This was another new light for the consultant. And it prepared him for what was to come next.

"It seemed to me that my only chance of escape was to leave him. But what reason could I give to the world for doing so? I had nothing to complain of as far as his treatment of me was concerned. He was always perfectly courteous. We were on friendly terms outwardly. I couldn't prove that he had been unfaithful to me; I wasn't even sure in my own mind that he had been, yet, although the letters showed me that he was pursuing one of his victims. What could I say? Was I to denounce him publicly as a scoundrel, and produce the letters? I might have ruined dozens of innocent men and women. And I might fail. I might find that the world sided with him instead of me. I knew him well enough to know exactly what he would do. He would say that I had spied on his professional work, that I had pried into the secrets of his patients and that jealousy had made me insane. And he would have found plenty of people to believe him. A wife who betrays her husband is not likely to be forgiven.

"If I left him I doubted if my own daughter would have come with me."

This was the first allusion the mother had made to her daughter's unhappy infatuation. And it was the last one. Sarah had begun to cry quietly. Now Mrs. Neobard put out her hand again and took her child's.

"You won't expect me to give you *all* my reasons for deciding that I must act as I did, Sir Frank. Perhaps you will think I really was insane. I don't know—after reading some of those letters that I found I sometimes feel it difficult to say who is sane and who isn't. I can only say I thought over everything time after time, as quietly as I could, and I always came to the same conclusion. I think what stuck in my mind most of all was the death of poor Miss Sebright. There was no doubt that he had murdered her, as surely as if he had given her arsenic. I thought he ought to die."

She said it without an effort, as though it were the most natural conclusion in the world.

"It looked like a providence to me that I had the poison ready. It was his own doing, you see. He had helped me to it through wanting it himself for his own wicked ends. I had taken it in self-defence, and there it was, ready to be used."

The listener remembered Shakespeare's lines, though he refrained from quoting them:

"How oft the sight of means to do ill deeds makes ill deeds done."

The master of human nature had anticipated the excuse of many King Johns. And in this case the excuse seemed genuine. In fact, the widow did not speak as though she meant to excuse herself; she seemed to be simply explaining the sequence of her thoughts.

"Then I came to a new difficulty, that I had never expected. I found I couldn't do it."

It sounded like confession. There was far more of apology in the tone with which she said this than there had been in her whole previous statement. For the first time there was moisture in her eyes.

"I had believed in him once.... I had loved him."

She broke down and ceased for a few moments. Tarleton watched her with real pity.

"I dare say you will find it difficult to understand me, Sir Frank, but I think most wives would. I hadn't changed my mind. I was still quite firm in believing that it was right to put an end to my husband, but I had to find someone else to do it."

The consultant nodded. It was all plain to him now. His theory had not been very far wrong, after all.

"I decided that I must try to discover one of his victims, one of the men who had confessed their secrets to him and were suffering in consequence, and give the poison to him. I didn't think of the appointment-book, unfortunately. The only way that occurred to me of getting in touch with the writers of the letters was to go to the Domino Club."

Tarleton felt astray again for the moment. There were more complications in the case than he had even yet grasped.

"I expect you know all about the Club. My husband had started it as a means of getting money out of his patients, but it caught on, and became quite a fashionable resort. It brought him something like £1,000 a year. Of course, his name didn't appear, but everyone knew he was to be met there regularly. He never missed a dance. The nominal proprietor of the Club was the woman who managed it for him, Madame Bonnell."

"Yes. I knew all that. And I know Madame Bonnell."

Mrs. Neobard's face betrayed some apprehension.

"Know her as a friend, do you mean?" she ventured.

"I know her well enough to think she could be a very dangerous one."

"Ah, then you *do* know her. I wish I had!... I went to her to buy a ticket of admission to the Club, as I wasn't a member. I didn't mean to tell her who I was, but she knew somehow."

"Madame Bonnell knew a good deal."

"Yes, I found that out, too, before I had done with her. She was all politeness; she pretended to think I was coming out of curiosity and treated it as a sort of joke. She promised of her own accord not to let Dr. Weathered know. Promised it playfully, you understand, as if it were of no consequence whether he did or not. What she really thought I can't tell, but she must have suspected something and meant to get me in her power.

"She deceived me completely. I asked her some questions about the people who came, especially the patients. I wanted to find out which of them came against their will, but I hoped she wouldn't see what I was driving at."

A sheep might as well have tried to hoodwink a wolf, was Tarleton's inward comment, but he thought he had interrupted enough.

"She answered all my questions so glibly and seemed so anxious to oblige that I was led on further and further. At last she said, 'You can see I am a friend, madam; why not trust me? I see you want to know your husband's enemies and I am willing to help you. This Club is full of them. Every time the doctor comes here I consider he takes his life in his hands.'

"I tried to draw back, but it was too late. She refused to let me go. She said, 'I must choose between you and your husband, madam. He is my employer, he pays me well, and if anything happens to him you may engage another manageress, and I shall lose my daily bread. If it is your object to preserve him from danger we can work together.'

"She must have guessed pretty well by this time that I had a different object, because she hardly waited for me to answer. Before I could make up my mind what to say, she went on: 'On the other hand, I have no friendship for Dr. Weathered. Of late I have sometimes wished that he were out of the way. The Club would do better without him in my opinion. He is unpopular. And always I am afraid of some terrible *esclandre*—some frightful scene or some exposure that would ruin the Club and perhaps injure my character.'"

In spite of the gravity of the situation Sir Frank Tarleton relished Madame's regard for her character, though he kept his enjoyment to himself.

"She meant me to feel that she was on my side, I could see. It seemed to be a pure matter of business with her. She was ready to help me to save my husband or to kill him—it didn't matter which, provided it was made worth her while. At the same time she let me see that I was in her power. 'It comes to this,' she said at last, 'that if you are not going to trust me I can't afford to trust you. You may have come here to pump me, to find out if I deserve your husband's confidence. In that case I must report this conversation to him for my own protection; I expect you to see that, madam.'"

It was all so clever, as clever as the advertisement about the letters, Tarleton reflected. He did not wonder that Mrs. Neobard had been overmatched.

"In the end I had to give in to her. I saw no way out, and it looked as if she would be perfectly willing to help me on her own terms. I undertook to transfer the whole property in the Domino Club to her on my husband's death, and she undertook to find one of his victims who hated him enough to kill him, if he could do it safely, and give him the secret poison. No one was to know where she had obtained it.

"I took the bottle to her the next day. The moment it was in her hands she said to me, 'I must have more than this, madam. I must have the letters you have found. They are your justification for planning your husband's death, and I must have them to show in my defence if I get into trouble for assisting you.'

"I had been weak enough to tell her nearly everything I have told you, because I couldn't bear to let her think that I was a bad woman acting from evil motives. Now I repented too late. As usual, she had a perfect answer to everything I could say. 'It comes to this, madam, that you have given me the means to commit a murder, and you have made these letters your excuse. If you decline to produce them I must doubt if they exist, and as an honest woman I shall hand this bottle over to the police.'"

Tarleton got out of his chair. If he did not yet know all he wanted to know, he knew all that this poor woman could tell him.

"Thank you. If I have your permission to use this information in my own way neither you nor your daughter need fear anything more."

The astonished woman stopped him on the way to the door.

"But after Madame Bonnell had got the letters she turned round and refused to go on with the plot. How did my husband die?"

"I am going to ask her that."

CHAPTER 20

THE FINGER-PRINT

When Sir Frank Tarleton walked into the room on his return from Paris the first thing he did was to put his gold repeater to his ear and make it ring out its musical notes. It was the sign of triumph.

He told me everything just as I have described it. Then he transfixed me with a question.

"I expect you to be as candid with me as Mrs. Neobard has been. Did you put this poison into Wethered's cup along with the opium?"

It was no more than I ought to have expected; no more than I had deserved. But it gave me a greater shock than I could have thought possible.

"Before God I am innocent of that!" I swore.

My chief received my oath without any indication of belief or disbelief.

"I don't blame you for anything else you did on behalf of Lady Violet," he said gravely. "Even if you hadn't been in love with her, as a man you could do no less than you did to save her from such a scoundrel. You were right to drug him and right to destroy his case-book. But you had no right to take his life."

I looked him in the face. I was too proud to repeat my denial.

"That has been my greatest anxiety in the whole business, Cassilis. I liked you; you knew it, and I think you should have confided in me."

"It wasn't my secret," I pleaded.

"I suppose that was the reason: yes, I accept that. It was a mistake, though, because you had no chance of keeping the secret. That is partly why I think it better for you to drop this kind of work and go in for private practice. You lack the first essential for a detective, my dear fellow; you can hold your tongue, but you can't hold your face."

I'm afraid I couldn't hold it then. It blushed in spite of me.

"I am a light sleeper, Cassilis, as you ought to know. The telephone bell woke me some minutes before you came into the house that first night. You moved as quietly as a mouse as soon as you heard it, but you see I was listening before it rang the second time and I had heard you come up to the front door and open it."

How silly all my precautions seemed now! My chief rubbed it into me with a touch of good humour.

"I gave you a hint that you might as well make a clean breast of it at once, but you didn't take it. When you came in to me with Charles's message your face showed me that you had something more on your mind than having gone out without letting me know. And you gave yourself away when you told me that you had been taken to the Domino Club by a Captain Smethwick. There is no such name in the Army List."

Blunder after blunder, he recounted them all. The theft of the case-book had pointed to the thief being a doctor. The omission of Violet's name from the list I had copied supplied the key to my motives, and my attack on Sarah Neobard left no doubt that I was in love with the girl she had denounced. My kind-hearted chief had willingly lent himself to my plans for meeting Violet at Tyberton, though he had tried to let me see he was not quite blind. He had followed the history of the Zenobia costume easily enough. And Violet's refusal to give up the name of her champion had told him more than it had told poor, dull-witted me.

"That is my best reason for advising you to start in practice for yourself, my boy. Consider what your prospects are with me. I am at the top of the tree now and my salary is a bare £1,500 a year. And if I make another £500 by my private work it's as much as I make. That's not enough for an earl's daughter to look forward to. You will make double as a fashionable doctor. You have the most valuable gift of all for the medical profession. You are a good listener. The people who will come to you, the patients who really bring in money, don't want to be cured. They like to fancy they are ill and they want to talk about themselves. Let 'em do it and charge them for it. With my influence and Lord Ledbury's you won't have long to wait."

I could only shake my head sorrowfully. "You are very good, sir; you are kinder to me than I deserve. But I have no right to think that Lady Violet will ever marry me."

Sir Frank gave me a queer look.

"Then I tell you this—if you don't marry her, *I will*."

Before I could recover from the start given me by this threat he was consulting his watch again.

"Charles ought to be here by this time. And I think he is. I shall be glad if you will come with us, Cassilis. We are going to the Domino Club."

I followed him thankfully into the hall, to meet Inspector Charles and a quietly dressed Frenchman who was briefly introduced to me as Brigadier Samson. I took the invitation to go with them as a token that my chief had acquitted me in his own mind at least. I was ignorant whether I ever had been under suspicion in the Inspector's, and I am so still.

We drove to the Club in the taxi that had brought the two police officers. We found it looking much more cheerful than on the last occasion. The new proprietress had evidently determined to make it a greater success than ever, in spite of the little cloud that had fallen on it. There were signs of renovation going on in the hall and new decorations had been put up in the ball-room.

The door was opened to us by the waiter Gerard, who looked as amiable as ever, but rather more subdued. The respectful glance he gave to Captain Charles seemed to tell of some intelligence between them. Gerard was closely followed by another man whose salute showed me that he was one of the Inspector's staff, in charge of the premises.

When Gerard, who had left us in the ball-room, returned to say that Madame Bonnell was ready to receive us, the French detective retained his seat. The other three of us were conducted into a smartly furnished parlour in which we found Madame enthroned in all the dignity of her new position. She had put on mourning for her late employer, but it was the sort of mourning a good modiste knows how to make a softener of grief rather than a perpetuation of it.

Madame Bonnell showed no trace of nervousness at our appearance. Like a good general, she had gauged her enemy in advance, she had anticipated his attack, and her plans of defence had been skilfully laid out. She received us in the manner of a courteous business woman who was only anxious to do whatever was asked of her.

I was conscious that my chief's keen eyes were on the look-out for any sign of recognition between Madame and me, as I came into the room. Fortunately she scarcely noticed me, and I think her indifference must have finally satisfied him that we were strangers to each other.

He came straight to the point.

"We have called on you, Madame, in consequence of the advertisement from Messrs. James, Halliday & James."

She heard this with composure. "What advertisement is that?"

Tarleton ignored the affectation of ignorance.

"It may save time to tell you that every person known to have been in correspondence with Dr. Weathered has been warned to take no notice of that advertisement." It was evidently news to her that the names of the correspondents were known to the police, and she looked less confident already. "Mr. Stillman has been informed that Dr. Weathered's executrix is the sole person entitled to deal with the letters, and he has now consented to allow a detective officer to sit in his outer office and refer any persons who may answer the advertisement to me. The same officer is opening all letters addressed to the firm."

By this time Madame Bonnell must have made up her mind that she had little chance of making anything out of the letters and that it was better for her to sacrifice them if she could do so without damage to herself.

"What has all this to do with me?" she asked cautiously.

"Mrs. Weathered informs me that she placed the letters in your possession and I am here to ask you for them."

Madame Bonnell did some hard thinking and did it quickly, too.

"Mrs. Weathered is a madwoman. She is not responsible for her actions, and her word is not to be believed. I am surprised that you should expect me to take such a story seriously. If you believe I have the letters, look for them."

It was a gallant last stand. She must have known that every inch of the premises had been searched already.

Tarleton smiled at her. He was beginning to warm to his work.

"If I am to take advantage of that permission, Madame, I shall have to ask you to accompany me to Newgate Street, where there is a female searcher. You probably carry the letters about with you."

A sudden spark, a very ugly and dangerous spark, was kindled in the woman's eyes at the mention of a female searcher. It went out again instantly. Madame folded her arms.

"If you believe what you say, it makes no difference. You say that Mrs. Weathered gave me those letters. Why isn't she here to ask for them back? I have a right to keep them till she does."

This was true, unfortunately. But Madame had just been betrayed into revealing her weak point, about which the representative of the Home Office had been pretty confident before. He now turned to Inspector Charles.

"I am afraid I must leave the matter to you, Inspector."

Captain Charles was quite ready.

"I must ask you to consider yourself my prisoner, Madame. The charge is one of conspiring with Arthur Stillman to obtain money from various persons by threats. Whatever you may say will be taken down and may be used in evidence against you."

She didn't wait for the production of the official note-book. Her hands were at the bosom of her dress.

"That charge is false and you know it. It is you who are using threats to obtain these letters, to which you have no claim. You are breaking the law, not I."

She was right, that was the amazing part of it, entirely right. But she handed over the letters. And she contrived to look rather anxious.

"Let me tell you that I only consented to receive those letters from Mrs. Weathered because I saw she was a dangerous woman and I wanted to prevent her from doing mischief. I meant to return them to the writers the moment I knew who they were. In my position I couldn't afford to do otherwise. I had to think of the reputation of the Club."

Against this there was nothing to be said. It was the second line of defence, of course. Tarleton was not the man to waste time in assailing it.

"Mrs. Weathered tells me she gave you something else beside those letters."

Madame Bonnell needed no preparation to meet this blow, which she had clearly been expecting. She heaved a sigh, apparently one of relief.

"Ah, I am glad she has confessed that! It has been a burden on my mind. I ought to have denounced her, I suppose, but I saw she was out of her mind, and I was sorry for her. I thought it would be enough if I took the poison from her and kept it in a safe place."

This was neater than even Tarleton had expected. I saw positive respect in his eyes.

"Then you have the poison still, Madame, untouched?"

"But yes. I placed it among my little aids to the toilet. You will find it in the cupboard you locked up, you remember."

"Perhaps you will oblige me by fetching it. Inspector Charles will unlock the door for you."

The Inspector's face fell as he rose to escort her. Perhaps he thought that Sir Frank was being deceived. They came back together, Charles carrying the little bottle, which he silently handed to the specialist.

Tarleton went through the form of wetting his forefinger, taking up a few grains of the gray powder and tasting it. His face told nothing.

"The powder now in this bottle is a harmless mixture of charcoal and common salt. The poison that killed Dr. Weathered was upasine."

Madame Bonnell raised her hands in admirable despair.

"*Mille tonnorres!* That wretched woman was more mad than I thought. She mistook this stuff for—what did you say, sir?"

The physician shook his head. "You do her an injustice. I have tested her story and I feel no doubt that she placed the real poison in your hands. I have seen the person from whom she took it and from whose brother I obtained some of it myself."

Again the first line of defence, a rather flimsy one, had been broken through. The second line was instantly unveiled.

"I have been robbed, then, that is what you mean? Some wretch has stolen the drug and filled up the bottle again to deceive me."

"It looks like that, certainly." Could I believe that this was Tarleton speaking? His voice remained perfectly steady as he went on. "Unfortunately, one of the Club servants, named Gerard, has told the police a different tale."

All at once Madame Bonnell turned very white. She began breathing in spasms.

"His story is that you threw out hints to him that Dr. Weathered was in danger of being poisoned, as you pretended, by enemies of his in the Club. At a later time you bribed Gerard to say that the doctor himself was afraid, and had given him instructions to watch over his drinks. What really happened was that your continued hints made Gerard watchful, and on the fatal night he did see something dropped in the doctor's cup by a dancer whom he described correctly. We know that it was a harmless dose of opium, a drug to which Weathered was immune, because he was taking it. Gerard reported what he had seen to you and you thereupon told him that it was what you had feared but that you had an antidote. You put this antidote, as you called it, into a fresh cup of coffee, and made him take it to the doctor. There is no doubt in my mind that he died in consequence of drinking it."

Madame Bonnell's perfect composure was gone. That angry spark had come back into her eyes to remain there. She clenched her teeth, and her words came through them like the click of castanets.

"Gerard is a bloody liar."

The next instant she recollected herself. She had still a third line of defence, a really good one this time.

"Are you going to tell that story to the world? Aha! I can tell stories, too. I shall have a fine tale to tell about His Royal Highness the Crown Prince of Slavonia; yes, yes. I shall tell how His Highness came to dance with poisoners and prostitutes, and people whose minds were fouler than any sink; and saw a murder committed under his eyes by his partner in the dance. Is it not so? And I shall recite much from all those letters I have read. I have a good memory, and I recite well."

Tarleton acknowledged the strength of this position.

"You are correct in thinking that the British authorities have reasons for not taking proceedings against you. Therefore, they propose to let you return to your own country."

"And give up my Club? Abandon my good fortune at its height? I am not a very great fool, Sir Frank Tarleton."

My chief raised a finger. Captain Charles sounded his whistle and Brigadier Samson stepped through the door.

Slowly the woman recoiled on herself, seeming actually to grow smaller in the act. The Brigadier gave her a careless nod.

"You have dyed your hair, Leonie Marchand, since I saw you last, but you haven't changed your finger-print, you know. And you are still wanted for the murder in the Rue Lausanne."

It was not a woman, it was a wild cat that sprang at Sir Frank with tearing nails and spitting teeth. I was just too late, but the French detective who knew the nature of the animal, was just in time; and he wasn't hampered by any false sentiment. His methods were not particularly pleasant to watch, but they were effective. I think Charles rather envied him.

The methods of the French criminal courts also seem to be effective. At all events when I read the newspaper report of the trial at which Leonie Marchand was sentenced to imprisonment for life, it contained no hint of any scandal about any royal personage.

Sir Frank Tarleton was none the worse for the little shock he had experienced, and for which he rather blamed himself afterwards. He ought not to have waited to see the arrest, he admitted to me, but he couldn't resist the temptation to see the real woman come out. He hadn't liked the sight.

"It lay between Madame and you from the first, as far as I could see," he explained to me, as we were walking away together down Tarifa Road. "I never believed the waiter's story for a moment. The idea that a man who knew his life to be in danger would go on coming to the Club and trust to a foreign waiter to prevent him from being poisoned, was ridiculous in my eyes. It was clear that the story had been put into his mouth by someone; and when Madame told a similar story, about Weathered having asked her to pour out his drinks herself, it was easy to see who was the inventor. It was a case of cleverness over-reaching itself. The theory that Weathered had been poisoned by one of his patients whom he was blackmailing was quite plausible in itself; as we know, it was very nearly being the true theory. If she had left it there and confined herself to saying what she said to Mrs. Weathered, that she knew he had enemies in the Club who would be glad of his death, I might not have suspected her. But when she took such pains to represent the whole place as a nest of assassins with herself and Gerard as guardian angels watching over the threatened man, I began to smell a rat.

"I had no suspicion of Mrs. Weathered; I don't see how I could have had at that stage. Madame Bonnell's motives were just what would make a woman of her stamp commit a crime. Sarah Neobard put it in a nutshell when she said she was a woman who would do anything for money. The Domino Club was doing well, and Weathered wasn't necessary to it any longer. In fact, he was beginning to be in the way. She spoke the truth, probably, in saying that she lived in fear of a scene of some kind. At the same time, I doubt if she would ever have ventured to poison him herself if the means hadn't been put into her hands. Here is the real murderer."

He took out the little bottle, which he had brought away with him. It was square-shaped and made of ground glass, the sort of bottle in which smelling salts are sold.

"I look on this case throughout as one of murder by suggestion. Armstrong did very wrong to leave this bottle in his sister's possession. The very precautions she took to keep it safely, as she thought, show that her mind was exercised by it. I shouldn't wonder at all if Weathered, who was a clever man in his way, actually did detect some latent fancies in the little woman's head as to how it might be used, and worked on them till he convinced her that they were serious. Then no sooner does he hear of the existence of the bottle than it fascinates him. An unknown drug, one whose effects will defy analysis—what a prize for a man who is fast sinking into a hardened criminal! Remember that if Armstrong had not happened to bring a sample of his find to me you might now be under sentence for the murder."

I shook as I recognized the truth of what he said. Even Tarleton's skill might have failed to demonstrate the presence of a strange drug unknown to the whole medical world.

"This accursed bottle next has the same effect on Mrs. Weathered. She is a good woman and she has been a faithful wife and a forgiving one. I believe every word of her story. I fully believe that she took the bottle with no intention to do anything but destroy it and its contents. But no sooner is it in her keeping than she succumbs to its temptation. She is fascinated by the idea of the invisible death it can deal. All kinds of motives and excuses spring up in her mind like spectres conjured up by a magician. So she becomes a murderess in intention, a murderess by proxy, one may say.

"Even Madame Bonnell, I think it most likely, had no idea of killing Weathered before this bottle came into her hands. She had committed one murder already and she seems to have had a narrow escape that time. She was a prudent woman, too, a woman to weigh risks carefully before taking them. I think it quite probable that her only idea at first was to use this bottle to extort money from Mrs. Weathered. But very quickly she was in its power. Then it was that she began weaving the romance of Weathered's revengeful patients, a picture only too well founded on fact. She may have hoped to find an enemy of Weathered's to do the job for her; however, you saved her the trouble. She saw her chance, and that night she had a double security. From first to last it is evident that she trusted to the Crown Prince's name to pull her through everything, and in a way it did."

"What made you think she had committed a crime in France, sir?"

"I didn't. It was a mere shot in the dark. I asked Charles to get her finger-print without her knowing, and I took it over to Paris on the bare chance that she might be known to the French police. It is fortunate that she was."

We were in Eaton Square by this time, after coming along the King's Road. My chief seemed to know where he was going, but he did not tell me till we had gone round the back of the Palace and come out in Piccadilly. When we crossed the road my heart began to beat quicker.

The dear old man had made up his mind to pull me through, and I suspect he did it as much for Violet's sake as mine. He must have seen that there was some obstacle between us, but he never asked what it was. He only gave me one hint before we reached the house.

"No man ever won a woman yet by making the worst of himself, Cassilis. If you haven't anything else to be proud of, be proud of being loved and show it."

The Earl, whom we found at home, was more than half prepared to listen to us. He had changed for the better, too, since he had taken Sir Frank's advice. He showed that he felt he owed a debt to him and another to his daughter, and was not unwilling to discharge both. It was my advocate who did most of the talking. He surprised and delighted me by telling my prospective father-in-law that I needn't throw up my post under him just yet. "Not till he is on his feet comfortably," he put it.

In the end the Earl said, "Well, I will see what my daughter has to say, Dr. Cassilis." And he rang the bell.

When Violet came in she saw why she had been sent for, before her father spoke. She had her answer ready when he put the question. "This young gentleman has come here to ask me for your hand, Violet. What am I to say to him?"

"He hasn't asked me yet," she whispered.

My dear chief sprang to his feet. "I think we had better leave these young people together, my lord."

We are together still.